The Unbelievers

Alastair Sim

MINOTAUR BOOKS

A Thomas Dunne Book
New York

A THOMAS DUNNE BOOK FOR MINOTAUR BOOKS.
An imprint of St. Martin's Publishing Group.

THE UNBELIEVERS. Copyright © 2009 by Alastair Sim. All rights reserved. Printed in the United States of America. For information, address St. Martin's Press, 175 Fifth Avenue, New York, N.Y. 10010.

www.thomasdunnebooks.com
www.minotaurbooks.com

Library of Congress Cataloging-in-Publication Data

Sim, Alastair.
    The unbelievers / Alastair Sim. — 1st U.S. ed.
        p. cm.
    "A Thomas Dunne Book."
    ISBN 978-0-312-62169-8
    1. Police—Scotland—Fiction. 2. Social classes—Scotland—Fiction. 3. Highlands (Scotland)—Fiction. 4. Scotland—History—19th century—Fiction. I. Title.
    PR6119.I455U53 2010
    823.92--dc22

                                        2010021269

First published in Great Britain by Snowbooks Ltd.

First U.S. Edition: September 2010

10 9 8 7 6 5 4 3 2 1

Dedication

For Muriel and Sandy Sim

Acknowledgements

I would like to thank the writers and friends who made the University of Glasgow such a fertile environment for my work on this book, and within that to offer special thanks to novelist Laura Marney, with whom I worked very closely on this book and other projects. My thanks also to the friends in Edinburgh with whom I have shared parts of this book. My wife Fiona Parker has unfailingly supported me artistically in my writing as well as in so many other ways. I hope that this book will be something that makes my two wonderful little boys, Christopher and Nicholas, proud.

Chapter 1

Inspector Allerdyce clung firmly to the leather-covered edge of the basket as he hung three thousand feet above the city. The chill west wind stung his eyes and his cheeks. He pulled his hat down more firmly as the wind caught its brim.

The pilot leant against the tiller, holding his jacket shut at the collar with his free hand. The gusty breeze couldn't drown out the steady whish-whish of the propeller behind them.

"What do you think, Allerdyce?" shouted the pilot.

"I beg your pardon, Professor Boyd."

"What do you think? Are you enjoying it?"

"Very much. Very bracing."

"It's windier than I expected."

"Sorry?"

"It's too windy," said the pilot. "We won't be able to make enough headway against the wind to get back to Bonaly. I'll try and put us down near Musselburgh."

"All right then."

"It's the engine that's the problem. I can only get 5hp out of it, and I can only carry enough water to make steam for 40 minutes."

"It's still very impressive."

"It's only the very beginning, Allerdyce. If I can build a lighter, more powerful engine I can build an airship that would carry passengers as quickly and reliably as a steamship, or even a train."

"I look forward to that."

"I'll start letting hydrogen out of the balloon in about 5 minutes to start descending. In the meantime, enjoy the view."

"Thank you."

The same wind that was stinging his eyes had blown away most of the smoky mist which hung over Edinburgh on a still day. Little wisps of white steam or dark grey smoke rose from factory chimneys or from locomotives, but were quickly dispersed. Far away, a white line against the horizon marked the beginning of the snow-capped Highlands.

Beneath him, Allerdyce studied the city which had changed so much, almost beyond recognition, in his forty-four years.

To the north of the rigid grid of the Georgian New Town, and to the south of the crowded warren of the mediaeval Old Town, the farmland had been partitioned into little green squares of garden and in each of them had been planted a square sandstone villa as a home for the newly-rich. The spires of new churches for every competing denomination, temples of respectability for the credulous polite classes, broke the monotonous chequer-board of gardens and houses. To the west, along the canal and turnpikes, and to the north-east, spreading along the parallel roads to Leith, dense tenements crowded darkly around the mills and breweries which employed the more fortunate of their inmates. The workers' places of devotion – the public houses and cheap brothels – were invisible from this height, but the vast black mass of the Calton jail promised retribution for their sins in this life, if not the next.

Allerdyce looked beyond the jail, over the roofs of townhouses and terraces, towards a patch of green parkland, dotted with the leafless skeletons of trees. He grasped the edge of the basket harder as he recognised it as the Warriston Cemetery. It was nine years since he'd stood there on another winter's day beside an open grave as a minister murmured funereal banalities. Nine years, but in his mind he was still there as Helen's coffin was lowered into the frost-hardened earth, the crows cawing impatiently from the trees.

He told himself it was only the wind which was making his eyes water. Wiping them with the back of his sleeve he looked away to where the sun glinted on the silver steel of the railway tracks beside the cemetery. He let them draw his attention away from Helen's grave, looking up the raw cutting of the railway to where first one branch joined, then another, before the tracks swung round to join the main line.

They're like a circulatory system, he thought, penetrating every part of the city, nourishing both the healthy parts and the cancerous tumours of deprivation and pollution. Alongside the tracks ran the telegraph cables, the nerves of the city transmitting the data – stock prices, orders for goods, news from the Empire and beyond – which informed its actions.

Modern science made the city's functioning, and even its malfunctioning, as predictable as a printing-press. Today, in 1865, in the twenty-eighth year of Her Majesty Queen Victoria's reign, human understanding of nature and society was surely nearing completion. Economic science showed the inexorable law by which wealth was generated by the poor and flowed to the rich. Social science revealed the inevitability that a sizeable segment of the poor would sink towards crime and depravity. Statistical science showed the precise extent to which this would happen. On a day like today, according to forensic mathematics, there would most likely be:

113 crimes against property in the street – pickpocketing or theft without assault.

76 burglaries by night.

48 housebreakings by day.

43 assaults causing bodily harm.

14 disturbances at public houses requiring the attendance of the constabulary.

7 cases of rape or sexual assault, disregarding any purely domestic disturbances.

3 abandoned babies found, dead or alive.

And 1 murder.

Chapter 2

Warner glanced over his shoulder, down the long carpeted corridor.

He was carrying a tray with a bottle of whisky, a siphon of soda and a glass, so there was no reason why any of the other servants should think he was up to anything. Even so, as he knocked gently on the door of his master's dressing room and softly turned the handle, he was grateful only to see the empty corridor and the gaslight reflecting against the glass of the paintings which lined it.

As he opened the door he heard the first tinny chimes of the clock which stood on the mantelpiece. He shut the door behind him as it struck for the fourth time, standing still until the twelfth ring had subsided.

The fire was lit in preparation for his master's return, though he could see on the table, curling up at one edge under the yellow light of the lamp, the telegram which had so agitated His Grace earlier.

He'd delivered it, sealed, when it had arrived from the telegraph office at four o'clock. Glancing at it later, after he'd helped his master to dress for dinner, he'd noted its promise of his master's absence.

He put the tray down on the table, covering the telegram. As he did so, he caught a glimpse of himself in the full-length mirror which stood beside the Duke's wardrobe. He turned to get a better look at himself, smoothing down his jacket as he did so.

Not bad, he thought, looking up and down at his slight, well-dressed figure. Especially in this light, not bad at all. His hair was neatly parted and its oiled gloss reflected in the dim lamplight and the flickering gold of the fire. He'd always liked the delicate darkness of his brows, the slimness of his nose, the paleness of his lips and the clear definition of his chin. He'd been lucky to have a complexion which had never been marked by pox, though tonight his cheeks looked, he thought, a little drawn, and the semi-darkness of the room seemed to accentuate the dark lines under his eyes, which still looked as bright and vigilant as a kestrel's. Standing here in a sober black suit, with shiny patent leather shoes and a neat black tie, he didn't see why he shouldn't be taken for a gentleman.

In fact, he thought, the only thing that distinguished a servant from a gentleman was money, and he could do something about that.

He crossed the room to his master's chest of drawers, which stood to the right hand side of the door. The way the door was hinged meant he should be hidden if someone opened it.

He only needed to open one drawer. Every night, after he'd dressed His Grace for dinner, he put away his master's daytime clothes and belongings – suit, hat, boots, shirt, riding-crop and wallet. He pulled the top drawer out a few inches, lifting it gently by the handles to stop it from scraping against the runners. He slipped his hand in and, brushing light silk handkerchiefs out of the way, closed it round the fat bulk of His Grace's wallet.

He eased the wallet out of the narrow opening, careful not to touch it against the wood, as if it was nitro-glycerine. He unfolded it, smelling the tang of old leather and the dryness of banknotes.

He checked the contents under the lamplight. From a quick flick through it he reckoned there must be about £250 in notes, stuffed in roughly and randomly in different denominations. Enough for a gentleman to live modestly for a year.

He didn't reckon that the old bastard was too careful about counting his money. He didn't need to be, seeing as he owned five coalmines and three estates. Even so, it didn't do to take too much of a risk, at least not all at one time.

Warner slipped a £10 note out of the wallet and into his trouser pocket. He was £10 closer to being a gentleman. He folded the wallet back up.

As he turned back towards the chest of drawers he heard a door open. It sounded as if it was opening at the near end of the corridor, where the servants' staircase came up. He froze.

Bugger. If they come in here and see me standing with the Duke's wallet in my hand I'm done for. If I put it away and make a noise they might look in here and wonder what's going on. He felt sweat on his back and in the palms of his hands.

The footsteps drew nearer, the floorboards creaking gently under the carpet with each pace. Before he knew he'd made a decision Warner had stuck the wallet back in the drawer and shoved it closed with a 'thunk' which he prayed hadn't been heard.

He picked up the tray – if the door was opened he could pretend to be arranging his master's drinks in anticipation of his return. His heart was pounding, though, and as he held the tray unsteadily he heard the glass chink-chink against the soda syphon in time to his racing pulse.

The light tread approached the door. He felt sure that the

clinking glass was ringing out his guilt to anyone who had ears to hear. He swallowed, hoping his voice would sound steady when he was asked to give an account of himself.

The footsteps passed by with what sounded like the swishing of a skirt. A little way down the corridor he heard a door open – he guessed it must be the door to the Duchess's dressing room or bedroom. Presumably her maid was taking her something.

He waited for a moment, feeling himself breathe again. If the maid did whatever she had to do and left quickly, then he could follow a couple of minutes later and no-one would know he'd been here. He stood, counting slowly up towards a hundred as he listened for any sign that the maid was coming back out, but all he could hear was a faint banging as if drawers or doors were being opened inside the room.

He'd reached seventy-three when he decided there was no point in waiting any longer. His hands felt steadier and the glass had stopped clinking. He might as well get going before anyone else interrupted him.

He opened the door and checked either way down the corridor before, carrying the tray in front of him, he walked steadily towards the servants' staircase.

. . .

Alice rushed into the small parlour in her white night-dress, holding a toy rabbit by the ears in one hand and a book in the other.

"Daddy, daddy, daddy, read me a story."

"Darling, I have to go out."

"Daddy, please, I've brought the book with me. Mummy said you'd read to me."

Allerdyce paused from pulling his boots on. He could hear the baby crying upstairs, and in the hall outside the parlour Albert was banging away at a drum with the full force of his three year old arms. Margaret must have sent Alice downstairs to get some peace while she tried to pacify the baby. For an instant he thought how blissful it would be to be at Professor Boyd's house already, with a glass of Boyd's excellent Burgundy and the company of his oldest friends. He checked that thought, recalling the chill and maddening silence of his house before Margaret and the children had saved him from his solitude. He knew he should cherish even their noise.

He looked down at little ginger-haired Alice, who was giving her best six year-old pout. If he had to guess, he'd say she was less than a minute away from a flood of tears if he didn't read to her.

"All right then. But only a little bit. I do have to go out very soon."

"Thank you daddy. I want to sit on your knee."

He lifted her up and sat her on his knee. It always amazed him that a whole human being, with all her moods and questions and smiles, could be so light. There was something so complex and wonderful about a child, and he chided himself for being in such a hurry to rush out to a Speculative Society dinner.

"What book did you bring, darling?"

She handed it to him.

"Ah, *The Water Babies*. A good choice. Where do you want me to start?"

"The beginning again."

She nestled herself against his jacket with her thumb in her mouth, squirming to get comfortable as he put his right arm around her. He opened the book dextrously with his free hand and started to read.

"Once upon a time there was a little chimney-sweep, and his name was Tom. That is a short name, and you have heard it before, so you will not have much trouble in remembering it. He lived in a great town in the North country, where there are plenty of chimneys to sweep, and plenty of money for Tom to earn and his master to spend. He could not read nor write, and did not care to do either, and he never washed himself, for there was no water up the court where he lived..."

The doorbell rang and Alice looked up. Allerdyce stopped reading and heard the maid's quick footsteps to the door. Damn, he thought, that can't be anything good. He put the book down and put his hands round Alice's chest, preparing to lift her from his knee.

The maid came into the parlour with an envelope.

"Message for you, sir. The lad said it was from Superintendent Burgess and required your immediate attention."

Allerdyce lowered his daughter to the floor. She kicked out helplessly into space as he did so.

"You said you'd read to me daddy! You said you would!"

"I'm sorry, pet, I'll have to read this. It sounds important."

"Daddy! Please!"

He opened the envelope with his thumb and took the handwritten message out. As he tried to read it Alice attempted to clamber back up into his lap.

"Will I take her up to her room?" asked the maid.

"Please."

The maid picked up the child and took her up the stairs. Allerdyce could hear her accusing sobs, and the baby's continued crying above the drumbeats in the hall, as he read the message.

'Allerdyce

I require your immediate attendance at the house of the Chief Constable, 38 Heriot Row.

Trusting that this finds you swiftly,

Burgess.'

He folded the paper away into the inner pocket of his jacket and finished pulling his boots on. As he took his heavy tweed coat off the coatstand in the hall and pulled it on he felt himself, yet again, assuming the mantle of duty. He opened the door and stepped, unnoticed, into the night.

...

Heriot Row was only five minutes walk away, up the steep, broad thoroughfare of Dundas Street. Not so much a hill, thought Allerdyce, as a social gradient, from his little two-storey tenement house in Cumberland Street, past the residences of bankers and solicitors in Northumberland Street, to the great terraced palaces of the Law Lords and Queens Counsel in Heriot Row.

It was a fresh night and he could see his breath in front of him as he climbed, inhaling the city's pungent blend of chill air and coal-smoke.

Whatever he was being summoned to must be important if both the Chief Constable and Burgess were involved. Nothing in the usual round of assaults, thefts and murders had merited the Chief's involvement.

He quickened his steps as he turned into Heriot Row. The

three-storied houses rose to his right, set back from the pavement, with well-lit steps leading up to double doors which, for the most part, opened into bright vestibules to receive guests. To his left, across the wide cobbled street, rose the dark shapes of the trees in the locked private gardens.

As he walked along, a closed carriage stopped a few doors ahead of him, and a footman dismounted from the step at the rear of the carriage to open its door. The footman held out his hand as two giggling young ladies, girls really, stepped down onto the pavement.

As Allerdyce approached the carriage the footman stood in the middle of the pavement.

"Can you wait there for a moment please, sir? There are a couple of gentlemen still to get out."

"I have urgent business. Let me pass."

Allerdyce tried to walk on but the heavily-built footman blocked his passage.

"If you please, sir. We don't want a scene."

Allerdyce was about to pull out his warrant card when two very young men got out of the carriage, pulling their top hats on as they descended. One, obviously drunk already, leaned against the other, punching him and laughing as the whole party crossed the pavement. He tripped on the second step, dragging his friend down with him. The girls seemed about to collapse with laughter as the footman rushed forward to help the boys up, supported them to the front door, and pulled the doorbell. An instant later, as Allerdyce passed, the whole party was safely inside.

He walked on past three more houses, checking the numbers as he went. He'd addressed plenty of correspondence to the Chief Constable's house – case reports, emergency requests for arrest

18

warrants, and the like – but he'd never had occasion to visit it. In fact, he'd probably exchanged no more than 20 words with 'Holy Joe' Stewart in his fourteen months as Chief Constable.

He went up the steps to the vestibule of number 38 and pulled the bell. Within seconds a butler opened it.

"Mr Allerdyce?"

"Yes."

"Sir Joseph is waiting for you. Please come in."

As soon as he was through the door a maid appeared to take his coat and hat.

"Sir Joseph is in the dining-room," said the butler. He ushered Allerdyce into the first room on the left, closing the door silently behind him.

Four men were sitting around a highly-polished dining table, large enough to have seated sixteen people in comfort. The light of silver candelabra glittered off the cutlery on the table – eight untouched place settings, Allerdyce noticed, each of them set for five courses – and off the crystal glasses. A huge bone-china tureen stood in the middle of the table, a Chinese pattern in blue against the white of the porcelain visible in the steady flame of the candles, a gentle plume of steam rising from the small slot at the edge of the lid from which the silver handle of a ladle protruded. Game broth, thought Allerdyce as he sniffed the air, wondering what he was missing at Boyd's house tonight.

Three of the men sat in evening dress, glasses in hand, at the far side of the table. Allerdyce recognised each of them. Lounging to either side of their host were Viscount Dunsyre, Her Majesty's Secretary for Scotland, and the nation's Lord Advocate, Lord Kinnordy. Dunsyre was about fifteen years younger than the Lord Advocate, probably only in his late forties and still fair-haired, but Allerdyce thought the fixed hardness and arrogance of their expressions could have made them brothers.

Between them, Chief Constable Sir Joseph Stewart was conspicuously sitting upright and holding a glass of water instead of the red wine of his companions. He smiled slightly at Allerdyce. If you just looked at him, thought Allerdyce, you might mistake him for a kind man. A concerned look had etched itself permanently onto his face, probably baked in by two decades of service as a colonial governor. With his ascetically hollow cheeks, close-cropped balding head and long, expressive hands he could have been mistaken for a mediaeval saint or mystic. His well-publicised support for charitable causes – reformatories for fallen women, gospel missions to the Zulus – might have affirmed that impression, but Allerdyce knew well enough that any convict or native who'd suffered under Stewart's governance of the Tasmania colony would have no such illusion (although the inquiry into his Governorship had notoriously found no surviving native to testify against him).

On the near side of the table, Allerdyce recognised Superintendent Burgess easily from behind, sitting upright in a worn-shiny grey suit which barely stretched over his powerful shoulders. His tight black curls reminded Allerdyce of a bull's head. As Burgess turned in his chair Allerdyce saw by the candlelight the familiar ruddy and broken-nosed face which would have fitted a prize-fighter better than a policeman.

"Thank God we found you," said the Superintendent.

"Now, Mr Burgess, I don't think there's any need for blasphemy, is there?" said the Chief Constable. "But Mr Allerdyce, welcome. We hear great things about you. Please take a seat."

Allerdyce sat down beside Burgess.

20

"I must apologise for insisting on your presence here tonight," smiled the Chief Constable, "but we find ourselves in a delicate situation which we hope, through your skills, we can resolve."

"Delicate?" The Lord Advocate choked on his wine. "More likely to be grossly indelicate."

Sir Joseph continued. "We had intended to meet here tonight to discuss some matters of public policy. In particular, we wanted to discuss with a close friend, with substantial mining and agrarian interests, how the organs of the state could best be used to combat the threat of industrial insurrection. I'm sure you agree, don't you, that in these dangerous times it is our duty to do everything we can to prevent the overthrow of the economic order on which our country's security rests?"

Allerdyce said nothing. Sir Joseph went on.

"Well, to be brief, this friend was unable to join us tonight. We received a note from his wife, delivered by special courier, just as we were about to dine. It said that she'd waited until the last minute before writing, in the hope that she wouldn't have to, but that her husband had failed to return home in time and that she regretted that they would have to present their apologies. She added that he'd not been home for some days and that she was increasingly concerned by his absence.

"Naturally, we're anxious to allay any concern that she may have for his safety, so we decided to invite Superintendent Burgess to advise us on how best to do so. He recommended you as the most efficient detective in our force, and we appreciate your kindness in coming here tonight."

Bloody hell, thought Allerdyce, you don't care about the murders of ordinary men and women but you want the full power of the police service at your disposal when a friend is late for dinner.

"Isn't it a job for a private investigator, sir?" asked Allerdyce. "Marital inquiries aren't normally part of police business."

Burgess shifted uncomfortably in his chair. Allerdyce saw the Chief Constable's eyes narrow further, though he maintained his thin smile.

"As I explained to the Superintendent, Mr Allerdyce, our friend is not exactly in a normal position in society, and normal methods may not be appropriate to this inquiry. It is important – for reasons of state as much as for personal reasons – that this inquiry is both discreet and thorough. I am certain, on the Superintendent's recommendation, that we can rely on you."

There was no point in further resistance, even if tracking down a stray husband was going to steal the time he needed for pursuing real criminals.

"Very well, sir."

"Splendid. I'll let the Superintendent brief you more fully." Sir Joseph turned alternately to his companions. "Shall we invite the ladies back in and dine, gentlemen? I think that's our business done. Oh, and Mr Burgess and Mr Allerdyce, thank you so much for coming. I don't think we need detain you any longer."

The Chief Constable opened the door to show the Superintendent and Allerdyce back into the hall. Instantly, the maid appeared with their coats and hats and they were smoothly ushered back into the night.

"I'm sorry," said Burgess, pulling on his gloves. "We have to do it. I know you're the best person for the job."

"Thank you for the compliment, sir."

"You probably think it's a waste of time, but we need to get started. I've asked for another sergeant to be assigned to you to replace Baird, and he should be able to help. If the message I sent has got to him successfully he should be up at the Police Office already."

"Thank you sir."

"So we'd better get there and get to work. It's not much of a way to spend Saturday night, is it?"

"No, but at least we're not out on the beat all night, sir."

"True enough. But Allerdyce, don't forget. We'll be crucified if anything happens to the Chief's friend. I think I'd rather take my chances on the streets."

Chapter 3

The Reverend the Honourable Arthur Bothwell-Scott BD (Ordinary) surveyed his sparse congregation.

The building had been expanded over the centuries from a simple late-Norman village church to its current magnificence, with a seating capacity of one hundred and fifty on the ground level and a further one hundred in the balconies, easily sufficient for every worker on the estate and their families to be dragooned into for the great festivals of the year. Marble memorials to generations of deceased Bothwell-Scotts lined the walls, which were punctuated by stained-glass windows endowed by his departed mother. When he'd first been given the living of Dalcorn by his eldest brother he'd enjoyed the way the clear light streamed in through the two hundred year-old plain glass of the great rectangular windows. Now, as a result of his departed mother's late fit of pious generosity (God rest her bitter and manipulative soul), fashionable Gothic arches had been installed and the interior was in perpetual kaleidoscopic twilight from the few sunbeams which struggled through the stained-glass reproductions of 'The Light of the World' and 'The Scapegoat'.

This Sunday, as every Sunday, only a handful of people sat in the hard pews of the main body of the church. The estate factor, out of professional duty, sat restlessly in his tweeds in a front pew beside his heavy crinolined wife. Behind him, scattered throughout the pews, were a handful of estate labourers and servants from the big house, their faces in varied expressions of leering contempt or vacant stupidity.

The rousing strains of psalm-singing penetrated the church, reaching it from the Free Presbyterian chapel which had been built two fields away, on a tiny pocket of land not owned by the Duke. Arthur reflected bitterly that anyone with any Christian ardour had left his church when he was appointed, and gone off to build their own chapel and choose their own minister. All that was left to him was the rump of people who were too scared of eviction or dismissal to risk the appearance of disloyalty to the Duke's family, and an endowment of 300 guineas a year.

He dutifully read the first lesson, hearing his thin voice resonate in the emptiness of the church, even though he expected it to benefit nobody.

"... and God said, let the earth bring forth the living creature after his kind, cattle and creeping thing, and beast of the earth, after his kind; and it was so..."

But, he thought, it wasn't so, at least if we're to believe Mr Darwin. Every living thing that we see, man or animal, is the result of a struggle to the death between the survivors and those species or people who fell, defeated, by the wayside.

Arthur did not, this morning, feel like one of the successful competitors in the fatal game of natural selection. He looked across at the Ducal aisle, where velvet-covered seats were roofed over by a damask awning surmounted by the armorial bearings of the

Dukes of Dornoch. He felt a pleasing warm softness as he looked towards its sole occupant, his cousin and sister-in-law Josephine, Duchess of Dornoch. She smiled at him while delicately stroking the lace gloves which she held in her naked, alabaster hand, and for a moment he thought his life's work was worthwhile if it was sustaining her precious spirit. Guiding and comforting her should be enough object for any man's work. It was only a shame that that task had fallen, first and foremost, to his brother William.

He returned to the lesson.

"… and the rib, which the Lord God had taken from man, made He into a woman, and brought her unto the man.

"And Adam said, this is now bone of my bones and flesh of my flesh: she shall be called Woman because she was taken out of Man.

"Therefore shall a man leave his father and mother, and shall cleave unto his wife: and they shall be one flesh.."

A story, he thought, so sadly unrealised in his own life.

As he read he noticed the door at the back of the church open and two strangers come in. One of them was slimly built with youthfully dark hair when he took off his bowler, but with a face whose deep shadows and slight smile suggested the depth of experience of an older man. The other was broad and tall as an oak, with a thick black moustache and sideburns, wearing the brass-buttoned blue tunic and black top-hat of the Edinburgh City Police. They took their places in the rear pew.

Arthur paused in his reading, wondering whether something of such gravity and immediacy had happened that he should interrupt the service. The slimmer stranger nodded, and he took it as a cue to continue. As he read on, though, he wondered what could have brought the police to this empty church and whether there might even be some hidden offence in his own past that led them here. He searched his memory, but in a life of monotonous innocence he could only remember the occasion where he had failed to intervene to stop William from beating a disobedient spaniel. Nonetheless, he hurried through the service before descending from the pulpit to greet the strangers.

Josephine was already with them when he reached the back of the church. She introduced them, touching him lightly on the arm.

"Arthur, I took the liberty of suggesting to Inspector Allerdyce that he might meet you here. He'll explain why he needs your help." Her soft American accent was freighted with gentleness and sorrow. She took her lace handkerchief out of her sleeve and dabbed at the corner of her eye. "I'm sorry I can't stay. I find that I'm too weighed down with grief and must retire to bed."

She smiled wanly at him. "What a silly, weak woman you must think I am. I just thank Providence that I have your spiritual guidance to fortify me." She glided past and through the door, which was held open for her by a liveried servant. Arthur detected the faint floral scent of her perfume as the chill wind blew in.

He shook the Inspector's hand, wincing at the firmness of the policeman's grasp.

"Please, Inspector, I'll be delighted to help you in any way I can."

"I appreciate that, sir. May I introduce my colleague Sergeant McGillivray?"

The tall sergeant bowed. As he did so, Arthur noticed the purple ribbon on his chest.

"Victoria Cross, Sergeant? I must say, it's an honour to meet you."

"Many other brave men deserved it more than me, sir." Arthur was struck by the force of the sergeant's clear Highland diction.

"I hardly think a Victoria Cross is an excuse for modesty, Sergeant. Where did you earn it? The Crimea? India?"

"India, sir. Lucknow. A bad business. I prefer not to dwell on it."

"Very well, and I'm sorry to have caused you discomfort. Shall we retire next door to the manse and I'll see how I can help you?"

...

Arthur led them through to the parlour. A fire had been lit in preparation for his return, and a decanter of sherry had been set out on top of the embroidered lace cover of the little round table at the window. The room still felt chilly, though, and the single sherry glass must, he thought, look pathetically inhospitable. He pulled the braided bellcord beside the fireplace.

"Won't you take a seat, gentlemen?"

"Much obliged," said the Inspector, sitting on a delicate silk-upholstered Chippendale at one side of the fireplace. The sergeant stood for a second until Arthur motioned him towards the matching chair on the opposite side of the fire, and the huge policeman sat gingerly as if scared that his frame would break it, holding his top-hat in front of him on his lap.

An elderly manservant came in and bowed.

"Wilson, would you be so kind as to help these gentlemen to a refreshment. Tea, gentlemen? Or perhaps something a little stronger?"

"Nothing thank you, sir. We need only detain you very briefly," said Allerdyce.

"Very well."

The servant bowed again and left, pulling the door silently behind him.

"How," continued Arthur, "might I be of assistance?"

Allerdyce took his notebook out of his pocket and flicked through several pages before speaking.

"We were hoping you could help us, sir, with a missing person case."

"How intriguing? I most certainly will help you if I can. Who is it?"

"Your brother, sir, His Grace the Duke of Dornoch."

"Good grief!"

"You are surprised, sir?"

"Surprised, Inspector? I should say so. I had heard nothing about this. My brother is a man of the highest public profile. I cannot see how he could possibly go missing."

"The Duchess is most concerned, sir. She says he has not returned to Dalcorn House for three nights, and no-one in the household knows of any business that would have required his absence. We wondered whether you might be able to indicate some possible lines of enquiry."

"Lines of enquiry, Inspector? Such as?"

"Well, sir, perhaps you know of a place your brother was in the habit of frequenting? Somewhere where we might be able to find someone who has had recent sight of him?"

Arthur paused. The only places he could think his brother might have gone were thoroughly dishonourable, and he was unsure that he should mention them. The detective, though, must have read his mind.

"I can promise you, sir, that all enquiries will be made in the strictest confidence."

Arthur stood up and paced the room. He strode over to the little table and put his hand on the stopper of the sherry decanter. Deciding not to pour himself a drink he turned back to face the policemen.

"Inspector," he said, "I appreciate your discretion, but I judge it appropriate that what I have to tell you should only be shared between gentlemen." He motioned towards the sergeant, who glanced at Allerdyce.

"I should prefer it strongly if you permit the sergeant to stay," said Allerdyce.

"Very well, then."

Arthur linked his hands behind his back and looked out the window for an instant, where the great bare branches of the parkland's oaks and elms stood motionless in the cold winter's day. He turned his attention back to his visitors.

"My brother is not a good man," he said. "It is a profound grief to me – both personally and professionally – that I have been unable to persuade him to adopt a Christian mode of life.

"Obviously, I grieve for his own soul. If he had shown the slightest signs of regeneration I could believe that my prayers for his salvation were having some effect. But, as it is, I have no such grounds for hope and I have become increasingly resigned to the expectation that my brother has irrevocably shut his heart against Our Saviour, and has consigned himself to the flames of eternal torment.

"I must also confess to grief – and, I freely admit – anger that my brother has not treated the Duchess with the consideration she deserves. Their marriage brought together the two branches of my family which were thrust asunder for four generations, but William has behaved towards her as if the estrangement still continued. He has spoken of Josephine most insultingly in front of strangers, and she has confided to me the cruel mistreatment which she has suffered from him in private."

"Most unfortunate, sir," said Allerdyce. "And may I ask how this relates to his disappearance?"

Arthur wrung his hands. As he did so, he imagined himself crushing a tiny figure of his accursed brother between them.

"William has often boasted to me, with no consideration to my holy office, about his exploits in Edinburgh. From time to time – not infrequently – he will creep out of Dalcorn House by the servants' entrance in the dead of night and walk across country to Dalcorn Station, whence a late train can bring him to Edinburgh in half an hour. Once there he can spend his time and money in gambling, dog-fighting and whoring until he returns to his concerned wife under cover of darkness the next night, with some incredible story about how confidential business had necessitated his absence."

"Very concerning, sir," said Allerdyce. "And would you be able to offer us any specific indication of the establishments His Grace has frequented?"

"I'm sorry, Inspector, but my brother did not confide those details to me or, if he did, I am unable to recall them specifically."

"I see." Allerdyce folded his notebook up and put it back in his pocket. "Trust me, sir, the information which you have been able to give us is most helpful. I don't think we need trouble you any further at this stage." The Inspector stood, and the sergeant followed his lead.

Arthur crossed the room to the bellcord and pulled it again.

"Tell me," he said, "are you concerned for my brother's safety?"

"At the moment we are only making routine enquiries, sir. I think it is far too early to make any gloomy suppositions."

"I'm most reassured to hear that, Inspector."

The servant opened the door again. Arthur shook hands with Allerdyce and accepted McGillivray's bow before they were ushered out and the door closed. Left alone in silence, except for the gentle crackling of the fire, he went back over to the table and poured himself a glass of sherry, his hand shaking as he did so.

If William was missing he must have come to harm in one of the debauched fleshpots he visited. He could be lying, injured, in a gutter somewhere. Or he could be dead.

God forgive me, he thought, turning back and looking into the leaping and twining flames. There is part of me that would rejoice at my brother's death, if only for Josephine's sake. She could be free of his cruelty, and I could more effectively be her rod and her staff as she walked along the hard roads of her earthly pilgrimage.

He knocked back a large mouthful of sherry. The alcohol made him feel warmer, and more resolute.

In my heart, he thought, I have become Cain.

Chapter 4

The fly stood on the gravel outside the manse, the horse stamping impatiently and snorting clouds of steam into the cold air.

"It's a fine day," said Allerdyce. "I should prefer to walk round to Dalcorn House if that's convenient to you. It's only half a mile."

"I should prefer that too, sir," said the sergeant.

Allerdyce walked over to the fly's driver.

"Wait for us at Dalcorn House, will you? I don't anticipate a long visit."

The driver whipped the horse's back with the reins and the fly pulled off, the gravel crunching under its narrow wheels. Allerdyce pulled his pipe out of his pocket, lit it, and tossed the lucifer onto the ground. He took a deep draw on the pipe to get it started before addressing the sergeant.

"So, what is your estimation of the Reverend Arthur Bothwell-Scott?"

"He appears to be a very pious gentleman."

"He's a fool, Sergeant, a fool."

"Rather a harsh judgement, sir?"

"Not at all. It's an immutable law of nature. Our friends the Bothwell-Scotts are merely the incarnation of a general principle. Send the bully into the army, the supposed intellectual into the law, and the runt into the church. The good reverend fits the model perfectly."

They walked on. Allerdyce heard the military crunch-crunch of his companion's footsteps on the gravel beside his own lighter, faster tread. It was a relief to have a sergeant again, after Baird had been dismissed a month ago. It was insane that Baird had been dismissed. He was a good policeman, with a keen sympathy with the criminal mind. It was mad to sack him for being caught, off duty, drinking with known criminals. Any decent policeman knew he often enough had to rely on rogues for evidence against other rogues, but when Baird had been reported to the Chief Constable he'd been dismissed on the spot.

Allerdyce told himself he'd done what he could for Baird. He'd appealed to Burgess, who was sympathetic but said he couldn't overturn the Chief's decision. He'd then broken the rules by writing a direct appeal to the Chief Constable, but the Chief had refused to see him and merely sent a note back saying that he expected the highest standards of moral conduct from his officers, without exception. So, Baird was dismissed, without compensation or pension. The money which Allerdyce had anonymously given Baird's family wouldn't sustain them for long, and he feared for them. It was difficult enough for a dismissed policeman to find employment, and there would be criminals out there waiting to take their revenge. Besides, Baird was a bad loss as a sergeant, and only time would tell whether McGillivray was a fit replacement. He cursed the Chief for a holy fool, throwing good policemen onto the streets and wasting detective time on tracking down a straying aristocratic husband. He cursed himself for being unable to save Baird.

The lane was overarched by the boughs of the great elms which had been planted at either side, their bare branches meeting high above like the vaulting of a cathedral. Above the noise of their footsteps Allerdyce could hear the high-pitched conversations of blackbirds and starlings. Through his pipesmoke he could smell the freshness of the mulching leaves, still a thick carpet which had lain beneath the trees since autumn and was gradually reverting to soil. One thing no-one could yet explain was why, despite its blind cruelties, the living world appeared so beautiful. He'd buried any last vestiges of faith when he'd lain Helen's body in the indifferent earth, but it was still hard to discard the superstitious feeling that nature was fashioned by some spiritual force of beauty and proportion. Either it was an entirely irrational reaction, or it belonged to some form of rationality as yet undiscovered.

They turned a corner in the lane, and a perfect pastoral vista opened up across open parkland, dotted with the occasional oak or elm, on which a small herd of Highland cattle grazed. To their left stood the pilastered bulk of Dalcorn House. Falling gently from left to right, bisecting the parkland, ran the white stone-chips of the great drive, down to the vast wrought-iron gates, topped with the Ducal arms, which stood open beside the little classical lodge-house. Beyond the drive, the lush grassland fell away towards a great enclosure wall, and beyond that the water of the Firth of Forth shone bright in the winter sunlight.

"This was once a village," said Allerdyce.

"Really, sir?"

"Yes, until about eighty years ago. I've been reading up about our wandering Duke's family history. Dalcorn House used to be oriented to face west, but when it was remodelled by a previous Duke he wanted the house to create the maximum effect on visitors approaching from Edinburgh, so he put the front at the east side and had the village demolished because it spoiled the view."

"Very consistent, sir."

"What's that, Sergeant?"

"Very consistent. I have some family connections with the Duke of Dornoch's estates in Sutherland. Quite a number of villages have been cleared away in my own lifetime, whether or not they were unpleasing to His Grace's eye."

"Of course, Sergeant, of course."

"Only, sir, His Grace's agents have created a different sort of park in Sutherland. You won't see cattle like this often on His Lordship's land. Practically the entire county is now one great sheep-walk."

"Most interesting."

Allerdyce looked at the tall sergeant, but could see no trace of resentment, or even of feeling, in his face. He looked like the simple personification of Duty. Allerdyce wondered, though, what stories of affliction might lie beneath the Highlander's impassiveness.

They reached the main drive and turned left, towards the great house. Allerdyce could read its history in its stone. At the centre, wide steps led up to great glass doors which were set into a Palladian front of pilasters and pediment. Above the triangular pediment, the careful viewer could make out some rougher stonework below the balustrade, perhaps remnants of the fortified towerhouse which had stood here for centuries before the Bothwell-Scotts had achieved their full notoriety and wealth.

To either side of the central block, a small wing had been added, two windows wide and three high, in the restrained style of Queen Anne.

Every newer feature of the house spoke of an explosion of power and wealth. The wings had been extended mightily, and a colonnade erected in front of them. At each end the colonnade turned sharply, grasping beyond the frontage of the house to give covered passage to two matching structures which sat to the left and right of the main building, slightly detached from its bulk. The vast windows of the building on the left hand side, stretching from the ground to the carved frieze below the roof, showed it to be the ballroom. A belltower sat in the middle of the ballroom's roof. Its partner on the right had tall black wooden doors in place of windows, and a ventilator set into the roof. It had to be the carriage house. Behind it, black smoke rose from a tall stone chimney – a furnace-house had obviously been installed to ensure that, whatever depths winter might sink to, His Grace need never fear the cold.

They strode up the drive towards the steps.

"Should we look for the side entrance?" asked McGillivray.

"Certainly not, Sergeant. We are the equal of any man and we bear the Queen's warrant."

They mounted the steps. Allerdyce went ahead of McGillivray. He tapped his pipe against the stonework to knock the embers out and pulled the bronze bell-pull.

They had waited at least three minutes, and Allerdyce was about to pull again, when a liveried footman, in eighteenth-century knee-breeches and bumble-bee striped waistcoat, opened the door.

"I regret that His Lordship is not at home," said the servant.

"I am aware of that," said Allerdyce.

"Her Ladyship is also unable to receive visitors."

"I have already spoken with the Duchess this morning. I would like to speak to His Grace's valet."

The servant narrowed his eyes, standing to block their passage through the door.

"Who may I say is calling and on what business?"

Allerdyce stuck his hand between the buttons of his coat and pulled out his warrant card from the inside pocket of his jacket. He showed it to the footman, who stepped back to let them pass.

They found themselves in a vast marble-floored entrance hall. To their left and right, double doors of darkly-polished wood, over twelve feet tall as if social status made the Ducal family into physical giants, stood closed. Ahead of them, a red-carpeted staircase, at least twenty foot wide, swept up to the marble-balustraded gallery which surrounded the hall at first-floor level. Spaced evenly around the walls of the entrance hall, white busts of all the previous Dukes of Dornoch stood on top of six-foot pillars, looking down on anyone who had the presumption to enter the great house.

The footman led them through the double doors to the left, and into an enormous sitting-room. Allerdyce looked around. It must have been a good eighty feet long, the floor covered by a Persian rug except for a strip of polished wood by the windows, to let servants pass through the room without wearing the carpet. The huge fireplace was dark, and the great iron radiators which were interspersed along the window side of the room could not fully dispel the chill. The crimson silk of the wallpaper was punctuated by paintings and by a great gilded mirror above the fireplace. Easy-chairs were loosely grouped round little rosewood tables.

Allerdyce whistled through his teeth as he took in the range of artwork in the room. It bettered – substantially – the quality of the collection in the new National Gallery in Edinburgh. It was the most astonishing collection of paintings he had ever seen gathered in one place. Whenever his eye caught one painting it was distracted by the sight of something even more exciting or valuable in the periphery of his vision.

The footman interrupted his musings.

"I shall fetch Warner down directly."

"Thank you."

The servant left, and Allerdyce decided to take a more systematic look at the pictures, starting beside the fireplace. The sergeant followed him.

"Look at this, Sergeant," he said, pointing to a portrait of a seated man with an extravagantly long powdered wig, which ran down to rest on the shoulders of a polished silver breastplate. A blue sash crossed the breastplate, and the man rested one hand on the head of a hunting dog which looked loyally up to him, while the other held a charter bound with red silk. Behind him, golden sunlight reflected on the sea and illuminated distant mountains. A small temple stood in one corner of the background, within which stood the shadowy figure of a boy holding a bow and arrow.

"Very handsome, sir."

"Do you think so? I think the artist has captured rather well the essential crudeness of the face."

"If you say so, sir."

"Anyway, what's significant here is the story it tells. You're looking at James, First Duke of Dornoch. He's been painted by Sir Peter Lely, who also painted King Charles II's portrait. The statue of Cupid in the background must refer to the Duke's willingness to allow his wife to be one of the King's mistresses. The charter he's holding, and the hills behind him, represent the Ducal title and the lands the King granted him in return. Until then, he'd had to make do with a Marquisate."

"It's a story we're familiar with in the North," said McGillivray. "Where I grew up in Sutherland the Duke and his family were known as *iarmad dhe adhaltrannas* – the children of cuckoldom."

Again, Allerdyce cast a sideways glance at the sergeant, who seemed to know more about the Bothwell-Scotts than one might expect.

He continued on to a picture three places to the right. A Madonna, her complexion pallid against the rose-pink and cobalt-blue of her robes, knelt to adore the chubby baby lying on a bed of herbs in front of her. The Madonna's face had the very slightest smile, which suggested coquettery more than prayerful bliss. Allerdyce looked at the plaque on the picture's gilded frame.

"Amazing."

"Sir?"

"The only Botticelli in Scotland. Priceless beyond measure."

"Can't say it's my taste, sir."

"Sergeant, we are looking at the one finest examples of Renaissance painting, here in this very room."

McGillivray moved on behind the Inspector, and stopped at another painting.

"I find this one more interesting, sir."

The painting showed a sheepdog standing on a shingle beach, looking down a sea-loch between steep hills as a sailing ship was silhouetted on the horizon.

"Mmm, Landseer," said Allerdyce. Very fashionable."

"There's truth in the picture, sir. When my oldest brother left with his family for Canada they couldn't afford the extra shillings for the dog, so she was left to fend for herself."

The sergeant's face was still impassive, but Allerdyce glimpsed through his words the tragedy of a family cleared off the land they'd held for generations and expelled to a foreign country. It was a story that had touched countless Highland families over the decades, but he knew it must have been harsh for every one of them.

The double door opened again and the footman who had admitted the policemen came in, followed by a sallow-complexioned man, only a little over five foot tall, dressed in a simple black suit with a white winged-collared shirt and a black tie. His face was as colourless as the Madonna's.

"Warner, sir, His Grace's valet, as you requested," said the footman.

"Thank you."

The footman showed no sign of moving.

"You may leave us now. I should prefer to interview Mr Warner in private."

The footman nodded and left the room, pulling the doors shut.

Warner looked from side to side at the policemen. His hand shook as he pulled a cigarette case out of his pocket then replaced it, unopened.

"Please, sit down," said Allerdyce. He sat in one of the easy chairs and indicated to the sergeant to do likewise.

Warner came over and stood in front of one of the chairs.

"What's this all about? I haven't done nothing wrong."

"Take a seat please, Mr Warner, this is just a private conversation."

Warner sat on the edge of the easy chair.

"You can't get me for anything. I've done my time."

"We don't want to 'get' you, Mr Warner. We just want to ask a few questions to help put our minds at rest about the Duke's safety. The Duchess has asked us to make enquiries."

"All right then."

Allerdyce unbuttoned his coat and took his notebook out of his jacket pocket.

"Mr Warner, would I be correct in assuming that, of all the servants at Dalcorn House, you are the one with the closest knowledge of His Grace's comings and goings?"

"Yes."

"When did you last see your employer?"

Warner paused for a second.

"Thursday evening. About quarter past seven o'clock. I had assisted His Grace in dressing for dinner, and laid out his bedclothes, and he dismissed me for the night."

"In what frame of mind was he?"

"Irritable. Quite normal."

"Can you think of any particular reason for his irritation?"

"His Grace has a quick temper with servants and women. He was annoyed that in inserting his collar stud I had pinched the skin on the back of his neck."

"Is that all? Had anything else happened during the course of the day to vex him, or to explain why he should choose to absent himself for three nights?"

"No." Warner's gaze shifted between the two policemen.

"Are you certain, Mr Warner? If your employer has come to any harm you may be invited to testify under oath in court. You wouldn't want to have been found to have withheld evidence, would you?"

"Do you think he's come to harm?"

"I didn't say so, Mr Warner, but I strongly advise you to tell us anything which may help us to find out."

Warner paused again before answering.

"There's one thing, but I don't think it's worth mentioning."

"Go on."

"A telegram arrived for him late in the afternoon which appeared to excite him somewhat."

"What did the telegram say?"

"I don't know. It arrived for him in a sealed envelope from the telegraph office, and I handed it to him unopened."

"What effect did it have on him?"

"A slightly queer effect. I saw him flush quite red and mop his forehead with his handkerchief as he leant against the mantelpiece of his study. He asked me to leave him."

"Do you have any idea who may have sent the telegram?"

"I said it was sealed. I don't know who it was from or what it said."

"Very interesting. And after the Duke dismissed you on Thursday evening when did you next look for him?"

Warner rubbed his chin and glanced at the floor before answering.

"On Friday morning at eight o'clock. I brought hot water and towels for shaving to his dressing room, then knocked on the door of his bedroom to inform him that I had done so. On hearing no answer I entered the bedroom to check whether he was present, and whether he had any needs."

"And, needless to say, he was not there."

"No."

"Were you surprised, Mr Warner?"

"No."

"Why not?"

"His Grace from time to time has pressing matters of business which require him, at short notice, to spend a night away from home."

"And you assumed that this was one such night."

"Yes."

"Did you think the telegram might be associated with his absence?"

"I don't know. I've told you, I don't know what was in it."

"And, Mr Warner, what do you know of the business which typically requires the Duke's sudden absence?"

Warner stood up.

"I don't know. I don't have to talk to you unless you have a signed warrant from a JP, do I?"

"No, this conversation is purely voluntary but it may be in your interests to assist us."

McGillivray stood up, towering over the valet. Warner walked over to the window. As he did so the sergeant stayed close to him, between the valet and the door.

Warner stared out at the parkland for a minute, then turned back to face the Inspector.

"Would you believe me if I said I knew nothing about the Duke's night visits to town?"

"No," said Allerdyce.

"But if I tell you anything I'll get sacked. I'll be thrown out with no character reference. I'd never be able to make an honest living again."

"Please, Mr Warner, sit down again. We have no interest in prejudicing your position. We are already aware from another party that the Duke has some sporting interests and some friends in the city that he likes to visit at night. We simply need some assistance in making enquiries at the places which he may have visited over the past three nights so that we can assure the Duchess of his safety. Can you tell us where these places are?"

"I could. But you'd never get in if they didn't know you. And if they smelled copper they'd knife you."

"Could you introduce us to these places, Mr Warner?"

"What's in it for me? They'd knife me if they knew I was introducing peelers."

"We might be able to offer an incentive. The Police Benevolent Fund could possibly stretch to £2."

"That's more interesting. But what if I don't?"

"There's a very large file of unsolved crimes in the basement of the City of Edinburgh Police headquarters. We also have an equally large file of known criminals, including former convicts whose sentences have been discharged. I'm sure we could find a crime which fits your skills perfectly."

Chapter 5

"I'm sorry Margaret, I have to go."

Margaret Allerdyce held baby Stephen to her shoulder, patting him gently on the back to help him release the trapped wind which was making him crotchety.

"You were out last night. You worked most of today. Now you're out again?"

"It's my duty Margaret. I have to."

"And what's so important that you have to spend Sunday night away from your family."

"It's a missing person. Quite an important one."

"Missing person? You didn't come to church with us this morning, you didn't get back from the Police Office until four o'clock, and now you're away again. Someone's more missing than that?"

"I don't want to go out. I'd stay at home if I could."

Margaret sighed and the baby gurgled.

"I know you would. I'm sorry. I just miss you. When do you think you'll be back?"

"I don't know. It could be quite late."

"If it's after ten o'clock I'd be grateful if you slept on the couch in the parlour. I'll have Millie make it up for you. The doctor's told me I need my rest, so I'd prefer not to be woken. I'm sorry."

"All right then."

"And Archibald, please look after yourself."

"I will."

She kissed him gently on the cheek. The baby started to cry again and Margaret turned away. Allerdyce watched as she slowly climbed the stairs, clutching the banister as if her legs didn't even have the strength to carry her frail body up to the landing.

Every day of his seven year marriage to Margaret he'd felt an impermanence, as if she might be torn away from him at any moment. Sometimes he'd almost persuaded himself that this was an irrationality, that she was young and healthy and he had no reason to fear. But now, watching how painfully slowly she was regaining her strength after the baby's birth, he knew it was permanance that was the illusion. In a vast, cold, chaotic universe of unimaginable force there was no reason why she shouldn't be carried off on any arbitrary day or hour, as suddenly and cruelly as Helen.

He also knew – and this chilled him even as he was pulling on his overcoat – that it would hurt less this time. There was something in him which had frozen on that winter's day in the cemetery, when he'd said his farewells to his first wife and to the God who'd let her die. Yes, he could say he loved Margaret and the children but there was some part of him, the part that had felt the keenest joy and the deepest sorrow, that had gone. He wished – he almost prayed – that he could feel the pain again, so that he could be released from a life of duty back into the agonies of love.

But right now, tonight, his duty was absolute. Find the Duke or face the consequences.

He opened the door and stepped onto the gas-lit pavement, pulling up his collar and turning his steps towards the East End.

...

Warner had chosen the Black Bull as a meeting place. It was set into cellars at the foot of Calton Hill, the darkness of the street made more profound by the great archway above it which carried the broad highway of Waterloo Place eastwards.

Allerdyce had to take his hat off to get through the low door. He'd left the bowler at home in preference for a shabby top-hat which he hoped would make him look like a gentleman who was out for an evening of dissolution. He'd put a black cloak on over his dark suit.

As he went down the steps into the public house he was assaulted by the stench of smoke, beer, whisky and vomit. He felt his boots sink into the damp sawdust on the floor.

He scanned the room, straining to see in the feeble light of the few gas jets which were set into the wall. The cellar was divided into high-sided wooden booths so that customers could conduct their business, whether criminal or sexual, in private. On the far side of the room, his eyes were drawn to the vast white bosom which spilled from the décolletage of the middle-aged landlady.

He looked into the first booth, where four men sat playing cards, with stacks of coins and a bottle of whisky on the table. One of them looked up at him and folded his hand of cards shut.

"Jesus, Inspector, what are you doing here?"

Allerdyce recognised 'Sharp' Blaikie, who he'd had to arrest three times for running illegal gambling a bit too openly.

"Nothing that need concern you, Mr Blaikie."

"I'm playing an honest game, Inspector. 52 cards to the pack, each and every one of them different. You can check them if you like."

"And I suppose the money on the table is just to buy the next round of drinks?"

"That's exactly right, Inspector."

"All right then, Blaikie, I never saw you here tonight."

"God bless you, sir."

Allerdyce looked into the next booth, where two young women in fashionable dresses were sitting with two men in evening dress. One of the women was vigorously kissing her man, while even in the dim lamplight Allerdyce could see her hand reaching into his trouser pocket for his wallet. The other took a swig from the bottle of champagne on the table with one hand while the other hand was hidden inside the fly-buttons of her partner, who lay back staring at the ceiling and groaning quietly. She looked round.

"Here, what are you staring at, you dirty bugger? Fuck off out of here."

"My apologies, madam."

He moved onto the next booth, and was relieved to see Warner and McGillivray already sat there, a pitcher of beer between them. The valet was still in the same clothes he'd been wearing earlier, minus the collar and tie. The sergeant was dressed as an artisan, wearing a blue canvas jacket over a collarless shirt of striped calico, and a red silk kerchief round his neck.

Allerdyce sat down on the wooden bench and Warner poured him a glass of beer.

"I'd drink to your good health," said Warner, "if I thought I could guarantee it tonight."

Warner looked the Inspector up and down.

"You'll do. You don't look too obviously like a pig, and your man looks all right. You'll be safe enough here, which is why I chose it. But you're going to have to be very careful in some of the places we're going to."

"Mr Warner has just been explaining the circumstances of his employment with the Duke," said McGillivray.

"I'm a good valet," said Warner. "I do my job as well as any man. But that wasn't entirely why the Duke appointed me."

"Go on," said Allerdyce, taking a mouthful of the bitter brown beer.

"He was looking for someone who could show him places that excited him, and arrange for him to meet people who could oblige his needs. He wanted me because I know my way around."

"Meaning?"

"Look, Inspector, you already know I've been in trouble. I used to manage the business interests of some ladies of pleasure – I did it fairly and the ladies were well rewarded for their work, but it's the sort of thing the law doesn't like. It's an enterprise where you learn all sorts of things about where to find your enjoyments in the city, and about the people who are looking for them. The Duke learnt that a friend of his was employing me as a valet, and that I was discreetly helping his friend to meet his needs. So he offered me more money than his friend was prepared to pay, and I went to work for him."

"So, you're his accomplice in his visits to Edinburgh on 'urgent business'? Why weren't you with him on Thursday night?"

"I don't have to be. I've shown him where to go, and now he's known in these places he can go when he likes. He doesn't need me unless I find out about some new entertainment he might enjoy, or unless he wants me to procure company for him and arrange a private appointment."

"So, you're going to take us to the places he frequents and maybe we'll find him?"

"I don't know, Inspector. It's not like him to go on a bender for three nights. You might find someone who's seen him, but I don't think you're going to find the Duke."

Allerdyce drained his beer and wiped his mouth with his handkerchief.

"The quicker we get going the better chance we may have of finding him," he said.

"All right then. But don't forget I'm taking a risk. I could get chivved for being with you. I need the two guineas you promised me, payment in advance."

"It's two pounds Warner, and cash on delivery. You get paid when we've found the Duke, or found out what's happened to him."

"Bloody hell, you peelers are the biggest crooks around."

. . .

The three of them shared a cab down Leith Walk, Allerdyce and Warner crammed on either side of the sergeant's bulk. The driver stopped at the Foot of the Walk, where the broad thoroughfare stopped and narrow lanes led between warehouses and tenements towards the dockyards.

The driver opened the sliding hatch into the cab's interior.

"I don't go beyond here at night," he said. "You'll have to walk."

Allerdyce paid him and stepped out into the cold. Down here, close to the sea, the gaslights struggled to shine through a damp mist.

"All right," said Warner, "here's the deal. I can get you into the Duke's favourite places, but I can't stay in there with you. If the Duke sees me with you I'm fired, and if your cover's blown I could be dead. What's your cover story?"

"I'm the manager of a brewery out looking for some sport, and the sergeant here is one of my draymen whom I've brought along for protection."

"That'll have to do, but watch your backs."

They crossed the road and went down a narrow lane which descended gently. They passed closed shops, and public houses from which singing and fighting could be heard. A drunk staggered out from the door of one of them and barged into Allerdyce, staring at him with confused hostility until the sergeant pushed the man out of the way and he tumbled helplessly to the ground. Soon, the dark bulk of the parish church of South Leith crouched against the night to their right, and Allerdyce heard the shrieking of drunken women from the graveyard. As he walked further into the darkness he clung to the knowledge that every pace was bringing him marginally closer to Royal Burgh of Leith police station, at Queen Charlotte Street.

"Down here," said Warner, indicating a darker, narrower lane which led off to the left.

Allerdyce followed the valet. The lane led away from safety in the direction of the Water of Leith, the filthy river which ebbed, near-stagnant, into the docks, bearing the effluent of the mills which had exhausted its power. Even here, Allerdyce could smell its sulphurous miasma, unless the smell was coming from the tenements which crowded four storeys above him, linked by washing lines from which sheets and rags hung limply in the night. As they walked along, he noticed that some of the windows of the crowded houses still had glass, while others were blocked up with paper or the wood from packing cases.

There were plenty of slums in the City of Edinburgh, and Allerdyce was familiar with every close and rookery of them. But here, across the Leith town boundary and in another jurisdiction, everything was tinged with alienness. His instinct for what streets a man could walk down in relative safety was disoriented, and when he looked at a passing rough he couldn't know whether he was a wanted criminal, a trusted informer, or simply a working man making his way home from the public house.

Warner turned right into a narrow close. Allerdyce and McGillivray followed him down the narrow passage into a courtyard, surrounded by tall buildings on each side. A low building, with a brightly-lit door, jutted into the courtyard from the far side.

"McGuigan's Sporting Arena," said Warner. "It's worth a try."

Warner spoke to the rough on the door and returned to the policemen.

"All right, you're in. It's a shilling each, payable at the door, and you'll be expected to buy a drink. And don't forget you're not looking for the Duke of Dornoch. He travels under the name of Willie Burns when he's in town at night."

"Well, Sergeant," said Allerdyce, "will you come with me? I needn't remind you of the circumstances of your predecessor's dismissal."

"You can't dismiss a brewer's drayman for having a pint," said the sergeant.

"Excellent."

Allerdyce paid the doorman for both of them, and they went down a narrow passage lined with posters for past sporting events. He could hear shouts from a crowd inside. "Come on, Griffin! Kill them all!"

The end of the passage opened into a large room. Allerdyce found himself looking down into a pit, in which a bull terrier was chasing rats against the wooden surrounds. Around the pit, in tiers like the anatomy demonstration room at the University, the crowd sat on wooden benches. The pit was illuminated from above by an eight-armed gas lamp. Beyond the pit and the seating a bar ran across the back wall of the room.

A bell rang and a man in the front row reached forward, lifted the dog up by its collar, and slapped it hard across its haunches.

"You have to do better than that, you useless cur."

The dog yelped as the man shoved it down behind the pit's surround.

"This is bigger than any dog-pit in Edinburgh," said Allerdyce, straining his voice above the boos of the crowd.

"Yes, sir."

"I think we'd better get some drinks, in the interests of authenticity."

The crowd in the benches was thinning as men made their way to the bar at the end of the bout. McGillivray led the way in pushing through the bodies to make way for him and Allerdyce to get to the bar. As they negotiated their way through the crush Allerdyce noticed the variety of humanity which had been drawn to the pit. Gentlemen jostled with navvies. A party of red-tuniced soldiers had already reached the bar, some of them with their arms round cheaply-dressed women. To his left, he could hear sailors conversing in a foreign language which could be Danish or Norwegian. Ahead of him, an Irishman with a stout mongrel at his heels was demanding whisky.

When they reached the front of the crush Allerdyce ordered two whiskies and passed one to the sergeant.

The bell rang again, and the master of ceremonies called out from the centre of the pit.

"Ladies and gentlemen, please place your bets for the most anticipated bout of the evening. Champion ratter 'Tiny', newly arrived from Aberdeen, will attempt to kill fifty brown rats, specially brought in from the countryside, within the space of five minutes. If he succeeds, his owner will be presented with this splendid silver collar. If you believe this dog – a champion at sporting arenas throughout the country – will succeed, place your bets now."

"I suppose we ought to place a bet," said Allerdyce, "to avoid being conspicuous."

"Definitely, sir."

"What do you think of the dog?"

"Looks like a good prospect to me, sir."

They had to wait again as the crowd members pushed forward to the betting table which had been set up in the pit. Eventually Allerdyce found his way to the front.

"A shilling on Tiny, please."

"A wise investment," said the master of ceremonies, pocketing the money, "and a pleasure to welcome a new gentleman to the arena."

McGillivray put fourpence on the dog to win and they took their places on the bench second-nearest the front. The benches gradually filled as the crowd finished their betting. A tattooed man with a bloody apron hammered the surviving rats from the previous bout with his spade, then scooped them up into a sack with the rats the dog had killed, before spreading fresh sawdust over the blood.

A man looking like a down-at-heel farmer stepped into the ring, holding a Jack Russell by the collar.

"Ladies and gentlemen," said the master of ceremonies, "please welcome Tiny's second, Lucy."

The farmer tied the Jack Russell by a short leash to a post in the centre of the pit then stepped back out again. A boy stepped in, holding a hessian sack by the neck. The sack seemed to be heaving and squirming of its own accord. The boy opened the sack and tipped the rats onto the sawdust.

"Here," said one of the soldiers, "how do we know that's fifty rats? You could have slipped a few extra into that sack for all we know."

"This sporting arena has always been known for honesty and probity," said the master of ceremonies, "and if you wish to enter the ring and count them you are welcome to do so."

"All right, just get on with it," said the soldier.

The rats momentarily sat dazed on the sawdust before seeing the dog tied in the middle. They scurried to the sides of the pit, climbing up on each other in little heaps which kept rearranging themselves as rats tried to climb to the top of the heap, only to be clambered over by their rivals for survival. The Jack Russell barked and strained at its leash.

Allerdyce scanned the faces of the crowd. He'd seen the Duke's portrait in Dalcorn House, and had a photograph of the Duke in his pocket. Every possible facial type seemed to be represented among the men sitting and shouting on the benches, clean-shaven, sideboarded or bearded; every hue from workmens' nut-brown weatherbeatenness to the pallor of late-stage tuberculosis; every gradation from sobriety to near-paralytic drunkenness. But no-one had exactly the white hair, jowly face, and mouth twisted by permanent contempt which was apparent from the images of the missing Duke.

The farmer now brought a brown-and-white Staffordshire bull terrier into the ring. Its tongue lolled lazily from its mouth.

"Ladies and gentlemen," said the master of ceremonies, "please welcome Champion Tiny."

The farmer placed Tiny on the sawdust and the men stepped out of the pit. The dog sat down for a second and scratched its ear with its back paw.

"Get on with it, for Jesus' sake," shouted the soldier. "I've got a guinea on you!"

The Jack Russell was now straining and barking in the direction of the Staffordshire. Tiny stood up, yawned, and sauntered over in the direction of a pile of rats. As he approached the pile the rats dispersed to either side.

"That dog's been doped!" shouted the soldier.

Tiny looked up in the direction of the man who was shouting. He stretched his paws in front of him, yawned again, and looked from side to side at the rats. The Jack Russell yelped incessantly at him.

Damn, thought Allerdyce, that's another shilling wasted.

Without warning Tiny ran hard against the wooden side of the pit. The impact of the dog's head against the wood sounded like someone had struck it with a mallet. When the dog turned round he had a rat between his teeth. He shook it from side to side then let it drop, looking for the next victim.

The rats were cowering, more thinly distributed now, against the bottom of the wood. Tiny started to chase them round and round the ring, doubling back on himself every few seconds, each time catching a rat who'd failed to turn quickly enough. One by one he massacred them, the white patches on his muzzle turning bloody.

"That's more like it!" shouted the soldier above the cries of the crowd.

The rats were thinning out now. Only about twenty survived. As if by common agreement they changed their tactic, dispersing themselves thinly over the floor of the pit, except where they were in range of the yapping and snarling Jack Russell.

The tactic failed. Tiny stopped and looked around, before choosing a particular rat, launching himself at it with an explosive burst of his bulky muscles. Despite his bulk, he could twist and turn to match any rat and soon another handful were dead on the sawdust, a couple of them still with limbs twitching desperately despite their broken backs.

Allerdyce fingered the change in his pockets, anticipating his winnings. Maybe he could treat Alice to the special edition of the *Water Babies* with coloured engravings.

Pay attention, he thought. You're not here to enjoy yourself. You're here to find a missing person. He turned his attention away from the ring and back to the crowd. For an instant, his eyes met those of man he hadn't seen before. He nudged the sergeant.

"Look, over there. Far side of the ring. Do you think it could be him?"

"Where, sir?"

"About five rows back. Seven people in from the right."

"Hard to say, sir. Might be."

"Keep an eye on him. Best be discreet – we'll try to get him at the end of the bout. But if he makes a move before that we'll have to catch him."

He looked back at the carnage in the ring. The surviving rats appeared to look at each other before reverting to forming a single writhing pile against the wood. Tiny launched again and again into the pile, each time pulling out a single rat, crushing it in his jaws, and tossing it aside.

Finally only one living rat, a thin black creature whose rapid breaths were visible in its sides, faced Tiny. Tiny launched himself against the wood at it, but the rat jumped up and seized the dog's muzzle. It sank its teeth into Tiny's nose and blood flowed down. Its front claws clung to the dog's cheeks while its rear feet and tail swung from side to side as the dog shook its head to dislodge the rat, banging his head against the wood.

"Here," shouted the farmer, "get that rat away from my dog. It's not a farm rat, it's a sewer rat! It'll give him blood poisoning!"

The rat clung on as the Staffordshire tried to paw it off. The Jack Russell barked and jumped, pulled back to the centre of the ring by his leash.

The bell rang and the master of ceremonies stepped back into the ring.

"Ladies and gentlemen, after a fair fight I declare that Champion Tiny has failed to clear the ring of fifty rats in the prescribed time. All bets are forfeit."

Blast, thought Allerdyce.

The crowd booed. The farmer stepped into the ring to retrieve the Staffordshire. He seized the rat with a leather-gloved fist and crushed the life out of it.

"That wasn't a fair fight!" shouted the soldier. "That was a dirty rat!"

"He's standing up, sir," whispered the sergeant. "I think there's about to be trouble. Better try and apprehend him now."

The policemen slipped out of the benches and went over to the bar. A handful of other customers were making their way to the bar too, but most of the crowd stood behind the soldier and his mates, who were arguing with the master of ceremonies to get their bets back.

The white-haired jowly man had nearly reached the bar when McGillivray seized his shoulder from behind. He turned to face Allerdyce.

"Are you the Duke of Dornoch, going by the alias of Mr Willie Burns," asked Allerdyce.

As Allerdyce waited for an answer his heart sank. Surely the Duke couldn't have sunk so low, his eyes glazed, his mouth half-open with stinking breath, phlegm caked in the bristles of his unshaven chin?

"Sir, I must ask for an answer. The whereabouts of His Grace is a matter of substantial concern."

The man opened his mouth as if to speak, exposing the rotting black stumps of his teeth, then threw up gently over his chin and threadbare frock-coat.

"Not our man?" asked the sergeant.

"Don't think so. Let's just check with the barman."

The man staggered as McGillivray propelled him towards the bar.

"Do you recognise this man?" asked Allerdyce.

"Never seen him before, sir," said the barman. "I'll have him thrown out if he's bothering you."

60

"No. It's all right. Would you recognise a Mr Willie Burns?"

"Certainly sir. A most sporting gentleman. I thought he'd have come to Tiny's bout but there's been no sign of him."

There was a shout from the pit and Allerdyce looked round to see that the master of ceremonies had been pushed to the floor and the soldiers were holding him down while the punters recovered their money. The man with the shovel was coming up behind the crowd. As Allerdyce watched, he started to lay about the crowd with the spade to try and reach the prostrate MC.

"Come on," he said to McGillivray, "I think we're finished here."

The policemen left the vomiting drunk leaning against the bar and slipped back out along the corridor, having to push themselves against the wall as the doorman rushed in to join the trouble. As they reached the darkness of the courtyard they could still hear the mayhem behind them.

Warner was waiting, smoking a cigarette.

"Is that all your fault?" he asked, nodding towards the arena.

"No," said Allerdyce, "it's a purely sporting disagreement."

"Glad to hear it."

"So where do you suggest we look next?"

"Just follow me."

Chapter 6

They went back through the vennel into the narrow street and turned right, towards the river. After a few minutes they found themselves standing on The Shore.

Allerdyce looked up and down the cobbled, dimly-lit street. Warehouses stood darkly in the night at either side of the stagnant tidal river which formed Leith's inner harbour. The darkness was interspersed with bright light from public houses, from which he could hear shouting and singing, and the feeble glow from the windows of the tenements which were crammed in beside the warehouses. The tide was out, and he could see the dark silhouettes of small ships resting on the tidal mud, their masts tilting at crazy angles as the boats leant against the harbour wall. He thought they looked like creatures out of their element, like the fish he'd seen caught by rod and line which were left to flail and suffocate in the poisonous air.

The stench was worse here, a toxic mixture of industrial effluent, faeces and rotting seaweed. The smell of crime, thought Allerdyce, breathing deeply. This is the manure which feeds it.

They turned right again, walking along the street towards the docks and the sea. After a few paces they stopped at a closed door with a lamp above it. Allerdyce squinted in the lamplight to read the sign by the door.

'Mrs Allingham's model lodging house for ladies. Hourly rates available.'

"I'd better check inside here myself," said Warner.

"Very well," said Allerdyce.

"I'll need to give the proprietrix a small gift if she's to help. Five shillings should do it."

"Go ahead."

"I haven't got five shillings on me, Inspector. You'll have to help."

"Oh very well. But it's on account." Allerdyce fished the coins out and gave them to Warner.

"Mean bugger."

Warner disappeared into the lodging house. Allerdyce and McGillivray stood under the lamp, rubbing their hands and shifting from foot to foot to stave of the night's chill. Allerdyce took his pipe out of his pocket and lit it.

What would Margaret think, he wondered, as he drew on the pipe. What would she think if she knew the sordidness he saw daily, if she knew that he came back to her from the depths of poverty and depravity?

And what will Burgess think if we can't find the Duke? The tobacco momentarily tasted bitter as he thought about the recriminations which would follow failure. It was absurd that he was being held responsible for a missing husband, but he'd pay for it if the old bastard wasn't found soon.

A scantily-dressed woman, in a ballgown with a fur-edged cloak wrapped loosely round her shoulders, came along the pavement from the docks. She stood under the lamplight, and Allerdyce noticed that the thickly-caked make-up on her face had started to crack.

"Good evening, gentlemen," she said, fluttering long false eyelashes at Allerdyce, "won't you come in out of the cold."

"Not tonight, thank you, madam," said Allerdyce.

"But you're both so handsome in your own ways. I've entertained two gentlemen at the same time before, you know. Or is the big one just your minder? We can leave him out here if you want."

"I'm sorry, madam," said Allerdyce, "We are simply waiting for a friend."

"Well move along a bit then," said the woman. "It's bad for trade having you hanging round the front door like policemen."

McGillivray coughed as the woman disappeared into the lodging house. Allerdyce checked his watch.

"Warner's been in there a while," said the sergeant.

"About eight minutes."

"Can't take him that long to make enquiries. Do you think we should go in and check? He might have scarpered out the back door."

"Give him another couple of minutes," said Allerdyce.

They hung around for another few minutes, Allerdyce drawing on the warm pipe smoke. Eventually Warner emerged.

"I've been thorough," said Warner. "The proprietrix hadn't seen His Grace since last weekend, and I was fortunate that his favourite girl was in and didn't have a visitor. I was able to interview her and she gave the same story."

An in-depth interview, thought Allerdyce, saying nothing.

"There's another haunt along here that's worth a try," said Warner.

They walked on, crossing a wide street beside a lifting bridge, before turning under a low arch into a warren of sheds and workshops.

"The Timberbush," said Warner. "There's a public house in here which His Lordship sometimes favours."

They came to a bright doorway above which a sign proclaimed 'The Sailor's Arms' with a picture of a muscled mariner.

"There used to be a glass window," said Warner, "but it got smashed so often that they bricked it up."

"A bit rough, is it?" asked Allerdyce.

"I'd prefer not to accompany you inside, if that's all right."

Warner spoke to the doorman who, despite the cold, was wearing only a sailor's white canvas trousers and short-sleeved top. The doorman nodded.

"You're in," said Warner. "I'll wait for you. Best not to stay in there too long."

Allerdyce squeezed past the doorman, followed by the sergeant. His first impression was of the humidity and noise of the place as he tried to edge his way towards the bar. His ears tried to tune into the different conversations as he pushed his way through the crowd, but the wheezing of an accordion and the scratching of a fiddle at the far end of the room, and the tuneless singing coming from there, made it all the more difficult. Even when he could tune in on individual voices in the general clamour he was little better off. He listened uncomprehendingly to a broad voice with long open vowels before realising that the man was speaking English in the Norse accent of Shetland. Other voices were Scandinavian, Dutch or German, with some stranger tongues which he guessed were from the further reaches of the Baltic. Occasional sentences of English would float above the aural Babel.

Looking around, he saw that while most of the clients were in the simple outfits of sailors or stevedores there were a handful of gentlemen. As he reached the bar he looked to the right and his eye briefly caught the squinting gaze of a moustached gentleman in evening dress, his arm round the waist of slim, blond young man in a white calico shirt.

Damn, thought Allerdyce, it's Jarvis. By some bizarre misfortune Inspector Jarvis of the City of Edinburgh Police, the man who'd informed on Sergeant Baird and who 'always got his man' whether or not the accused was innocent, was in the same bar at the same time.

Allerdyce turned round to McGillivray.

"Get out of here now," whispered Allerdyce. "It's for your own safety. I'll explain later."

"No," said McGillivray, standing still behind Allerdyce.

"Please, just go," said Allerdyce. "You could lose your job if you stay. I can make enquiries on my own."

"Sir," whispered McGillivray, "I believe you may be in grave danger here. I choose to stay."

Allerdyce looked along the bar. Jarvis had disappeared, but he couldn't be far away.

He ordered two whiskies and passed one back to the sergeant.

"I'm looking for Willie Burns," he shouted to the barman. "I was told I might find him here."

The barman winked at him peculiarly, then glanced at a sailor who was standing three places along to the left at the bar, his tattooed arm muscles bulging prominently below the short sleeves of his sailor's shirt.

The sailor pressed his way through the crush to stand alongside Allerdyce. He put his arm around Allerdyce's waist.

"Looking for Willie Burns are you?"

"Yes."

Allerdyce tried to shift his body from the sailor's grip, but found himself clasped tighter.

"You're in the right place. There's a lot of gentlemen looking for willie here and you've just found it."

He kissed Allerdyce on the cheek.

"For a guinea you can have whatever you like, all night. I'm yours."

"You misunderstand me," said Allerdyce, struggling against the sailor's vice-like grip.

McGillivray was standing immediately behind the sailor. He put his arm around the sailor's neck and squeezed. Allerdyce heard a throttled sound from the sailor's throat and felt a haze of spittle on his face. The sailor fell gasping to the floor.

Allerdyce felt his arms clasped by McGillivray and his feet lifted from the floor as the sergeant pushed him through the crowd towards the door. He was thrust past the doorman into the darkness and landed at Warner's feet.

"I did try to warn you," said Warner as Allerdyce picked himself out of the dirt.

McGillivray had turned back. He pushed the doorman aside and stood in the doorway as the sailor, now with a bottle in his hand, rushed at him. He waited until the sailor was practically upon him before punching him hard in the face, sending him flying back into the crowded bar.

"Run, sir," said the sergeant, coming back into the darkness.

"Follow me," said Warner.

As they started to run, going back through the arch and onto the Shore, they heard angry voices behind them. They doubled left then right, before Warner led them up some tenement stairs.

"Where are you taking us?" gasped Allerdyce.

"I don't think they saw us come up here," panted Warner. "I think they'll run past."

"I hope you're right."

McGillivray stationed himself below them on the narrow stairs. The angry voices below them grew louder, then more distant. Allerdyce found himself starting to breathe more easily.

"Do I get my two pounds now?" asked Warner.

Allerdyce's look was entirely wasted on the valet in the darkness.

Chapter 7

Allerdyce had only been at work for ten minutes, his head aching from last night's drinking and his shoulder and back aching from a night spent twisting and turning on the sofa after being thrown out of the public house, when he was summoned to see Burgess.

As he entered the Superintendent's office he wondered whether Jarvis had already spoken to him. Maybe he was about to be dismissed as summarily as Sergeant Baird.

He stood in front of the great teak desk while the Superintendent sat with his head in his hands looking at some papers. His face was invisible, apart from the lined forehead which receded back towards his tight black curls. After thirty seconds Burgess looked up at him, and Allerdyce saw his superior's face, its complexion ruddier than he had ever seen it.

"The Duke of Dornoch," said Burgess.

"Yes, sir."

"Have we found him yet?"

"No sir. I spent yesterday making enquiries and have found some leads. As yet, I have not physically located the missing person."

"Missing person? Blast, Allerdyce, can't you just leave your misplaced egalitarianism out of this? We are looking for the richest man in Scotland, a personal friend of the Lord Advocate, the Secretary for Scotland, the Chief Constable, and of anyone else who may choose to kick us arse over tip down the Canongate if he comes to any harm. He's not just a missing person, he's our personal nemesis if we don't find him."

"I will be pursuing further enquiries today, sir."

"You bloody better had. I've already had a message this morning from the Duchess enquiring about our progress. I don't have much to say to her, do I?"

"You can say that we conducted enquiries right into the night."

"I suppose that's something. If you can find the old sod I don't care how you do it."

"I appreciate that, sir."

"If anyone can find him, Allerdyce, I believe you can. But God help us all if he comes to any harm."

Dismissed, Allerdyce walked back to his room. His relief that Burgess had done no worse than bark at him faded when he saw Inspector Jarvis standing in the corridor.

"Come into my office for a second," said Jarvis.

Allerdyce went in. Jarvis checked up and down the corridor to see whether anyone else was around then entered and shut the door. The two men stood facing each other.

Allerdyce felt his pulse race. If the Chief Constable thought either he or Jarvis were frequenting places of ill repute – on the Sabbath of all days – without good cause they'd be finished. He tried to calm his breathing, reasoning that Jarvis was the one who should worry since he didn't have any obvious police reason for being in the sailors' bar. But it felt as if each of them had their hands round the other's neck.

"I don't think we need to say any more about last night, do we, Allerdyce?"

"No."

"I was conducting a clandestine investigation, of course. I presume that you and your man were doing likewise."

That'll be right thought Allerdyce, remembering Jarvis's embrace of the blond youth.

"Yes."

"So we understand each other then, Allerdyce? In the current climate merely visiting such places on business can give rise to mistaken inferences. But we can't all afford to be holy if we're going to do this job. Neither of us will have any occasion to mention it to the Chief, will we?"

"No, Jarvis."

"Fine. I appreciate your discretion. It's so important that we can trust each other."

Jarvis opened the door and Allerdyce left. Going down the corridor he looked back and saw that Jarvis was standing looking at him. Trust, he thought. Not a word that sits easily with Inspector Allan Jarvis.

He walked down the stairs into the duty room. Sergeant McGillivray was sitting in uniform at his small desk. Three constables were hanging around waiting for their orders – one of them sitting on a hard chair reading a newspaper, another polishing his boots and a third studying the noticeboard. At the far side of the room the desk sergeant, Henderson, was leaning against the public counter filling in a ledger while he waited for business.

"A word in my office please, Sergeant McGillivray."

"Yes, sir."

The sergeant followed him back up the stairs to Allerdyce's

cramped office. Allerdyce shimmied neatly between the filing cabinets and his desk and sat down. The sergeant stood to attention on the other side.

"Please, Sergeant, take a seat."

"Thank you, sir."

"And thank you, Sergeant, for your courage last night."

"No more than my duty, sir."

"But our Duke is still missing."

"I was thinking, sir. If we could find the telegram which the Duke received before he disappeared we might learn something."

"Yes. I was thinking the same."

"Failing that, sir, I suppose we'll have to spend another night in bad company in Leith."

"Perhaps, Sergeant. But before we pursue either course there is one other enquiry I want to make."

"What's that, sir?"

"I'm afraid it's an enquiry I have to make entirely alone."

...

Allerdyce got down from the omnibus at Stockbridge. He looked over his shoulder as the driver whipped the horses and the wheels rumbled away over the cobbles. There was no reason why anyone should be following him, but the chance encounter with Jarvis last night had shaken him. He was relieved to see no-one he recognised.

He crossed the Water of Leith – running fresh and clear here as it tumbled out of the Dean gorge three miles upstream from the mills and harbour of Leith – and walked under the trees of its left bank for a hundred yards before turning into the handsome

Regency terrace of Danube Street. Each house proclaimed wealth and respectability from its sober, classically-proportioned frontage, but Allerdyce knew that at least one of the front doors, its brassware gleaming like its neighbours', hid a secret life.

His hand was shaking as he pulled the doorbell. Every time he came here he felt himself drawn back towards those awful months after Helen had gone, when he'd doubted whether he was in fact sane. But, by some luck or miracle, his visits here had started a healing which would never be complete but which had at least stopped him from losing his mind.

After a few moments the maid opened the door.

"Mr Allerdyce? We weren't expecting you."

"I'm sorry to disturb you. Is Miss Antonia at home? I need to speak to her."

"Yes, I'll let her know you're here."

The maid asked him to sit in the parlour while she went upstairs to announce Allerdyce. He sat in the familiar chair beside the brandy decanter, looking up at the same paintings of nude gods and goddesses, and entwined nymphs and satyrs, which had blended themselves into his dreams and nightmares when he'd first come here. Even the smell – a rich blend of *pot-pourri*, polished mahogany and faintly lingering cigar smoke – was as it had been then.

"Miss Antonia is ready to receive you in her boudoir," said the maid.

"Thank you."

He went up the stairs, feeling the deep red pile of the carpet springing under his feet, and along the landing to Antonia's room. As he stood at her door he inhaled the unique blend of wood-polish and musky perfume and felt his pulse quicken. He knocked gently and let himself in.

Antonia was sitting in front of the mirror at her dressing table, tossing the long curls of her blonde hair over her shoulders as she dabbed perfume under her ears. A book was open in front of her. She had an embroidered silk Chinese dressing gown on, birds and the figures of little men against a sky-blue background. The gown fell loosely open at her throat, exposing the dark golden cleavage which disappeared into the lacy whiteness of her undergarment.

Allerdyce reflected on how seldom he'd seen her in daylight. The cold winter light from the lace-curtained window showed the shadows of lines which were masked by the amber lighting she used in the evening, and her face seemed a little thinner, but overall the nine years of their acquaintance had been kind to her. She turned to him and smiled.

"Archibald! An unexpected pleasure!"

"I'm sorry to disturb you, Antonia."

"Not at all, Archibald. I was worried, you know."

"Worried?"

"When you didn't come to see me after your Speculative Society dinner. I'd been looking forward to seeing you, but I thought something must have happened to you."

"Some sudden business came up. I'd have sent my apologies if I could."

She stood up and took his hands.

"I know you would, Archie, But I do rely on you to keep me in touch with the great current of ideas. You have no idea how isolated a woman in my position can feel from intellectual life. Come and sit by the fire."

They sat in silk armchairs at either side of the hearth. Allerdyce was uncomfortably conscious of Antonia's large white-linened bed in the corner of the room, the bedclothes turned down to show the plump white pillows. It was years since he had lain there, not since those weeks of madness, but the temptation was still strong. There was no absolute moral reason why he shouldn't yield, no vigilant and narrow-minded God who'd punish him, but his duty to Margaret was clear. It would also feel like a betrayal of Antonia – he told himself that they had discovered in each other a shared interest in the life of the mind and that it was through sustaining her in that intellectual life that he could best support her as a friend. It was almost like being a missionary for his sex, trying to show that a man could have a relationship with a woman which was neither carnal nor domestic. If he could hold to that belief he could persuade himself that continuing to see Antonia was the right and dutiful thing to do, but it didn't feel sufficiently right that he could ever tell Margaret about it.

"I ought to say," added Antonia, "that I have a gentleman caller due in twenty-five minutes. I'd like to see you for longer, but I'm afraid this will have to be a rather short conversation."

"That's all right."

"So how was the dinner? You told me that Alexander Bain was going to be speaking on criminal psychology. I was looking forward to hearing about it."

"I didn't go."

"That's a shame."

"I know. He's done some brilliant work. He's bringing together social influences, observed behaviours and phrenological analysis to create a typology of crime. If he's right, we'll be able to diagnose the criminal character in early youth and treat – even remedy it – accordingly."

"Phrenology?" Antonia giggled behind her hand.

"I know, practically everyone thought it was bunkum when I was at medical school."

"Maybe they changed their minds later? I mean, after you'd had to leave."

"It's more recent than that. There's been a lot of work to systematise it and relate it to what happens to patients when particular parts of their brains are destroyed by injury or disease. Bain's even persuaded John Stuart Mill that the science is sound."

"A persuasive gentleman then. Something important must have happened to tear you away from hearing him."

"That's what I wanted to ask you about, Antonia. I was just getting ready to go when I was called to the Chief Constable's house and told to look for a disappearing Duke. His wife is worried that he's been away from home for a few days, and the Chief thinks it's a matter of importance to the State that we find him."

"Not quite your usual calibre of business, Archie. One man temporarily missing, no-one injured."

"I know. Frankly, I resent being used as a private detective for the aristocracy. But the fact is he's still missing. I've tried to track him down in the disreputable haunts he's known to have frequented, but no-one's seen him. I don't think he wants to be found."

"And so you thought you'd ask me? In case he'd visited this 'disreputable haunt'?" Antonia pulled her gown more tightly around her.

"I have to ask you, Antonia. It's important."

Antonia looked straight at him, her lips thin and her delicate hands clenched in her lap.

"It hurts me, Archibald. It hurts me because it exposes the inequality in our friendship. You're a policeman, I'm a whore. You could have me closed down or arrested if you chose. I want to be your friend, Archie, not your informer."

"I'm sorry I asked."

"But you'll be in bad trouble if you don't find this Duke?"

"Yes."

"All right then. I'll help if I can. Who is it?"

"William Bothwell-Scott. The Duke of Dornoch."

Antonia breathed in sharply. She was holding her hands together, thought Allerdyce, as if she was trying to stop them from shaking. She stood up and went over to the window, the light bleaching the goldenness of her complexion. Allerdyce stood and went over to her.

"Are you all right, Antonia?"

She turned and smiled thinly at him.

"Yes, Archie, quite all right."

"I thought you shuddered."

"Sometimes I wish you were a less acute student of human nature, Archibald. I confess that that name caused me a moment of pain."

"May I ask why?"

"It is a pain which I buried long ago and which I have no wish to resurrect. But in answer to your immediate question, I have no knowledge of the gentleman's recent whereabouts."

"I'm sorry to have upset you."

She touched him gently on the arm.

"You were only doing your duty, Archie. But please, leave me to compose myself before my next visitor arrives. And Archie, next time you come please come as my friend and not as a policeman."

Chapter 8

Allerdyce and McGillivray shared a second-class compartment on the Edinburgh to Queensferry train. The Inspector opened the window a few inches to let his pipe smoke out and to breathe in the fresh air, but as they went through the Haymarket tunnel more steam and smoke leaked in than out. He coughed and wiped a fleck of soot from his eye as the train pulled into Haymarket Station.

"Did you find anything out, sir?" asked the sergeant.

"Pardon?"

"From your private enquiries?"

Allerdyce blinked hard, his eye still watering from the soot.

"No, Sergeant. It was a false lead."

"Bad luck, sir."

Allerdyce wiped the black fleck from his finger onto his handkerchief.

"Inspector Jarvis caught sight of us in the bar at the Timberbush," he said.

"That's very unfortunate, sir."

"He says he was there on police business. He assured me he would say nothing to the Chief."

"That's good, for what it's worth, sir."

"You don't trust his word?"

"I would trust the word of any man who had earned it," said McGillivray. "It's no secret, sir, that Sergeant Baird's dismissal has caused some discontent downstairs. We didn't see any cause for Mr Jarvis to inform on him. Some of the lads think Mr Jarvis was just trying to ingratiate himself with the Chief."

"I'm sorry. How is Baird?"

"Quite low, sir. He's lost his pension and hasn't found employment. The lads downstairs are all helping his family – we're each putting a little money aside for them each week, but it's barely enough to put food on their table."

"I hadn't realised. A little trade union."

"We can't call it that, sir, on pain of dismissal."

"I understand."

"Baird and his family would have been evicted from their rooms if they hadn't received an anonymous donation."

"Really?"

"And may I say, sir, that the lads are very grateful for that anonymous help and proud to serve with you."

The train pulled out of the station and rattled and swayed over points, the cords of the window-blinds slapping against the glass.

"It's a bit rough, sir."

"I know. I doubt the railway company spend anything on maintenance."

"No, I mean about Baird, sir. It was the same in the Army – good men left to shift for themselves after years of loyal service. There were seven VCs awarded in India to comrades in the Sutherland Highlanders. I know that one of those men is in the workhouse, and another has turned to crime."

A strong yeasty smell cut through the mellow aroma of Allerdyce's pipe smoke as the train passed a brewery. The smell faded as the train passed briefly behind houses and an engine-shed before reaching a patchwork of market gardens, fields, farmsteads, and the big houses which titled families kept for their visits to the capital.

"I heard that your Victoria Cross was for saving a man's life, Sergeant."

"Yes, sir. Though I also had to take a man's life in the action, sir. It's something I hope not to have to do again."

"Lucknow, wasn't it? What happened?"

"It was a day from hell, sir. I still wake up sweating, thinking I'm back there."

"I'm sorry. You don't have to tell me."

"There's no harm in talking about it, sir. I'll tell you what I can remember.

"We'd opened a breach through a wall into the mutineers' fortress. Captain Monro led us through it. As we came forward a horde of sepoys rushed at us waving sabres and firing rifles. Others fired down from every wall and rooftop, or jumped down on us with swords and knives."

"Were you wounded?"

"I was grazed by a spent bullet. I saw Captain Monro fall in front of me, and the hole in the back of his tunic from which the bullet had exited.

"As he fell I saw a sepoy holding his rifle over the captain, about to bayonet him. I took my sword, thrust it hard into his stomach and ripped it upwards.

"What I remember most, sir, is the look of puzzled surprise on that lad's face. I reckon he must have been about seventeen years old, and I suppose he thought he was fighting for his country. He just stood there startled for a second as his guts spilled from his abdomen then smiled at me, as if he was apologising, before falling dead."

"That's a hard memory, Sergeant."

"It is, sir. I was hit twice more before we got the Captain back to safety behind the breach. I can barely remember the rest of that day's fight. I must have killed or wounded other men that day, but it's that lad's smile that I see when I shut my eyes."

McGillivray looked out the window at the bare winter fields. The carriage rocked over points as the branch to Dalcorn and Queensferry swung away from the main line. He turned back to the Inspector.

"You know, sir, being in the army made me value life more highly. I've seen enough of death. It's the hardest part of this job for me, sir, knowing that some of the people we apprehend will be hanged."

"It's the law, Sergeant. It's how society prevents the disease of murder from spreading. If you have a gangrenous foot you have it amputated before the infection can spread further."

"Indeed, sir."

"And in cases of less inevitably fatal disease, like typhoid or theft, you isolate the patient in hospital or in prison in the hope of recovery. It's a system which makes scientific sense."

"I suppose so, sir."

The train passed a single tree standing in the middle of a field, its bare branches spreading like arms. Allerdyce was silent for another moment, drawing on his pipe.

"There's a case that still comes back to me in my own dreams though, Sergeant. It was about a young boy – thirteen years old – who was convicted of murdering his father."

"Did he do it, sir?"

"Oh yes. He admitted as much to me. In any case the neighbours had heard the whole thing through the walls of the room they shared in a lodging house in St Mary's Wynd."

"So why trouble your conscience about it, sir?"

"Because I don't think the boy I arrested deserved to die."

"Why?"

"The father had been abusing the boy with insults and blows since the boy's mother had died. The neighbours said his abuse had been growing steadily worse. One night the father came back from the public house and beat the boy so badly with a poker that he lost the sight of one eye. Then he buggered the boy. When the man fell asleep, dead drunk, the boy cracked his head open with the poker. The boy's advocate pleaded that the murder was excused by the provocation he had received, and that the boy was at worst guilty of culpable homicide. But the judge directed the jury only to consider whether the boy was guilty of murder – he obviously didn't think the lower orders should get away with killing each other. Since the father was indisputably dead at the son's hand, the jury found him guilty."

"And the boy was hanged, sir?"

"A week later in front of a jeering crowd in the Lawnmarket. I was bitterly sorry, Sergeant. I had interviewed the boy before he was charged. I had no doubt that he had the potential to grow into a useful citizen once he was free from his father's influence. If I could have let that boy walk away without charge I would have done so."

"You did your duty, sir."

Allerdyce sighed.

"I suppose I did, Sergeant. But sometimes doing your duty to the law doesn't seem to do justice to the people you encounter."

...

The policemen stepped out of the train at Dalcorn station. It wheezed away from the platform as they stepped into the telegraph office.

The clerk, thin with balding black hair slicked back over his scalp, put his glasses on and looked up at them.

"Police? Here?"

"Routine enquiries," said Allerdyce.

"Routine's about all that happens here. I'm not sure that I can help much."

"We want to enquire about a telegram that arrived last Thursday afternoon, addressed to the Duke of Dornoch."

The clerk took his glasses off again and wiped them on his grey handkerchief.

"The Duke gets a lot of telegraphic correspondence."

Allerdyce leant on the counter and looked into the clerk's eyes.

"Well, can you check what he received last Thursday afternoon? It may be of some importance."

"All right then, but I doubt you'll find anything interesting."

The clerk went to a shelf at the back of the office. He looked along it for a few moments before pulling down a box file. He brought it over to the counter and leafed through it. Allerdyce tapped his pipe impatiently against the counter as the clerk methodically studied each paper.

"I thought you said this was routine," said the clerk as he fingered the papers.

Allerdyce stuffed his pipe back into his pocket, tapping his fingers against its stem while he waited.

At length the clerk pulled out five sheets of paper.

"All right then, here's carbon copies of all the telegrams that went to the big house on Thursday. Five about business transactions which I can't pretend to understand, one to tell a servant that her mother was very ill, and one more personal one for the Duke. All quite normal."

"May I see? Perhaps the personal one first?"

The clerk shuffled the papers so that it was at the top and passed them to Allerdyce. He read it, the sergeant looking over his shoulder.

'MINE ALL MINE STOP

MEET AT THE WELL AT MIDNIGHT STOP

ENDS'

"And you say that's a routine message?"

"Oh yes. The Duke used to receive lots of these."

"Every day? Every week?

"Not quite as often as every week. Slightly irregularly. Sometimes four or five weeks – or longer – would go by without any such message. This was the first one for some time."

"Very interesting," said Allerdyce. "No name is given by the originator, but the message was sent from the telegraph office at Waverley Station in Edinburgh."

"Yes."

"I should be very interested to see all the similar messages which you have on record."

"It may take me some time to find them all," said the clerk.

"Just find them. We'll be back. The sergeant and I have to visit Dalcorn House now."

Chapter 9

The front door of Dalcorn House was answered more quickly this time. The same footman opened the door.

"I suppose the Duke is still not at home?" asked Allerdyce.

"No."

"Is Mr Warner at home?"

"Yes."

"I should like to see him directly."

The footman led them straight into the long parlour where they'd sat before, then went to fetch the valet. Warner appeared two minutes later, dressed immaculately. The footman left them, and Warner stood facing the policemen, one of the little tables between them.

"You're expecting your master's return?" asked Allerdyce, looking Warner up and down.

"I have to. If he caught me unprepared I'd be dismissed."

"And do you have any specific reason to expect that he will return today?"

"No."

"You told me that a telegram had arrived in the afternoon shortly before he went missing, and that you had no knowledge of the contents of that telegram."

"Look, Inspector, I've been helpful, haven't I? I've done my best to help you find him. I don't know what you want from me now."

Allerdyce took the copy of the telegram from the inside pocket of his jacket and put it on the table.

"Read that."

The valet picked it up.

"Bloody hell."

"What's that, Warner?"

"I thought he'd stopped getting these. I used to find them in his room from time to time."

"And?"

"I knew he was going out late into the gardens sometimes, and that it was related to the telegrams. I didn't know why. I didn't know who he was going to meet. It might just have been straightforward – maybe he met some lover by moonlight for his excitement. Sometimes I thought someone might have been meeting him to collect blackmail."

"Who could blackmail the Duke?"

"I don't know. I suppose he wouldn't want it generally known that he'd had a child with some woman, or that he'd had carnal relations with some sailor, but that's only a guess. I don't know who'd want to do that."

"So why do you suggest it, Mr Warner."

"It's just an educated guess. You've seen the sorts of places he goes. I don't know anything more specific than that."

"Really, Warner?"

"Yes really."

"And why didn't you tell us about these telegrams before?"

"I've already said. I didn't know what was in the telegram. I thought all this had stopped."

Warner put the telegram back on the table and Allerdyce picked it up.

"Well, Mr Warner, clearly it hasn't." said the Inspector, "I think we should take an immediate look at the well referred to in this telegram."

...

Warner led them out of the house by a back entrance. The parkland extended as far to the rear of the house as it did to the front. A lawn, bounded by walks of sycamore and elm, stretched for quarter of a mile towards dense woodland. Nearest to the house, a square of lawn had been made perfectly level for bowls or croquet. Further away, about halfway towards the woods, a low round wall surrounding an area no more than five feet wide sat in the middle of the lawn. There was a paved area with stone benches around the wall.

They walked up to the wall. As they approached, Allerdyce noted its peculiar decoration, a frieze of cherubs with pick-axes, lanterns and barrows.

"Here's the well," said Warner.

Allerdyce looked with disappointment at the paving round the well. If it had been grass he might have been able to detect footprints, even now.

He looked down into the unrelieved darkness.

"How deep is it, Mr Warner?"

"I don't know. About fifty feet, maybe more."

"And is there still water in it?"

"Yes."

Allerdyce picked a stone up from the paving and dropped it

down the well. He waited but heard no splash.

"Are you sure there's water down there, Mr Warner?"

"Absolutely."

He hollered down but heard no reply.

"That's peculiar."

"What?"

"There should be an echo from the water."

The sergeant peered over the wall.

"There could be an obstruction, sir."

"Yes."

"If Mr Warner can provide me with a rope and a lantern I can go down and check."

"Are you sure, Sergeant?"

"I've set charges underground in the Crimea, sir. I'm sure I can do it."

"All right then."

Warner led the sergeant off to fetch equipment from the workshop at the back of the coach-house, leaving the Inspector alone, staring into the inky blackness of the well. His mind couldn't help picturing a body jammed awkwardly between its narrowing sides. He shivered as he thought about reporting to Burgess that Scotland's richest man, missing for four nights, had been found. Dead – when Allerdyce had specifically been charged with his safety.

Steady on, he thought. There's no reason to think the worst. Maybe an animal has fallen down the shaft and got stuck. Perhaps some vegetation has blocked it. The Duke is quite likely still away drinking and whoring. But he felt sick.

Warner and McGillivray returned with a block-and-tackle, a lantern and two ropes. They set up the tripod of the block-and-tackle over the well. McGillivray threaded both ropes through the pulley, tying one of them round his waist.

"I'll climb down now, sir," said the sergeant. "I'll rest as much of my weight as I can against the sides of the well but I'll need you and Mr Warner to hold the rope I've tied to myself. Let it out slowly as I go. I'll attach the other rope to the obstruction if I can."

The sergeant climbed over the wall and descended into the darkness. Allerdyce leant back on the rope, Warner behind him, feeling the hemp abrade his palms as he let it out, over the creaking pulley, a foot at a time.

"More rope, sir," echoed the sergeant's voice from the darkness.

Allerdyce felt the muscles of his arms and shoulders strain to tearing point as they lowered the sergeant further and further. Each time he let the rope out he feared it would tear away from him.

He heard a muffled cry and the clank of falling metal and the rope shot through his hands, burning skin from flesh. He grasped it tighter through the pain of searing flesh and felt his feet lifting from the ground as the rope hurtled over the pulley and into the darkness. Warner grabbed the waistband of his trousers and they brought the rope back under control.

"Are you all right?" shouted Allerdyce.

"Sorry sir, I slipped," said the voice from below. "I've lost the lantern but the obstruction broke my fall. I'll fix a rope round it."

McGillivray climbed back out of the well, Allerdyce and Warner pulling on his rope despite the pain. The hemp was stained red with their blood. McGillivray then pulled the other rope, and Allerdyce saw even the sergeant's muscles straining as he pulled the dead weight past the rocky outcrops and protruding roots of the well's shaft.

One last heave brought the obstruction fully clear of the well. Allerdyce looked on in horror.

It hung limply by a rope tied under its shoulders, its back towards Allerdyce. As it swung gently under the pulley block it came face to face with him.

The body's evening dress was in disarray, and the caked dark blood of a gash marked its forehead. The deathly paleness of the face was marred by the blue-green blotches of early putrefaction. But the white hair, jowly chin, and contemptuously twisted mouth were unmistakable. Allerdyce was looking into the glazed and unblinking eyes of His Grace the 7th Duke of Dornoch. Deceased.

Damn.

Chapter 10

The circle of light on Allerdyce's desk shrank away to nothing as he turned off the paraffin lamp. Some light still shone through the glass of his office door from the corridor, but behind him his window was dark and a chill draught penetrated the ill-fitting window-frame.

He squeezed between his desk and the filing cabinets, and picked his coat and hat off the coathook.

There was no point in staying here any longer. However long he stayed in the office the Duke of Dornoch would still be dead, and his murderer would still be at large.

Murderer.

He'd only been able to say that for sure in the past half hour. Mackay, the police surgeon, had handed in his report at half past nine. Allerdyce had smelt the formaldehyde on the doctor's hands, fresh from the morgue.

The report had taken two pages to describe a simple fact. It had detailed all the damage – both acute and chronic – which the flesh and organs of the Duke had suffered. It listed moderate cirrhosis of the liver, incipient ulceration of the duodenum, accumulation of fatty deposits round the heart, some calcification of the carotid artery, contusions of the spine consistent with sudden traumatic injury, bruising on the neck (uncertain whether pre- or post-mortem), laceration of the forehead and hands, probably post-mortem.

And a puncture wound caused by a small-calibre bullet which had grazed the lower left ventricle of the heart, causing some leakage of blood and loss of heart function, before lodging in the deceased's spinal cord.

Shot dead and dumped down the well.

He pulled his coat on and stepped out into the corridor, locking the office door behind him. He looked up and down the corridor, but saw only the shut, dark doors of the other offices.

He turned right, and went down the back stairs at the end of the corridor, to avoid having to pass through the orderly room and make conversation with the night-watch constables.

Stepping into the night, he turned his collar up and reflected on what must be his worst day so far as a policeman.

Scotland's richest man murdered, on his watch. The Duchess, thank God, hadn't been at home when her husband's body had been found, and the Chief Constable had taken it upon himself to inform her. But telling Burgess had been bad enough. He'd thought the Superintendent might be about to have an aneurism as he stormed up and down his office cursing Allerdyce, the Chief Constable, the Duke and himself for all their various parts in the debacle. And, after Burgess had dismissed him, it hadn't helped that Jarvis had made a special point of, smirkingly, conveying his commiserations on Allerdyce's failure to find the Duke alive. The worst thing was that Jarvis's insinuation had got under his skin, like a poison through a hypodermic needle.

He should go home now. He should present a brave face to Margaret. She had enough strain in her life, with the children and her own illness, without having to listen to his complaints.

She needed rest and quietness for her recovery, not a share of his own doubts and stresses. But right now, exhausted and defeated, he wanted to rest the weight of his tired self on the shoulders of somebody who had the strength to bear it.

He walked down to the corner of the High Street and the North Bridge and hailed a cab.

"Where to, sir?" asked the driver.

"Danube Street."

Allerdyce climbed in. He rested his head against the leather upholstery and stared blankly at the passing streetlights, feeling himself rocked towards sleep by the swaying of the cab's springs.

The cab rattled and juddered over the stone cobbles at the junction of the North Bridge and Princes Street. Allerdyce was jerked awake. He looked out and saw a little girl, maybe eleven years old, standing under a gaslight and pulling up her ragged skirt in a pathetic attempt to attract a passing gentleman.

That's what we should be doing, thought Allerdyce. Protecting the poor and weak from exploitation by the real criminals of this world. And the sooner I find out who killed the bloody Duke of Dornoch the sooner I can get back to that work.

...

It was after eleven o'clock before Allerdyce let himself back into his own house, aware of a strange alloy of discontent and and relief within himself. It was a feeling so mixed that he could find no single word for it.

Antonia had, as always, taken an intelligent and sympathetic interest. She'd had the maid bring up ointment and bandages, and had washed and dressed his raw, burnt hands herself. She had given him a generous measure of the brandy he felt he'd needed, and the flush of the alcohol and the kindness of the firelight had made her look as as inviting as he'd ever known her. But he'd detected a reserve in her after he'd told her that the Duke had been recovered, dead, from the well. She had asked him if he wanted to lie with her, as she had done from time to time since those awful months when he'd eased the madness of his grief with her. Tonight, though, it had sounded formulaic, and he'd felt it stripped bare as a proposal for a business transaction rather than an act of friendship and love. It had felt easier than before to say no, and to leave.

Now, he chose not to go into the parlour of his house and lie down on the sofa. Late as it was, he walked gently up the stairs, hearing only the softest flexing of the wood of the narrow steps. He opened the door to the bedroom and heard the quiet chirruping of baby Stephen talking infant nonsense to himself in his sleep and Margaret's rhythmic, shallow breathing.

He took off his clothes and let them fall randomly to the floor, lifting the blankets and creeping into bed beside her. As the steel mesh of the bedsprings creaked Margaret's breathing was interrupted for a second then settled back to its former rhythm. He put his arm around her, feeling her thin, feverish body under his hand.

His mind still wrestled with the conflicts of the day, and its anticipation of the difficulties of tomorrow. But there was a clearer sensation underlying the mind's noise now, a feeling which he could capture in a word.

Home.

Chapter 11

"No, Allerdyce. No."

"Sir, I need to interview the deceased's widow and brothers. They may be able to make inferences from the telegram."

Superintendent Burgess stood at the window of his office, side-on to Allerdyce, the grey light from the overcast sky making him look old and sick.

He turned back to face Allerdyce, who stood at the opposite side of the great desk.

"Look, Archibald, I'm sorry I blew up at you yesterday. I know it's not your fault that someone decided to kill the Duke. If Dr Mackay's right, he was probably dead for three nights before I even sent you to look for him."

"Yes, sir."

"And take a seat, for God's sake, man. It makes me uncomfortable to see you standing there like a schoolboy about to get a thrashing."

The Superintendent sat down in his leather swivel chair. Allerdyce sat on the simpler chair at the other side of the desk. Burgess put his head in his hands and rubbed his eyes before looking up again and speaking.

"I'd want to do the same thing as you right now, Allerdyce. I've been a policeman for over twenty years and I know the value of a quick follow-up."

He clasped his hands in front of him. His mouth was clenched as if, Allerdyce thought, he was in intestinal pain. Allerdyce wondered whether the Superintendent was suffering from gallstones or whether it was just the strain showing. Burgess continued.

"I was a bloody good Inspector in my time, Allerdyce. So if I was in your place I wouldn't want to be sitting here. I'd want to be out there speaking to everyone who knew anything about our deceased friend. I'd be battering doors down and calling in grasses and making it generally known that anyone who knew anything and didn't tell me was in very serious trouble indeed."

"Yes, sir."

"But this is different. This is political."

"It can't be that different sir, surely. We have a murder victim, and a killer still at large."

"As a straightforward man, I agree with you, Allerdyce. But it isn't that simple. For a start, we don't actually have a murder victim."

"What? So who did Sergeant McGillivray pull out of the well? Didn't Mackay find a bullet in the man's spine? We most certainly have a murder victim, sir."

"Not in public we don't. The Chief has spoken to the Lord Advocate and the Secretary for Scotland. They've agreed that it would be better if, for the moment, the death was described as accidental."

"Why?"

"Partly out of concern for the delicacy of the Duchess's feelings. They think her highly-refined feminine nerves may not currently be able to stand the shock of discovering that her beloved husband was murdered."

"She already knows that her husband's body was found down a well. If she can stand that she should be able to stand the full truth."

"Quite, Allerdyce, and as a married man I can't say that I've ever felt that my wife has suffered from a delicate mental constitution. Quite the reverse. But our masters are modern men with modern notions of feminine psychology, so that's what they've decided."

"So, no interview with the widow?"

"Not by you. The Chief Constable has conveyed the force's condolences and promised every possible help in investigating the accident that led to his untimely death. He'll handle any further communication with the Duchess."

"He said it was an accident?"

"That's what it says in the newspapers today. It's what the Lord Advocate told them."

Burgess pushed a folded copy of 'The Scotsman' across the desk. Allerdyce took it and unfolded it. He ignored the front page, with its advertisements for theatre shows and drapers' shops, and turned to the news pages inside.

As usual, the first stories were dispatches from America. Sherman had at last taken Charleston from the Confederates, and the city had been burnt to the ground. From New Zealand came news of the continued Maori rebellion. At home, Parliament was still debating giving the vote to the better sort of artisan, and the textile mills of Galashiels and Hawick were closed for a second week by a strike. Only after these stories was there a brief news item about the Duke.

Allerdyce folded up the paper again and passed it back across the desk.

"I suppose it's not strictly untrue, sir. After all, the Duke did suffer from cardiac failure, even if it was caused by a bullet."

"The politicians aren't just concerned about the Duchess's mental welfare. They said it was important, in these inflamed times, to ensure that undesirable elements didn't get the impression that the pillars of society could be torn down so easily. So, Allerdyce, as far as the public are concerned there's no murder."

"And if there's no murder there's no murder investigation? Surely the politicians don't want to leave a Duke-killer at large?"

"I didn't say that, Allerdyce. They'd like the murderer found.

They're not keen to expose the family to embarrassment in court, so they'd be content if a non-judicial way were found of securing justice."

"Non-judicial?"

"Come on, man, I don't have to explain myself. If the murderer turns out to be one of the low-life types you say the Duke was consorting with, they'd be content for them to disappear quietly rather than telling all the sordid details in court."

"What do you think, sir?"

"I'm not an imaginative man, Inspector. I like it best when we catch criminals and send them to court."

"So do I, sir."

"I don't think we need to throw the laws of Scotland out of the window just yet. I'd like you, quietly and discreetly, to carry on with your investigations. Tell me when you think you're getting somewhere and we can make a judgement about how to proceed."

"All right, sir. But it's going to be difficult if everyone thinks the Duke's death was an accident."

"Not everyone, Allerdyce. The Chief has told the Duke's brothers what happened. You can interview them if you want – but not until after the funeral. The Chief gave his word to the family that they needn't be disturbed until they'd observed all the decencies of burial."

"And in the meantime the killer could have left the country."

"Let's hope for our own sakes, Allerdyce, that he hasn't."

. . .

Arthur walked down the aisle with Josephine, her arm slipped

99

through his. He could feel the trembling warmth of her flesh, even through her thick silk and crepe. Her wide skirts brushed his ankles, and as he glanced sideways he could see, through the obscuring veil, her angelic complexion, the straight delicacy of her nose, and her soft, moist grey eyes. A single tear glistened on her cheek.

This was not how it should have been. In a just world, he would have been able to lead her out of the church as his bride, dressed in radiant white and with her veil thrown back, instead of supporting her as she walked, draped heavily in unreflective black, towards her husband's tomb.

He'd kept the service as short as he could. Partly, he'd felt intimidated by seeing the church completely full for once, and full of the richest and most powerful men in the country. He'd thought for a moment that if a Fenian or a Communist had taken a notion to they could have lobbed a bomb into the church and obliterated three members of Her Majesty's Government, five Dukes, four Marquesses, and an uncertain number of Earls, Barons, and captains of industry. He'd scanned their hard, handsome faces and felt their impatience with the hymn-singing and prayer-saying. He'd wondered whether there was a single true Christian amongst them.

Also, it would have been difficult to give a long eulogy to a man with as few virtues as his brother. He'd said what he could about William being a man who cherished the land (just as well, he thought, since he owned so much of the counties of Linlithgow and Sutherland), who devoted his energies to God's creative work of clothing and feeding the poor and keeping them warm (if they could pay for the wool, oats and coal generated by the Ducal estates), and who was a passionate admirer of beauty (and prepared to pay for it, whether it was a picture or a prostitute). After that there didn't seem to be much to say.

As he and Josephine progressed up the aisle the members of the congregation bowed their heads respectfully. Behind them, six servants in their new mourning suits shouldered the lead-lined mahogany coffin.

Another servant opened the door at the rear of the church and they stepped out into the clear morning chill. He felt Josephine shiver and pull her body closer to his. For an instant, before she pulled gently away again, he felt her stays brushing his elbow and felt the subtle movement of her breast beneath them.

They turned left from the church door, and he heard the heavy crunch-pause-crunch of the six pall-bearers' slow march along the churchyard path between the tombstones, some clear and modern, others ancient with skulls and hourglasses as *memento mori*, towards the Bothwell-Scott mausoleum at the far end of the churchyard.

The mausoleum had been built in the model of a Greek temple, like a miniature Parthenon, with pillars supporting a triangular pediment. Behind the pillars, a blank sandstone wall was broken only by a small iron door which, today, stood open.

There was only room in the mausoleum for the closest family and essential servants. The pallbearers took the coffin in before the family were admitted. Arthur let Josephine in first, before bowing his head to get through the low door into an interior which was in three-quarter-darkness, lit feebly by a lantern which had been hung on a chain from the roof. The damp chill inside the mausoleum was, he thought, literally sepulchral. As his eyes adjusted to the darkness he seemed to be looking at a filing cabinet for the dead. Ahead of him, along the back wall of the mausoleum, was a honeycomb of niches four feet wide by three feet high. Most of the niches were dark and empty, but some – eleven, Arthur thought – had already been filled and were blocked off with plaques on which the incumbent's name and dates were carved. His brother's coffin had been slipped into its niche, with no plaque as yet. At a conservative estimate, he reckoned there was enough space to accommodate generations of Bothwell-Scotts until Judgement Day, or at least 2,200AD.

He shivered as he looked at William's coffin. Who's next, he thought? He imagined his own body being slipped into its final resting place by indifferent servants. And what if there was some terrible mistake? What if signs of life had been hastily unnoticed? This dark mausoleum was like a grave in itself, but what if he was screwed down in a lead-lined coffin, beating helplessly against the metal until he suffocated? His breathing was fast and shallow and he felt as if he might suffocate right now in this cold place.

Josephine clasped his arm more tightly.

"Are you all right, Arthur?"

"I'm sorry Josephine. Just a pang of grief."

He saw his two surviving elder brothers enter, silhouetted against the daylight of the door. Frederick removed his plumed Brigadier's hat to stoop through the door. George followed, taking off his silk top hat.

"Get on with it," barked Frederick. "Haven't got all bloody day, you know."

"Steady on, Fred." Arthur heard George's softer tone. "We have to observe the decencies."

"Bloody religious mumbo jumbo."

Arthur looked at his brothers in the dim light as they took their places at the far end of the coffin. George, blandly handsome, smiled with his usual polite indifference, immaculate in his black suit. His patent leather shoes caught a reflection of the lamp which hung above the coffin. Frederick, his red tunic tight across his stomach, fidgeted irascibly and Arthur heard his spurs jingle and his scabbard scrape the floor.

Despite the chill, Arthur felt a sweat break out all over him as the image flashed back into his mind of a previous time he'd been thrust into a dark, damp place by his brothers. When he was nine years old he'd told his mother that he'd seen William and Frederick pestering a maidservant. They had got their own back by holding him upside down in the well behind Dalcorn House, George looking on. He seemed to be back there now, seeing the far-off reflection of the water at the bottom of the well and hearing his own pathetic cries as he struggled helplessly. He remembered Frederick's comment to William echoing down the well – 'Get on with it' – and the grip on one of his ankles being released. He didn't know whether they'd have let him drop if a gardener hadn't seen them. He felt dizzy and swaying. Josephine put her arm around him to stop him falling.

"Arthur, I think you're ill."

"I'm sorry."

Pull yourself together, he thought. This is ridiculous. You can't let yourself be weaker than a woman who's just been widowed. Josephine's touch seemed to transmit some strength and comfort to him.

"Well, then," grumbled Frederick. "Pray or something."

He mumbled his way through the ordained words to send William on his way to eternity, gasping for breath between the phrases. At last it was done. He half-ran past his brothers and finally breathed freely as he reached the open air.

Farewell William, he thought. May God judge you as you deserve.

But, standing shivering outside the mausoleum, death and hell seemed uncomfortably close to his own body and soul.

Chapter 12

Allerdyce stepped out of the Police Office into the thin grey drizzle, the sergeant at his side.

It was curious how on a damp February day, even though most things looked duller and the spectrum of colour of the sky and the buildings ranged from drab to dun, the cobbles of Parliament Square had a bright oily sheen. Looking closely he could see prismatic spreads of colour on the cobbles, like a chromatography image, presumably from the coal fumes and other pollutants which were held in suspension in the filthy rain.

He drew on his pipe and exhaled, looking at the statue in the middle of the square. In the misty dampness he could almost see the clouds of breath from the great bronze horse which pawed at its plinth between the classical façade of the law courts and the dark bulk of St Giles Cathedral, perpetually waiting for a command from the armoured figure of King Charles II which sat astride it.

Two advocates in long scholars' robes and white periwigs, holding parchments tied up with red silk, crossed the square in front of him, conferring quietly. A carriage rumbled over the cobbles and halted. Allerdyce saw the tall, gaunt figure of High Court judge

Lord McLaren step down. Ahead of the carriage, the windowless 'Black Maria' van from the Calton jail was discharging shackled prisoners, men and women, with bowed heads and shuffling feet as they trooped into the court building in their heavy serge prison outfits.

"Don't fancy their chances much," said the sergeant, "if they're up before McLaren."

They emerged into the broad square, crowded with canopied market stalls, at the west side of St Giles. There appeared to be more stall-holders than customers, warming their hands and shouting an occasional desultory cry to passers-by to come and buy their fine sheet-music, straight from the music-halls of London, or the new cheap edition of Mr Dickens' most popular works. A dancing bear was hauled briefly to its feet, groaning, as two ladies passed, before subsiding back to the damp cobbles.

As they crossed the square a one-legged man emerged, on crutches, from between two stalls. He wore a Glengarry bonnet from which matted red hair stuck out underneath, a filthy red soldier's jacket with no buttons left and braid that was hanging off by threads, and a kilt so worn and grey you could hardly make out the tartan.

The man held out a tin cup and rattled the coppers in it.

"Spare a few pence for an old soldier, gentlemen, crippled in Her Majesty's service."

Allerdyce walked by, holding his breath against the stink of filth and whisky and brushing the man's outstretched cup out of his way. He stopped and turned as he heard the sergeant's stern voice.

"Who are you?" asked the sergeant, looking down at the stunted veteran.

"Private James McNeill, if it please."

"Your regiment?"

"The 91st, Sergeant. Argyll Highlanders."

"Which company?"

"Captain Ewart's, sir."

"Stand to attention as you address a senior non-commissioned officer, Private McNeill."

The veteran attempted to stand straighter, his hands shaking on his crutches. The sergeant continued.

"Where did you serve?"

"Cape Colony, Mr Sergeant sir, the Crimea, India."

"Where are your medals?"

"Pawned, Sergeant, to put some thin broth on my table and pay for my poor bed."

The sergeant's face relaxed slightly.

"Tell me, McNeill, if you were in Captain Ewart's company you must have known a young private by the name of Aeneas McGillivray of Strath Naver."

The veteran knitted his brows for a second before giving a broad smile, exposing the rotting black stumps of his teeth.

"Oh yes, Sergeant, I remember him well. A charming man, and most gallant."

"Were you with him when the Russians abandoned Sebastopol?"

"I was, to be sure, Sergeant. He was a brave man that day. A true Highland hero."

McGillivray stood to attention. He slapped the veteran hard on the face. The veteran's crutches scrabbled for grip on the slippery cobbles as he hopped sideways to maintain his balance.

"Jesus, Sergeant, what was that for? That's no way to treat an old comrade."

"You are a coward and an impostor, Mr McNeill. You have no title to the uniform which you disgrace."

Allerdyce's shock at the sergeant's violence held him back for an instant. He wondered whether the sergeant was about to kick the supposed veteran's crutches from under him. He stepped forward to intervene, but McGillivray stood stock still as the cripple turned, spat on the cobbles, and swung away on his crutches.

"What was that about, Sergeant?"

"That man is a fraud, sir. He never served with Her Majesty's armed forces."

"Are you sure?"

"The 91st don't have kilts, sir. And the man had the temerity to claim to know my youngest brother, who served with the 93rd. He claimed to have been with my brother at the fall of Sebastopol, when poor Aeneas had been dead for seven months before that event."

"I'm sorry, Sergeant."

"I expect he bought old bits of uniform from a rag dealer and tried to learn enough about the regiment to pass himself off as an old soldier. We could arrest him, sir, for personation." The sergeant looked towards the impostor, who was swinging his way towards the High Street.

"Sergeant, we have murder to solve. Interviewing the deceased's brother must take priority. "

"Very well, sir."

They resumed their progress up towards the Castle, climbing up the broad slope of the Lawnmarket between the tall, thin frontages of the ancient six-and-seven storey tenements. The sergeant's anger was barely visible, though Allerdyce thought there was still the faint trace of an unusual hardness in his face. He wondered for a moment whether he should caution the sergeant for striking the beggar, but supposed that breaches of military honour raised passions that mere civilians could never fully understand. They walked on in silence.

They passed the spot in the Lawnmarket where, until so recently, public hangings had been carried out until they were removed to the discreet privacy of the death cell in the Calton Jail. Allerdyce paused as his mind saw again the abused thirteen-year-old-boy. He'd kicked and gasped at the end of the rope for ten minutes in front of a jeering crowd to try and hold onto a life that had given him so little. Allerdyce shuddered. At least it was progress that the public were no longer able to watch that degrading spectacle.

Passing the Gothic extravagance of the Tollbooth kirk, its spire and pinnacles already a sooty black barely twenty years after the Queen had laid the foundation stone, they mounted the steep wynd of Castle Hill.

"Did you come across Brigadier Bothwell-Scott when you were in the army?" asked Allerdyce.

"I was never favoured with a direct word from him, sir, but I knew him well enough by his actions in the Crimea."

"Such as?"

"I regret, sir, he was not well regarded by the men. He was briefly in active command of our regiment and led us rather poorly."

"What happened?"

"It was a shambles, sir. He led us up the heights at the River Alma. We couldn't see the Russians but their shells were landing among us. Men next to me were falling with arms or heads blown off. When we got to the top we saw a line of Russian riflemen waiting for us. We were about to charge them when he told us to stop."

"Stop? Why?"

"He'd mistaken them for the French. He thought they were our allies, and that they'd reached the heights already."

"What happened then?"

"They fired straight into us, sir. We lost eighty good men before Sir Colin Campbell rode up and told Colonel Bothwell-Scott to hand over his command."

"You must have lost good friends."

"I did, sir. Unfortunately, that that was the least of the trouble we had from him. Having been removed from active command of soldiers in the field, he was made responsible for the distribution of supplies. Lord Raglan promoted him to the rank of Brigadier so that he didn't feel humiliated.

"It was in that capacity, sir, that he killed more men by neglect of his duty than he could ever have killed in battle."

As they passed the Ragged School they heard the rhythmic chanting of times-tables. McGillivray continued.

"Sir Frederick's entire challenge was organising the forces available to him so that supplies were unloaded from ships, transported to front lines which were no more than five miles distant from the harbour at Balaklava, and distributed according to need. He completely failed in this."

"We read in the newspapers that there were problems with supplies," observed Allerdyce. "I don't recall why it was so bad."

McGillivray looked grimly ahead, his jaw clenched. It was a moment before he spoke.

"Thousands of men died because, we heard, the Brigadier was too drunk to do anything to organise the supplies. We heard he'd taken his removal from command very badly, and that he punished as insubordination any attempt by anyone else to remedy the situation. I don't know the truth of that rumour, sir – all I know is that there were ships full of winter clothes and food lying rotting at anchor in Balaklava harbour with no-one stirring a finger to unload them. And when I think of my poor brother Aeneas dying of hypothermia in the sleet in the trenches before Sebastopol, I can't help thinking that a woollen overcoat and a bowl of porridge would have been enough to keep him alive. It's a bitter thought, sir, but it's un-Christian of me to blame any one man."

Allerdyce looked at the sergeant. He wondered how much grief and resentment this proud, dutiful man was carrying. He felt sorry for having to bring the sergeant face-to-face with the man he held responsible for his brother's death. But duty was duty, and had to be done.

...

A young officer showed them into the Brigadier's vast office in the Governor's House of the Castle and left them waiting.

The dark wood panelling was interrupted by paintings of old generals in various attitudes of disdain or anger, and lines of red-coated soldiers advancing into different eras of slaughter by sword, musket or artillery. The huge wooden desk supported a sword, laid lengthways on a stand, a decanter of whisky and a glass, and some papers. Behind the desk was a portrait of the unsmiling, heavily-moustached features of Brigadier Sir Frederick Bothwell-

Scott sitting in full Highland dress as he scowled at the artist, and above that the glazed eyes of the stuffed-and-mounted head of a ten-pointer stag.

Allerdyce sat drumming his fingers against the desk. He started to whistle gently – a banal little tune from his last visit to the music-hall that he couldn't quite get out of his mind.

At last the silence was broken by the muffled flushing of a water-closet. A few seconds later a hidden door opened in the panelling, to the right of the Brigadier's portrait. The 8th Duke of Dornoch emerged, his red tunic undone, still fastening the fly buttons of his tartan trousers.

"You must be the policemen?"

"Yes, sir."

"Know who did it yet?"

"No. We'd like to ask you some questions."

"Well, it bloody well wasn't me so I don't know what I can do for you."

The Brigadier sat down. He was the exact facial image of his portrait, except that the artist had not fully captured the broken veins and the redness of his complexion. He poured himself a whisky and sat back.

"Sir," asked Allerdyce, "do you have any idea who might have killed your brother?"

"I'm not a bloody detective, am I? How should I know?"

"Can you think of anyone who might have a particular resentment against him?"

"You don't get to a position of honour in society without people resenting you for it. But no, I can't think of anyone who'd specifically want to murder him."

Allerdyce took an envelope out from the inside pocket of his jacket. He opened it and took out the telegram which had arrived on the afternoon of the Duke's disappearance. He held it out to the Brigadier.

"Does this mean anything to you, sir?"

The Brigadier took it and, for a couple of seconds, appeared to have difficulty focussing on it before he read it out loud.

"'Mine all mine. Meet at the well at midnight.'"

"So? Can you shed any light on the message, sir?"

The Brigadier furrowed his brows and squinted again at the telegram. He turned it round, and turned it upside down, as if he could shake some truth out of it. At length he punched the air and seemed, for an instant, to smile.

"I have it, gentlemen. It's obvious."

"Is it sir?"

"Well it is to me. I think I should be appointed to the detective force. I clearly have more aptitude for it than you gentlemen."

Allerdyce tried not to let his face reflect the insult. The Brigadier continued.

"My brother's body was recovered from a mine shaft, wasn't it?"

"We understood it to be a well, sir."

"You were not fully informed, then. The shaft in which my brother met his end is decorated as an ornamental well, and has water in it, but it was originally a mine shaft.

"As you know, my family have substantial mining interests on our estates in Linlithgowshire. Some of the reserves have been worked for many centuries. The 'well' from which William was recovered was a mediaeval mineshaft – a bottle mine is the correct term I believe. The grounds at Dalcorn are riddled with these shafts, but that's the only one that's been kept open. A sort of memorial."

"So," asked Allerdyce, "how does that lead us to the murderer?"

"Think about mines, gentlemen. Is there anyone connected with the mines who has a resentment against my brother? I can think of one clear person."

"Who is?"

"James Semple of the Amalgamated Fraternity of Scottish Miners. He's the seditionist who led my brother's miners out on strike when market forces meant he had to cut their wages. He got dismissed for it, of course, along with the other strikers and he and his family were thrown out of the company's cottage. We made sure that every mineowner and factory-owner in Britain knew not to offer him employment. These were the wise precautions my brother had to take to avoid the spread of industrial sedition. Mutiny is mutiny, whether it's in the army or in the mines. It's only a shame that we can't blow the industrial mutineers from the cannons."

"So you think Semple would want to kill your brother for revenge?"

"I suppose so."

"Why do you think he would arrange to meet your brother at midnight, on your brother's estate?"

"I don't know. Presumably you fellows can fill in the details. That's what you do, isn't it?"

"I think we might need some more evidence to be able to charge Mr Semple."

"Well, thrash it out of him then. That's what we do in the army. And hang him quick. The worst you'll have done is to rid the world of another verminous socialist. He's got be punished for what he's done."

Allerdyce shifted in his chair and flicked over another page of his notebook.

"How has your brother's death affected you, sir?"

"What sort of a bloody impertinent question is that?"

"Merely one asked from professional interest, sir."

"Well, it's a bloody awful thing to happen isn't it? But you get used to death in this job, and it isn't all bad."

"Not all bad?"

"I'm sorry for William, of course, but it's been an upturn in my own fortunes. I'm getting a promotion out of this – the army thinks Dukes should rank at least as Major-Generals. And I can't pretend that I don't welcome having the entire revenues of the family's properties."

"The entire revenues, sir? The late Duke made no provision for the Duchess in the event of his death?"

"No. Why the hell should he leave anything to that fallow bitch?"

Allerdyce lifted his eyebrows. The Brigadier continued.

"My brother managed to avoid marriage for as long as he decently could. He's a wise man – I've managed to avoid marriage entirely and I can't say I feel any the worse for it. But William had the responsibility of perpetuating the family line hanging over him, as our mother reminded him more and more forcibly from year to year. She didn't want the estates passing to a bastard or a stranger. So she ground into him the notion that he had to get married. She also harangued him to recognise the wisdom of marrying his cousin Josephine – she was the sole heir to the fortune which her side of the family had made in America. It would bring the money home to where it belongs.

"Well, gentlemen, the whole thing was a bloody disaster

from start to finish. Generations of fine breeding had generated a narrow-hipped bitch who couldn't drop a living child. She was seventeen years old when William married her, she's twenty-seven now, and she's never pupped. There isn't going to be any fortune either – it's all gone in the American wars. And she's turned out to be an opinionated shrew. The whole thing was a complete bloody disaster, gentlemen, a daily curse on all our lives. I've a good mind to turn her out of Dalcorn House so that I can enjoy my property in peace."

Allerdyce grasped at the lead which the Brigadier had, probably inadvertently, thrown.

"You mentioned that your mother didn't want the estates to pass to a bastard, sir. Did you have anyone particular in mind?"

The Brigadier knocked back his whisky and poured some more.

"How the hell should I know? William was a man of the world. It's his business what he got up to. I've told you who must have killed William – what else do you need to know?"

"You've suggested James Semple, sir. I just wonder whether there are any other connections with the family we should know about?"

"I've told you everything you need to know. Now, just run along and catch that bloody seditionist if you'd be so kind. I have work to do here." The Brigadier took some papers in his hand, squinted at them, and shuffled them into a different order.

Allerdyce folded away his notebook and stood up to leave. The sergeant followed his lead. The Brigadier tottered unsteadily to his feet. He leant forward over the desk, supporting himself with one hand and holding the glass in the other, and peered at the purple ribbon on McGillivray's chest.

"Victoria Cross?"

"Yes, sir," answered McGillivray, standing straight.

"Where?"

"Lucknow, sir."

The Brigadier sat back down, heavily, sloshing whisky out of the glass onto his tartan trousers.

"Ha, India. Bit different from the Crimea. I didn't get anything from the Crimea except this bloody sword from a Russian officer. Not a single medal for all the work I did to clothe and feed an entire bloody army. And that was a proper bloody war. And then Colin Campbell goes spreading medals around like bloody confetti in India, just for putting down a few darkies. Rather devalues the thing, don't you agree?"

Allerdyce looked towards the sergeant. McGillivray's face had gone quite white, and the colour drained from his lips. His fists were clenched. Allerdyce worried for a second that the sergeant might actually reach across the desk and strike the Brigadier.

McGillivray slowly raised his hand and Allerdyce braced himself to intervene between the two soldiers. But the sergeant opened his fist and raised his open hand in a military salute.

The Brigadier staggered back up from his chair and, sloppily, returned the salute. McGillivray about-turned and marched out of the office.

The Brigadier, leaning forward on the desk, addressed Allerdyce.

"The lower ranks can be splendid when they're loyal, but once they go bad they need to be exterminated. I trust you know how to deal with Mr Semple."

Allerdyce looked the Brigadier in his rheumy eye but saw no reaction. He turned and followed the sergeant out the room.

Chapter 13

Rock House clung to a ledge on the lower slopes of Calton Hill. Allerdyce noted that its frontage was angled so that the residents had a view along Princes Street and towards the Castle, rather than across to the looming bulk of the Calton Jail. The seventeenth-century simplicity of the large house was marred by an ugly brick-built extension which, famously, had housed the photographic studio of Hill and Adamson. George Bothwell-Scott QC now owned the house and the studio of the photographic pioneers.

Allerdyce and McGillivray were shown straight through to the studio, where the advocate was tinkering with a screwdriver at the innards of a complex camera. He glanced up briefly as the policemen came in.

"I'll be with you in a second, gentlemen."

He turned his attention back to the brass spindles and cogs, leaving Allerdyce and the sergeant standing.

So, thought Allerdyce, this is the famous advocate, equally at ease as a defender or a prosecutor, who used to earn the highest fees of anyone at the Scottish bar. George Bothwell-Scott was still a young man, no older than his early forties, but he had retired from the law, and it was rumoured that he'd become unbalanced.

Looking at him now, absorbed in his work, he didn't look

mad. His blond hair was neatly parted and macassared, his pale moustache was neatly trimmed, and his shirt-sleeves were rolled up to reveal lean, muscled forearms. The lines under his eyes suggested insomnia, but there was nothing in his appearance that would confirm the rumour that he was addicted to laudanum.

Neither did the room show signs of madness. The French windows admitted as much light as was possible on a dreich, pallid winter's day. Various sizes of camera, their wood and brassware highly-polished, sat on shelves. Where the light was best, augmented by a large skylight, a comfortable chair and a pot-plant sat in front of a painted backdrop of a trellis with vines and flowers. A camera and tripod pointing towards them to capture the portrait of a person who wasn't there. Framed examples of photographic portraits and landscapes hung on the walls. The only peculiarity was the largest picture above the fireplace, a photograph showing a shaft of light from the skylight cutting across an empty chair.

George Bothwell-Scott replaced the cover of the camera and turned his attention to his guests.

"So sorry," he said. "How may I help you?"

"We'd like to ask you some questions about your brother William's death," said Allerdyce.

The photographer looked momentarily puzzled.

"Death, gentlemen?"

"His murder, sir. In the well. At Dalcorn."

"Ah yes, of course. William's passing-over. But please, gentlemen, we mustn't think of it as a death. It is merely a changing. A moving-on from the physical to the spiritual life." He smiled gently.

Allerdyce corrected his first impression. George Bothwell-Scott was quite possibly mad as a hatter after all. Nonetheless, he might know something useful. He pressed on, determined not to mention the content of the telegram in case it prejudiced George's views.

"We were hoping, sir, that you might be able to suggest some people who may have had particular resentments against your brother. It would help us greatly with our enquiries."

"Of course, gentlemen, I'll be happy to offer any assistance I can. Please, be seated."

They sat at the other side of the table from George, the boxy camera between them.

"Let me move that out of the way," said George. He picked the camera up. "It's a marvellous thing. Do you know anything about photography, gentlemen?"

Allerdyce thought about the struggle he'd had to get a family photograph with Alice and Bertie and baby Stephen in the commercial photographer's studio at Canonmills. The poor man had had to bribe them with sweets and amuse them by holding a toy elephant above the camera before they'd sat still long enough for the exposure. The result had been magical – Margaret sitting smiling with the baby on her lap looking happy and well, and Alice and Bertie staring open-mouthed towards the elephant as if they'd seen an angel flying by. He'd had a miniature version of the photograph made for an extra sixpence, and carried it everywhere with him in his wallet.

"No sir, I'm no photographer."

"You should be. It's the most fascinating thing I've ever done. You see life so differently when you perceive it through a lens."

"I'm sure, sir."

"Take this contraption here. It's one of my favourites, when I can get it to work properly. It's a magazine camera. It's got ten dry collodion plates in it. Wind it up, press the button, and it'll expose each plate in turn. If I point it, say, at a carriage going down a street I'll get images from moment to moment of its progress. And then if I mount the pictures on magic lantern slides I can project each one in turn, at the same speed as they were taken, and re-create the progress of the carriage before your very eyes. It's a whole new concept of time, gentlemen – the ability to revive an actual series of events whenever you choose to."

"Very interesting, sir, but I wonder if we might address ourselves to your brother's passing-over. We're anxious to find out who did it before he helps anyone else to pass-over prematurely."

"Of course."

George put the heavy camera back on the shelf beside its fellows and re-joined the policemen. Allerdyce pulled his notebook out of his pocket.

"First of all, sir, and without any regard to the practicality of whether they could have committed the murder, can you think of anyone who would have wanted to harm your brother?"

"Not specifically, no."

"Are you sure?"

"No-one comes to mind immediately."

Allerdyce paused, looking straight at George, judging whether an embarrassing silence might draw out some suggestion which the advocate had initially suppressed. McGillivray stared at him too, his arms folded. George gave a slight, guileless smile and Allerdyce continued.

"All right then, sir, perhaps we can look at this by a process of rational deduction. Can you think of anyone who might feel particularly ill-treated by your brother?"

"Well, yes, lots of people. He's had to do some harsh things, but the wisest people have always recognised that they were utterly necessary."

"Such as?"

"I'm afraid our father had left the modernisation of our estates woefully incomplete, particularly in Sutherland."

"You mean clearances, sir?" asked McGillivray. Allerdyce glanced at his sergeant, anticipating another tense interview.

"Rather a crude word, I think," said George. "When William inherited the Sutherland estates most of the tenantry had already been moved off the unprofitable land in the middle of the county – but our father had stuck for too long with the unsuccessful experiment of re-settling some of the people in new fishing hamlets on the coast. It was a poor idea – the crofters weren't going to take easily to the sea, even if they'd had the capacity and inclination to learn, and the whole enterprise made a frightful loss. People were drifting away anyway – and I'm afraid when the blight came in '47 and '48 some people passed-over from hunger – but it fell to William to take the necessary decision to close the whole enterprise down. It simply wasn't sustainable."

"So, you think someone who got cleared out of the coastal hamlets might have wanted to take their revenge?" asked Allerdyce, glancing again at the sergeant.

George looked into the space above the Inspector's head, towards the skylight, for a moment before speaking.

"Actually, no. I don't think that's the most likely situation. Most of the survivors are re-settled in Canada and probably quite happy."

"Not all of them, sir," observed McGillivray.

"Well, that's as maybe. But I think there might be someone else with a resentment."

"Being?" asked Allerdyce.

"The estate factor. Patrick Slater. I think he felt rather hard done-by."

"Why?"

"He'd been quite vigorous in implementing William's policies. He'd taken two months to clear the villages of maybe three thousand people in all. You can't do that without causing a little bit of upset, when tenants find the bailiffs piling up their furniture outside their houses and setting fire to the roof. It's always better to get these things over with quickly, even if it doesn't seem so at the time."

"My family had some acquaintance with Mr Slater, sir," said McGillivray. "In fact he served the Duke's eviction notice on my own father and brother."

"How very interesting," replied George, with a slight smile of supercilious indifference. "Of course it was slightly unfortunate – and not humanly predictable – that the county got such a sustained spell of bad weather in November – you don't normally expect storms and blizzards to set in that early. A certain number of tenants perished in the elements. I believe some more of them perished on the winter passage to Canada, but that was utterly outside William's control."

"My own father passed away on that voyage," said McGillivray, looking impassively at the advocate.

Allerdyce felt his cheeks redden. Again, the sergeant's few words hinted at an agony of pain and loss. It didn't serve the investigation well, however, if McGillivray's private grief made the witness embarrassed or cautious about the conversation. He glanced at the sergeant, holding his hand up slightly to motion him to keep silent.

George, though, seemed singularly unperturbed.

"How unfortunate, Sergeant. But not my late brother's responsibility."

"So," asked Allerdyce, "why would Mr Slater resent your brother if he'd been so loyal in carrying out his orders?"

"Well, Inspector, the law has increasingly intruded into the relations between landlord and tenant. One crofter, who'd lost his wife, took it into his head to inspire a prosecution against Slater. Mr Slater ended up in the High Court in Edinburgh, accused of culpable homicide for the energy with which he'd pursued the evictions.

"It looked briefly as if the trial might cause serious harm to the family's reputation. Mr Slater chose to forget his loyalty to his employer and blamed William for having given him so short a period within which to carry out the evictions. He claimed, completely unfairly, that William had even approved his methods. He even wanted William called as a witness.

"We were fortunate at the trial that the judge – Lord McLaren – was an old family friend. He quickly saw the absurdity of dragging a Duke into court as a witness, and reached the proper conclusion that Mr Slater was entirely responsible for the methods he'd chosen."

"So, what happened to Slater?"

"Found guilty. Sentenced to fourteen years transportation."

"And when was that?"

"1850. I forget the month."

"So, Mr Slater may already have returned to these shores, if he has survived so long?"

"It's possible, Inspector, but I don't know. For all I know he's dead, or decided to stay in Australia."

Allerdyce folded away his notebook and shifted uneasily on his seat. Again, a Bothwell-Scott had quickly fingered a favoured suspect, but had said nothing useful about the rifts which were hinted at within the family. They might be saying what they really thought, or they might be closing ranks.

"May I enquire, sir, about certain family matters?" he asked. "Purely off the record, of course, but it may help to illuminate the background to this case."

The advocate looked momentarily troubled.

"Family matters? In what sense?"

"I would simply like to understand a little more about the recent history of the Bothwell-Scott family. Your brother Frederick referred to a division in the family which was supposed to have been healed when the late Duke married the Duchess."

George Bothwell-Scott relaxed.

"I'd hardly call that division recent, Inspector. In fact, it goes back to 1745."

"The Jacobite rising?"

"Precisely, Inspector. Like so many other families, we were uncertain about the possible outcome of the conflict, so we hedged our bets. The judgement at the time was that the Jacobite cause was more likely to prevail, so James, the heir to the estate, raised a regiment to fight for Bonnie Prince Charlie while, for insurance, his brother Charles accepted a commission in the Government forces."

"Very prudent, sir."

"Well, they ended up facing each other at Culloden. If they'd been in one of Walter Scott's romances I suppose there would have been a reconciliation on the battlefield, perhaps with one of them cradling the other in his arms when he died. I'm afraid the outcome was more prosaic. James was taken prisoner and tried. He could have been hanged, but he was sentenced instead, like a common soldier, to be banished and sent into indentured labour in the West Indies. Of course, the Government confiscated his right to inherit the titles and properties he expected, in favour of his loyal Hanoverian brother Charles."

"And how," asked Allerdyce, "might this be relevant to the late Duke's marriage?"

"Well, Inspector, the reversal in James Bothwell-Scott's fortunes was not permanent. When he arrived in Jamaica he was, to all intents and purposes, a slave. He was sent to work for the owner of a sugar plantation. The plantation owner, though, was a Scot of good family who instantly recognised that James was of noble birth. He was spared the hard manual labour under the torrid sun which killed so many others, and put to work very successfully as manager of the plantation's business.

"Naturally, that kept him indoors a great deal, in the company of the plantation owner's only child, a daughter. Nature took its course, and the plantation owner granted James his freedom so that they could marry. James became heir to an estate which his own skills had rendered highly profitable."

"How very fortunate."

"That was only the start. It was James's son who saw that there were even bigger profits to be made from cotton. Cotton-growing land was cheap, the climate was slightly better than Jamaica so you didn't need to replace the slaves as often, and the new mechanical weaving machines meant it was the fabric of the future. He sold the Jamaican plantation and acquired an estate near New Orleans. The estate prospered, and the American branch of the family came to rival our own in wealth."

"And was there contact between the two sides of the family during this time, Mr Bothwell-Scott?"

"Very little I'm afraid, Inspector. I think James was rather resentful at losing his original inheritance, and the old family story is that as he left Britain he pronounced a curse that our line would become extinct. I don't think I believe that – we're still going strong, well except for poor William, over a century later. But our American cousins nursed a grievance for decades."

"So why the reconciliation? Why did your brother marry Josephine?"

George Bothwell-Scott sighed.

"It was our dear, departed mother's idea. I don't think William liked it, at first, but she was right that he had to marry. She felt it was high time that the two sides of the family came back together. I think she liked the idea, too, that we would have a property empire which spanned the Old and New Worlds. Also, I have to say that Josephine is a most splendidly handsome woman."

"So why was the late Duke resistant to the idea, Mr Bothwell-Scott? It does appear admirably rational."

George looked up at the skylight again before answering.

"William felt there were certain… impediments in the way of his marriage."

"Impediments? Of what sort?"

George leant forward and whispered to Allerdyce.

"I can't tell you. William might hear."

"What?"

"Ssssh. We must be quiet. I think I just saw his spirit."

"Really sir?"

"Yes. In the light from the skylight, just above you."

Allerdyce looked round, but only saw a patch of grey winter light.

"Are you sure, sir?"

"The spirits are all around us, Inspector. Look at the picture above the fireplace. What do you see?"

Allerdyce looked again at the large photograph.

"I can see the seat you use for posing photographic portraits, sir, with a beam of light falling across it."

"No more than that?"

"No, sir."

"Let me help you."

George stood up and went over to the picture. Allerdyce followed, the sergeant behind him. He felt the heat of the fire through the thick wool of his trousers as he looked at the strongly contrasted light and shadow of the portrait-sized photograph.

"Look closely into the beam of light, Inspector."

Allerdyce peered closer. The quality of resolution was fantastic – you could see the specks of dust floating in the light, caught in an instant of their slow eddying in the air.

"What do you see now?

"I can see dust particles in the light, sir."

"What pattern do they make?"

"I can't see a pattern."

George smiled gently.

"Not everyone sees it at first, Inspector, but it's as clear as day to me. If you look for long enough you'll see the clear pattern of a woman holding a child. I've felt the spirits around me since my poor wife died giving birth to a daughter who only survived her by hours. I've seen their spirits around me many times, to my great comfort, and I've been experimenting for years with different lenses and filters and exposures, and different coatings for my photographic plates. This picture is my first complete success at capturing their spirits in a permanent portrait."

Allerdyce could still see nothing but the random flux of airborne particles, but he felt he ought to humour the deluded photographer. He would have sought comfort in fantasies himself after Helen's death if he'd retained the ability to believe in any supernatural agencies.

"It's most remarkable, sir."

"Isn't it? And I know I can do more. Sometimes the spirits appear to me at night, a shimmering silver-white phosphorescence before my eyes. It's not always Matilda and the baby, in fact it's not always anyone who's passed over. Peoples' spirits can wander where they want when the conscious mind is asleep, and even Josephine has appeared to me on occasion."

Did she say anything useful about her husband's murder, Allerdyce wanted to ask. He felt obliged to be more tactful to at least try and get a glimmer of insight into the 'impediments' the late Duke may have felt.

"Do the spirits ever say anything to you, Mr Bothwell-Scott?"

"Sometimes I hear a soft angelic singing, like the ringing of distant bells. Sometimes they speak gentle words of comfort."

"Has your brother's spirit ever said anything to you?"

George touched him on the arm and whispered.

"Please, Inspector, William's here with us. He's angry already and I don't know what he'll do if he hears us talking about him."

"I'm sorry."

"That's all right. I'm trying to capture the night-spirits on film too. I've got a camera set up in the darkroom, on permanent exposure. The red light I use to develop my plates in silver nitrate is too dim to make an image on the photographic plate, but I believe the light of a spirit will be sufficient to be captured by the collodion."

The prospects of getting anything further of any use out of George Bothwell-Scott seemed remote in the extreme. Allerdyce nodded to the sergeant who was still staring into the picture.

"Thank you very much for your time, Mr Bothwell-Scott. It's been most useful. And please, do tell us if you get any useful information from one of your spirit visitors."

"Yes, Inspector, I will. And I wish you every success in finding Patrick Slater."

. . .

Allerdyce stood in front of Rock House, pulling on his hat against the continuing drizzle.

"What a bloody waste of time."

"Do you think so, sir?" asked McGillivray.

"Utterly. We get his half-baked theory about an estate factor who's probably dead or in Australia, and we get his ramblings about fairies or whatever. And we're told the deceased Duke has not in fact gone into the obscurity of death but is suspended in the air in the same room as us. What a load of bloody nonsense."

The sergeant was silent for a moment before answering.

"I wouldn't be so sure, sir. There's plenty of stories from where I grew up in Sutherland about the actions of spirits. And I had a mightily queer feeling myself when my father died – I seemed to see his face receding into the night-time waters like a setting moon. I didn't find out for months that the night I'd seen that vision was the night he died."

"I'm sorry, Sergeant. I'm sorry that this investigation is bringing back painful memories. I'd avoid that if I could. But I simply refuse to believe in fairies and spirit-visitors."

"That's your privilege, sir."

"So what about Mr Slater, Sergeant? The estate factor? He's obviously known to you."

"Every crofter in Sutherland thought he was the devil in a suit, sir. When he wasn't putting the rents up he was throwing people out of their homes. People liked to imagine that the Duke didn't know how harsh Slater was, and would have reined Slater in if he'd known. I never believed that. I think he was doing exactly what he was ordered to."

"So do you think he could be a suspect?"

"Perhaps, sir. But I wonder about the 'impediment' Mr Bothwell-Scott mentioned. There's clearly something important we're not being told. Perhaps it'll lead us to our criminal."

Maybe it will, thought Allerdyce, though we've already heard enough the Duke's oppressions to understand why a man might want to kill him.

What would he do when he found the suspect? He shuddered at the Chief Constable's talk of 'non-judicial' solutions.

That would have to be a problem for another day. First find the truth.

Chapter 14

"Another crumpet, Josephine?"

"Thank you, Arthur. I don't know what I'd do without your kindness."

He buttered a crumpet for her and passed it to her before topping up the tea in her cup.

It was amazing how Josephine could make the simple, and potentially coarsely physical, act of eating a *patisserie* into something delicate and beautiful. Her mourning veil was cast back from her face. Her downcast eyes, so dark and solemn, glanced demurely at him with the merest flutter of her eyelashes as she opened her lips of palest coral and gently seized the confection between her teeth, pulling almost imperceptibly at its doughy flesh before the merest morsel, glistening with melted butter, disappeared into her mouth and the slightest movement was discernible in her white throat. Arthur felt a warm flush of blood round his body which must be inspired by his desire to help this angelic creature of God.

"You've been more than kind, Arthur. I've had no-one else to turn to." She smiled, but her face spoke of affliction rather than joy.

"It's my simple duty and my inestimable privilege as a Christian, Josephine, to provide comfort where I can."

"Your quotations from the Holy Bible have been most helpful to my meditations, and a great strength to me. I've pondered long, Arthur, on the beautiful story of Ruth, left to mourn her widowhood in a strange land. It's brought me much comfort to think how Ruth found protection from a kinsman, and how the kinsman's kindness won her as his wife."

Arthur's heart leapt and he thought he would spill his tea. Could Josephine, through the Holy Scriptures, be suggesting that he might hold out some hope of winning her affections? Or was it absurd, a symptom of a too-fevered mind, to think that a widow in the depths of mourning could be suggesting any such thing to a poor, hesitant clergyman? Was it sinful of him even to think of the possibility of affection with the woman who, so recently, had been one flesh with his brother William?

Josephine continued, her smile fading.

"There's another passage that's come to my mind in recent days, Arthur. It's the beautifully simple statement, from the twenty-second chapter of the book of Exodus, that 'ye shall not afflict any widow'. I find that the Lord is bringing that passage into my awareness rather often at the moment. What can it mean?"

He put his teacup down on the table and leant forward to look into Josephine's troubled eyes.

"I don't believe the Lord has given you these words in vain. They must have been given to you to grant you confidence that, whatever your current troubles, He is with you. But Josephine, it pains me to think you may be under any affliction and I would be honoured if you would share it with me."

She took her handkerchief out of her sleeve and dabbed at the corner of her eye.

"It's so wrong of me to consider myself afflicted in any way.

For the most part I've only known kindness from your family. Your own dear mother was so anxious to welcome me into it, and your brother William always ensured that I was provided for. If William was ever harsh to me it was only because, poor man, he was so bitterly disappointed at my failure to give him the heir he so dearly wanted."

"That was hardly your fault, Josephine. It was very wrong of William to treat you inconsiderately."

"I do feel it was my fault, and that I was a burden to him. I wish I could fully have been the wife that he deserved. But, Arthur, I find myself subject to new afflictions which, even in the depths of my prayers, I cannot see that I fully merit."

"I'm sorry, Josephine. What is troubling you so?"

She looked straight at him, her eyes clear and firm.

"Your brother Frederick has told me to leave Dalcorn House."

Arthur felt a rush of rage. How could Frederick be such a heartless brute? Didn't he realise the deep sinfulness of casting a widow out of her home? He struggled to keep his voice calm.

"I'm very sorry to hear that, Josephine. I can offer no defence on his behalf."

"I would ask you to intercede with him on my behalf, but I fear there is no hope of his relenting. His heart seems set against me."

"I can only try. Has he suggested any way in which he might make other provision for you?"

"He's had the kindness to suggest that the north wing of Dornoch Palace could be opened up for me. It's thoughtful of him, but I can't go, Arthur. I've had to go to the Palace every autumn since I came here, to entertain guests when William invited houseparties to help him murder grouse and stags. I hate the place. It's always dark and cold and it's a complete charnel-house of antlers and taxidermy. And I know no-one there – it's two hundred miles away from the comfort you're able to give me."

"What else could you do, Josephine?"

"I suppose I could try and go back to Pappa. But I don't even know if that's possible – the Yankees are still blockading New Orleans and I don't know how I could get to the plantation or if the house is still standing. And even if I could get there, he's been utterly ruined by the war and I'd only be another mouth to feed."

"I must be able to do something for you. I can't let this family abandon you."

She leant towards him, her hands clasped in front of her.

"Arthur, you dear sweet man, you've done more than you know already."

"But please, Josephine, I must help you!"

He found himself, with unconscious boldness, clasping her pale hands in his, feeling their trembling warmth. She let her hands rest in his and smiled. He felt a pang of joy, and of a desire which he didn't know whether he should call sin.

"Perhaps, Arthur, there is one thing you could do for me."

"Anything. Please."

"There's a cottage on the estate, near the east lodge, which has been unoccupied for some months. It's nothing grand – merely the plain family house of a grieve – but it would suffice for my simple needs. I would still be able to benefit from your counsel and support."

"Are you sure, Josephine? It's hardly the proper residence of a Duchess."

"Arthur, please remember that I was brought up in a country where no distinction of rank existed between the orders of society. I would rather live simply among my friends than in exiled dignity.

I shall think of it as my dower-house, and God willing I may be happy there."

"Very well. I shall ask Frederick at least to have the decency to grant you that."

"Thank you."

The door opened and Arthur abruptly dropped her hands from his grasp. The servant appeared and bowed.

"What is it, Wilson? Can't you see that I'm engaged?"

"I'm sorry, sir, but the gentlemen from the police have returned. They are seeking a private interview with you."

"Well, tell them to wait."

Josephine stood up.

"No, Arthur, I should detain you no longer. You have been a great blessing to me."

She held out her hand and he kissed it before, with the soft rustling of black taffeta, she glided out of the room. The soft floral scent of her perfume remained behind her. Arthur breathed deeply, drawing in the scent as if by doing so he could absorb part of her heavenly being. He checked himself from the unfitting thought.

"All right Wilson, tidy the cakes away and show them in."

The servant piled the cakestand and the cups and saucers onto a tray and took them away. A minute later he appeared with the policemen. Arthur stood to welcome them.

"Good afternoon, gentlemen. I had not expected you."

He chose not to extend his hand. The sergeant bowed slightly, but Inspector Allerdyce's smile looked like the cunning grin of a hungry wolf. The policemen remained standing.

"What may I assist you with?"

The Inspector answered.

"We were hoping that you might be able to clarify some points which your brothers made when we interviewed them. It could be of significant assistance to our enquiries."

"I shall help you if I can, of course. What, specifically, would you like to know?"

The Inspector took out his notebook and flicked a few pages back.

"You were most helpful, sir, in your frankness about your brother's slightly shall we say... sporting interests in Edinburgh at night. Sergeant McGillivray and I followed that up by visiting certain establishments. It was a most interesting experience."

"I shudder to imagine it, Inspector. And you think that whoever murdered William may have some association with his nocturnal life?"

"It's one line of enquiry, sir."

"And, as I said before, not one with which I'm able to offer much further advice. God has had the goodness not to tempt me with any desire to see these fleshpots of Babylon for myself."

"That's most generous of the divinity, sir."

Arthur did not like the Inspector's tone. It seemed entirely unfitting when addressing the dignity of the clergy. Even if he was a poor sinner, his holy office should be respected.

The inspector continued, peering at his notes.

"I seem to recall, sir, that you told us that His Grace did, however, boast to you of his exploits, so you have some vicarious knowledge of them."

"Yes, yes."

"We were intrigued to discover the diversity of His Grace's interests when we visited his favoured establishments. He appeared to have a liking for young gentlemen as well as young ladies. Does that conform with what he told you?"

"Yes, to his shame, it does. His tastes were quite Greek in their range, though I think his overall preference was for ladies."

"Do you think His Grace may have been open to blackmail?"

"It's possible. Though I think William would be more likely to tell any blackmailer to publish and be damn... I mean confounded."

"Do you know of any man who might be in a position to blackmail him?"

"No. Not specifically."

"Do you know of any woman who might be in a position to blackmail him?"

"No. I've told you, Inspector, he only spoke to me in very general terms about the dissolution of his secret life. I can't be any more specific."

The Inspector was still smiling but was looking him uncomfortably in the eye.

"I would ask you seriously, sir, to consider your answer. Is there no man or woman known to you who would have been in a position to blackmail your brother?"

"For heaven's sake, Inspector, can't you desist from this line of questioning? I have no more to tell you."

"All right then, sir, let's forget about His Grace's night visits. There are aspects of His Grace's life that still remain obscure to me. It has been suggested to me that he may have fathered an illegitimate child or children. Do I recall that correctly from our conversation with the Brigadier, Sergeant?"

"Yes, sir. He referred to the possibility of the estate passing to a bastard."

"Thank you, Sergeant. And remind me what George Bothwell-Scott QC said about his brother's marriage to the Duchess?"

"He said there were impediments, sir."

"Yes, Sergeant. 'Impediments.' Precisely."

Arthur felt his anger rise. How dare these men of no standing come into his house and accuse his family of scandal? His fists clenched but he felt the sweat in them.

"Inspector, I fail to see how your attempt to taint my family's honour relates to my brother's tragic death. If you have no further relevant questions I must ask you to leave."

He reached out towards the bellcord but the Inspector made a sign and the sergeant moved to block his way. He looked back at the Inspector.

"This is outrageous, Inspector."

"I'm sorry, sir, but I must insist on a few minutes more of your time. I am getting a very confused picture of your brother's life, but one which suggests that one way or another he may well have made himself vulnerable to blackmail. I find it hard to believe, sir, that you have no light to shed on my confusion. It would be unfortunate if, when you're called as a witness under oath in court, you had to admit to a lack of candour."

Arthur sat down and turned his eyes towards the window, away from the policeman's fixed, smiling gaze. He felt like a trapped hare. He was silent for a moment before turning back to face the Inspector.

"All right, Inspector, there was one further thing which I did not believe to be relevant."

"Excellent. The sergeant and I would be most grateful if you could share it."

"It relates both to the impediment of which you spoke, and to the suggestion that William may have fathered an illegitimate child.

"When I was a child, old enough to begin my lessons, I had a new governess whom I shared with my brother George. She was a handsome lady who must only have been in her early or mid twenties when she was teaching us, though she seemed very grand and unattainably knowledgeable to us.

"William was already nineteen years old and only at Dalcorn during the vacations from Oxford. All through my childhood he had been a bully, and I had often suffered taunts and beatings from him."

"Did you come to hate your brother, sir?" asked the Inspector.

Dear God, thought Arthur, is he trying to make even me a suspect?

"No, Inspector. I forgave him for all his errors."

"Very generous, sir. You were telling us about the new governess."

"I was. When she arrived William's behaviour took a turn, inexplicable to me at the time, for the better. Instead of berating every poor weaker creature who came within his orbit he became quiet in company, and instead of coming into the schoolroom to disrupt our lessons he would bring flowers and sit quietly and stare at the new governess. Often, they were seen walking together arm-in-arm in the grounds. It was a brief period when my brother's presence ceased to signify pain and trouble to me."

"Most enchanting, sir. I take it this state of affairs did not continue."

"No. Without warning, after a few weeks, I came into the schoolroom in the morning and found myself confronted by a withered old woman who said she was my new governess. I asked her what had happened to the kind governess. She caned me and said that Miss Mitchell had been sent away and wasn't coming back.

"Life resumed its usual rhythm of punishment and abuse and I tried not to remember kind Miss Mitchell. It wasn't until years later that it became obvious to me that she had been sent away because of William's affection for her."

"You said, Mr Bothwell-Scott, that this related to an illegitimate child and to an impediment to William's marriage."

"Yes. It was later still, after I had been ordained, that I learnt the full story.

"I think it was something about the clerical collar that made William feel he could confide in me when he was drunk, as if the Church of Scotland offered a Roman confessional. When I look back, I think I had occasional glimpses of a deep loneliness under his bluster.

"Anyway, just before he got married to Josephine he staggered in here, rolling drunk, and told me the wedding had to be cancelled.

"I asked him why.

"He said it was impossible for him to get married since there was only one woman he had ever loved and it wasn't Josephine.

"I told him to pull himself together, and that he'd made a public promise to marry Josephine and that mother would make his life unbearable if he didn't go through with it. I told him it was his duty.

"He took a long drink from his hipflask and stared into the fire before replying. He said that it wasn't as simple as doing his duty. He said that he had in fact been through a form of marriage with the woman he loved, and that she was Augusta Mitchell. There was therefore an absolute legal impediment to his marriage to Josephine."

"And yet he married?"

"I asked him whether he was entirely separated from Miss

141

Mitchell. He said yes, utterly, he had cast her aside completely on mother's instructions. I asked him about the circumstances of his marriage. He said that, shortly after she had been expelled from Dalcorn, he had arranged to go down from Oxford to London and meet Augusta Mitchell, and had eloped with her to Paris and married her there. I asked if he had taken, or intended to take, any action to bring this unsatisfactory state of affairs to an end. He said mother had barred all talk of divorce, in which he would have had to be the guilty party. Instead he had made a large financial settlement on Miss Mitchell in return for which she had surrendered her marriage certificate to him and he had destroyed it. The settlement was sufficient, in his judgement, to preclude any trouble from Miss Mitchell or her child."

"Child?"

"A daughter. I don't know her name."

"And you proceeded to officiate at the wedding of your brother, despite having been told that it was subject to an absolute impediment?"

"William came round the next morning and said it was all a fiction and that he'd been talking nonsense under the influence of too much drink and strain."

"Did you believe him?"

"I was uncertain, but I had his word and it would have been a grave disgrace to the family if we hadn't gone ahead. I think mother might have disowned us all."

"And do you have any idea where we might find Miss Mitchell?"

"No, none. She may or may not be alive. I can tell you nothing about her daughter either." Arthur stood, feeling his legs trembling. "I have never previously told any man this story, and I only do so now under the obligation to assist you in finding my brother's murderer. I must ask you to maintain the strictest possible confidence."

The Inspector put his notebook away.

"Thank you, sir, you have been most unexpectedly helpful. We will happily see ourselves out."

The policemen left, and Arthur rang the bell to get Wilson to bring him a large sherry. As he waited he thought about the slight chinks of likeability he had seen in William – his love for Miss Mitchell, his impulsive marriage to her, and maybe even a refusal to give in to blackmail which had led to his death at the well.

And yet, when he thought of Josephine's years of misery and abuse at his hands his heart hardened and he found it impossible to mourn.

And now Frederick had effortlessly assumed responsibility for tormenting poor Josephine, throwing her out of what had become the only home she had.

Anyway, one way or another God had a way of dealing with these things. As the Lord said in St Paul's letter to the Hebrews, 'Vengeance belongeth to me, and I will recompense'.

Amen – and let it be soon.

Chapter 15

Allerdyce thought he'd walked into the wrong meeting when he saw Inspector Jarvis seated in front of Burgess's desk. Burgess signalled Allerdyce to come in.

"The Chief Constable has asked Mr Jarvis to join us, Allerdyce. The Chief has given Mr Jarvis special responsibilities for counter-sedition and asked him to assist us with this case since it involves a senior public personage."

"I see."

"Purely advisory, Allerdyce. Nothing to undermine your role as investigating officer."

That'll be right, thought Allerdyce. I suppose the Chief just doesn't quite trust Burgess and me to do his dirty work for him. He gave a sidelong glance at Jarvis and saw the faintest hint of a self-satisfied smirk.

"So," asked Burgess. "Where are we? Do we have a murderer yet?"

Allerdyce outlined the evidence from his interviews with the Duke's brothers – their identification of James Semple and Patrick Slater as suspects, their reluctance to volunteer information about the dead Duke's discarded wife Augusta Mitchell and her daughter, and the almost innumerable range of men and women who could have blackmailed the Duke about his sexual conduct.

"What do you think about the blackmail possibility, Allerdyce?" asked Burgess.

"I'm not sure, sir. Blackmail's a parasitical growth. It depends on the continued survival of its host."

"And the rest of the people identified?"

"Too early to say, sir. I'd like to find out more about them, and interview them if possible. As yet, we don't know where they are, or even if all of them are still alive."

"What do you think, Mr Jarvis?"

Inspector Jarvis smiled thinly, but it didn't reach his eyes which focussed on Allerdyce.

"I think I can help Inspector Allerdyce to find the prime suspect. We've had our eye on James Semple for some time because of his work to stir up industrial insurgency in the mines. It would make perfect sense for him to murder a leading mine-owner as part of his revolutionary plot."

"Jarvis, I think you're leaping to an assumption," said Allerdyce. He felt himself standing on top of a greased slide that led straight towards a 'non-judicial outcome' with no pause for evidence and judgement.

"Well, Allerdyce," said Jarvis, "I've always thought of you as a bit of a socialist, but you surely don't want to protect revolutionaries from justice."

"I don't, Jarvis. I just don't think we're in a position to say Semple is necessarily a strong suspect."

"You surely wouldn't object if I enabled you to interview Mr Semple? I could arrange that."

Burgess looked across the desk at the two men.

"That sounds fair enough doesn't it, Allerdyce? And do you think you can arrange it, Mr Jarvis?"

"I'm sure."

"Allerdyce?"

"Yes. All right. But I don't want us to do anything to him which isn't supported by good evidence."

"Of course not. Thank you, gentlemen."

Allerdyce stood. He let Jarvis leave the room first. Looking at Jarvis's back he hated every macassared hair and carefully-tailored thread of his rival. He thought of Sergeant Baird, jobless and destitute to serve Jarvis's ambition. He thought of each poor soul convicted on the basis of Jarvis's meticulously and inventively manufactured testimony. Christ, he thought, with Jarvis on the case what hope of justice is there for any of us?

...

Jarvis had briefed Allerdyce on how to find James Semple. A paid informer in the union had told Jarvis that Semple was going to speak at a meeting of miners at an inn in Winchburgh in Linlithgowshire. The informer would infiltrate Allerdyce and McGillivray into the meeting, and the policemen would have to seek their opportunity to seize the trade unionist and hustle him out the back door of the inn where Jarvis would be waiting to spirit them all away.

Finally, Jarvis had passed a revolver across the table.

"Put this in your pocket, Allerdyce. You may need it for personal protection if the men suspect you're police. A constable from Glasgow was beaten senseless outside a union meeting last November when the men found out who he was."

Jarvis had gone on ahead of Allerdyce and the sergeant. He'd said he wanted to remain invisible, as far as possible, since once his face was known he'd be the target of seditionist plots. So Allerdyce was left feeling the unfamiliar bulk of the revolver in the pocket of his stinking working man's jacket while the third-class carriage rattled and swayed its way through the darkness.

He and McGillivray were the only passengers to alight when the train drew up at Winchburgh station. He looked up and down the platform for the informer who was meant to meet them, but there was no-one visible in the dim gaslight except for the train's guard. After an instant the guard blew his whistle, climbed back into his compartment, and with a hiss and a squeal the train pulled away, leaving the policemen on the deserted platform.

"So what do you think we should do?" he asked McGillivray.

"Wait a while, I suppose. Maybe our contact is on his way."

"Do you think Jarvis has set us up to fail? Do you think he's sent us out here for nothing?"

"It wouldn't surprise me at all."

They stood for a couple of minutes more, their breath forming clouds in the chill air.

"Damn that man Jarvis." Allerdyce kicked the gravel of the platform, the unfamiliar weight of the steel-capped boot giving him an unaccustomed force. "He promised us the contact would be here."

"Maybe we should try and find the meeting ourselves. I don't know if we'd get in, but it may be worth a try."

"All right then. Let's walk into the village."

They left the platform and turned into the unlit lane which led up from the station. On the far side of the lane, behind straggling hawthorn branches, the moon reflected in the still water of the Union Canal.

Their footsteps were soft on the beaten earth of the lane, but

Allerdyce could still hear the heavy, regular paces of his companion. He turned around as he heard a lighter, less regular pace behind him, his hand reaching into his pocket and touching the body-warmed metal of the revolver.

Even in the moonlight he recoiled instinctively from the thin, rat-like features of the man who'd crept up behind them, his face the only patch of lightness against his dark bonnet and his shapeless black clothes. His hand closed firmly around the handle of the revolver as he wondered for an instant if Jarvis's plan had been discovered – or deliberately disclosed – and whether he was facing a trade union enforcer instead of the informer he was meant to meet. He said the password that Jarvis had told him, ready to pull the pistol out if he had to.

"Unity and brotherly love."

"All right." The informer walked up to them. He took his hands – weaponless – out of his pockets and Allerdyce let go of the gun. "I'll get you in. You'd get lynched if you just tried to get into the meeting by yourselves."

"Thank you."

"But if there's going to be trouble – and it sounds to me like you're going to cause some – I won't be any part of it."

"I wouldn't expect you to be."

The informer looked McGillivray up and down.

"Christ, he's a bit big to be a miner, isn't he? He's going to stand out a mile. Can't you leave him outside?"

"My colleague has to come in with me."

"All right, but it's going to take some explaining. Let's walk."

The set off up the lane. The informer kept talking.

"The men at the meeting are all from the shale mine here. Semple's come to stir them up. He's wanting to cause a strike. The fools will probably listen to him but they're mad if they think they can win."

"Why are you helping us?" asked Allerdyce. He couldn't shake off the feeling that the informer might be leading them into a trap.

"Because striking's useless. I was on strike once for two months, but after weeks of eating whatever rubbish we could find on peoples' middens we had to go back. There's always a score of men wanting your job if you're not prepared to work. We've a wee girl now, she's already sick, and I need to work to feed her. And I'm being paid for this."

Bribery. That sounds like Jarvis's way, thought Allerdyce. But he couldn't help picturing the informer's girl coughing consumptively in a damp, dark miner's cottage while little Alice slept in her comfortable bed.

They turned from the lane into the mean main street of the village. Single-storey cottages fronted directly onto the tarmacadam, without any tree or garden to relieve the drabness. With no streetlights, they walked by the pale moonlight and the occasional crack of light from a window. A dark mound rose behind the houses, silhouetted against the starry cobalt of the sky. It looked like a hill, but Allerdyce knew it must be the smoking spoil-heap of the mine. A handful of other drab figures shuffled, stooped, along the road towards the only well-lit building in the street.

They reached the building and saw the sign 'The Artisan's Arms' above the door, with the emblem of the compass and set-square.

"Semple's pretending he's a worker on the tramp," said the informer. "This inn's a house of call for unemployed mining

149

engineers. They walk round the houses of call across the country, and if they're union members they'll get a meal and a bed for the night at the union's expense, and get told if there's any vacancies locally. It's a good way for an agitator to get round the country."

They followed a short, limping man into the bar. Only a couple of men were ordering drinks. The limping man went straight past the bar to a door beside it, whispered something to the heavily-built bearded workman who stood at the door, and disappeared through it. As the door opened Allerdyce could briefly hear a murmur of voices.

The workman stood in front of the door as they approached it.

"Who are these men?" he demanded of the informer.

"Fraternal visitors from Lodge Polkemmet."

"All right. Pass, brothers."

The door opened into a large hall with a stage at one end. Miners in worn dark jackets and moleskin trousers, each with a dark bonnet and wearing heavy boots or clogs, stood murmuring and coughing, some of them spitting phlegm into brass spittoons on the floor. Allerdyce glanced behind him to the door, wondering whether, if any trouble broke out, he and the sergeant could get out and past the doorman before they got a kicking. The sergeant's presence beside him was some reassurance, but the fact that McGillivray towered a good six inches over anyone else in the room could only increase their conspicuousness. The revolver felt more like a danger than a security, too, as they threaded their way through the crowd behind the informer, the pistol's weight banging against people as he squeezed past.

They got towards the front of the crowd, looking up at the stage, which was bare except for a couple of wooden chairs at one side and, at the back, a great red banner with the words 'Amalgamated Fraternity of Scottish Mineworkers: Lodge Winchburgh No. 23' embroidered above a gold laurel wreath which enclosed the representation of a crossed pickaxe and shovel with a paraffin lamp radiating painted yellow light above them.

Allerdyce still couldn't see how they could safely apprehend James Semple and get him out of the building. Presumably he would appear from the door at the back of the stage, beside the banner. But how could they see him privately?

The informer must have been reading his mind.

"I'm on the area committee, so it's my job to tell Semple when to come out. I'll tell him that you want to pass on fraternal greetings from your lodge after the meeting, and he'll see you in the back room behind the stage."

"Thank you."

"I'll get on with it now."

The informer climbed up the steps at the edge of the stage and went into the back room. The murmur from the crowd was growing louder. One voice, high and clear above the murmur, started chanting.

"Semple. Semple. Semple."

Other voices, hoarser and deeper took up the call, and soon the whole was roaring, shaking with the pounding of boots and clogs.

"Semple! Semple! Semple!"

Allerdyce took up the chant to blend in, feeling its unfamiliar mesmeric power as he called out and stamped his heavy boots on the floorboards.

At length, the door at the back of the stage was opened by the informer. Semple entered and stood at the centre of the stage, the informer creeping behind him to take his seat at the side.

Semple, nearly six foot tall with tousled blond hair, jacketless and with his shirtsleeves rolled up to show his wiry forearms, stood still for a second and let the acclamation roll over him before raising his hands for silence. He scanned his audience for a moment before speaking.

"Brethren, I thank you. You do me great honour by inviting me here tonight, to assist in your courageous struggle against oppression."

"Down with the mineowners!" shouted the man who'd started the chant. "Equal pay for all!"

Interesting, thought Allerdyce, he's been planted to manipulate the audience.

Semple held his hands up again.

"Thank you brother, thank you. You've summarised my speech so well that perhaps I need not continue, but with your assent I will.

"Brothers, there is little I can tell you that you do not already know. You know, because you live it daily, the grinding oppression which is forced on you by the mineowners and the managers. You know the burden of toiling underground, in dampness and darkness, for ten hours a day, six days a week, for barely a pound a week. You know the dangers of death you face daily, whether from the explosion of firedamp or the collapse of a mineshaft roof, for a pittance which will barely feed your children until they, too, are old enough to be enslaved by capital and consigned to a living death in the mines. In this very mine, not a year ago, you lost four boys, none of them older than fifteen, when a roof collapsed on them."

There was an angry murmur and a groan from the crowd. Semple continued.

"The mineowners steal from you even while they are killing you and your children. You feel a just anger at the theft of your wages when the managers extort, from each miserable pay packet, a deduction for the costs of the very tools you use to hew their wealth from the ground and for the costs of the miserable cottages they compel you to rent from them. That theft is compounded by the larceny of the bosses' insistence that you buy the very essentials of life from the overpriced company shops run by their agents."

Allerdyce glanced at the faces around him. They had a lean-ness, a hardness, which you seldom saw among the slum-dwellers of Edinburgh. Their hollow-cheeked pallor seemed to be animated by anger. Listening to Semple, he could feel a spark of their anger in himself. Steady, he thought, you're here to do a job.

Semple's voice rolled on, clear, poised and rational. His tensed arms and clenched fists showed a passion underlying his words, as if he was looking for a mineowner to come up and fight him on the stage.

"You know new oppressions daily. Where, in previous years, you were barely able to subsist on five shillings a day, you are now told by the Lothian Paraffin Company that 'market circumstances' mean that your wages are necessarily reduced to four shillings and sixpence and may have to fall further, to a bare four shillings. When in previous years you were expected to mine a ton of shale a day, and a ton was reckoned at an honest twenty hundredweight, you are now told that the Lothian Paraffin Company regards twenty-two hundredweight as the substance of a modern ton.

"In the name of all that is decent and honest, in the richest nation this world has ever known, amidst prosperity for the capitalist bosses that King Midas himself could never have imagined, how can this be?"

A voice from the back of the hall – a different one – shouted.

"Shame! It's a bloody scandal!"

Another voice started

"Shame on the capitalist bastards!"

A chant started.

"Shame! Shame! Shame!"

The boots thundered against the floor again, and this time Allerdyce was quick to take up the chant. As he chanted he felt how easily the passion and rhetoric could sway a man.

Semple raised his hands and quieted the audience again.

"Comrades, often we feel powerless in the face of such oppression. Singly, we can be dismissed, blacklisted, turned out to starve. Sometimes even our victories can seem hollow – we rejoiced when one of the worst of the mineowners, our neighbour the Duke of Dornoch, met a fitting end, but without pause he was replaced by as black an oppressor.

"But, comrades, a new dawn is fast approaching."

Semple reached into the back pocket of his trousers and pulled out a worn-looking red book.

"Comrades, every working man who can read should have this book. 'The Communist Manifesto.' In it, our international leader Karl Marx tells us that in the war between workers and capital, a war waged for so long with unequal weapons, victory can be ours, and inevitably will be ours as the capitalist system is engulfed in the flames it has fuelled with oppression and injustice."

Not if Jarvis has anything to do with it, thought Allerdyce.

"The capitalists have known for decades that victory lies in unity. They have formed combinations to agree on the prices of goods, and on the wages they will pay to the workers, so that they can assure themselves of the maximum profit with the minimum cost and without the inconvenience of competition. When we come together to demand a living wage, we are denounced as an illegal combination and the forces of the state – from paid informers to mounted police and oppressive judges – are ranged against us."

Allerdyce shifted uneasily at the mention of informers, looking towards the rat-like man on the stage, who seemed even paler than he had before. Semple continued.

"Comrades, patiently and carefully, meeting by meeting, we have built the unity among working men which will be our unassailable weapon in the revolutionary struggle which is coming. Our work here is part of an enterprise which crosses all boundaries of nationality and belief, seeing common cause between workers everywhere in the overthrow of the capitalist system and the state apparatus which supports it.

"Fellow-workers, you are right to want to strike against the cutting of your wages by your bosses. You would be right to strike to demand double, nay triple, the wages which you are paid for the daily risk of your lives to build capitalist fortunes. Across Scotland, and beyond, your brothers in the mines and factories are also right to want to strike.

"So, comrades, strike! Strike when the union gives you the word, and I promise you will be supported.

"Brothers, what I am proposing is not simply that you strike alone against the Lothian Paraffin Company, but that every miner in Scotland, of coal, ironstone or shale, will rise in a co-ordinated general strike whose only outcome can be complete victory!

"I ask only for your shortest period of patience while the final arrangements are put in place.

"Comrades, arise! You have nothing to lose but your chains!"

The hall was rocked by a thunderous, stamping cheer. Through the chaos of applause a clear voice started singing:

> *Arise, ye workers from your slumbers,*
> *Arise ye prisoners of want;*
> *For reason in revolt now thunders*
> *And at last ends the age of cant.*
> *Away with all your superstitions,*
> *Servile masses arise, arise.*
> *We'll change henceforth the old tradition*
> *And spurn the dust to win the prize.*

A few voices joined in the chorus:

> *So comrades, come rally*
> *And the last fight let us face.*
> *The Internationale*
> *Unites the human race.*

As the chorus was repeated more workers joined in, until a mighty tide of sound was rolling from behind Allerdyce. He glanced sideways to see that the sergeant was singing lustily, his hand over his heart.

Finally, as the singing subsided, Semple disappeared backstage. The rousing chorus over, the hall rang to the loud and angry conversation of the miners. Occasional words drifted out of the general hubbub – 'strike', 'unity', 'blacklegs', 'bastards'.

The informer came down from the stage and edged his way through the crowd towards the policemen.

"All right, you can present your greetings to Semple now. I'll introduce you, then you're on your own."

He led them up the steps to the stage. As he mounted the

steps, Allerdyce couldn't help thinking that he was acting as an unwilling agent of the mineowners in apprehending Semple. His heart felt like lead. This is serving Jarvis, not justice, he thought. It's oppression.

The informer opened the door at the back of the stage and showed the policemen in.

"Brothers from Lodge Polkemmet, Mr Semple. They want to pass on their fraternal greetings."

"Fine."

Semple was standing at the table the centre of room, splashing his face from a bowl of water beside which stood a pitcher. He picked a towel from the back of a chair. As he dried his face and hands Allerdyce noticed the door in the left hand wall and the window to the outdoors darkness, praying to his non-existent god that the door wouldn't be locked.

Semple put the towel down.

"Polkemmet, eh? How stand things there?"

Allerdyce was relived that the sergeant responded, in his more authentically working-class accent.

"Tense, Mr Semple. The men are only waiting for your word to strike."

"Is that so? I think we're really going to do it this time. The whole country united."

Semple looked the sergeant up and down.

"You're like me. Too big to be down the mine. What do you do?"

"I did learn to mine, Mr Semple, in the Crimea. But I'm employed at the pithead as a banksman."

"You poor sod. I don't know how anyone can live on a banksman's 3 shillings a day."

Allerdyce was conscious that he was procrastinating while the sergeant improvised. He gave the sergeant a nod and McGillivray came close to Semple, standing behind him. Allerdyce moved to stand as close as he could to Semple, conscious that the corner of the table was still between them. He spoke softly, in case anyone was listening through the door, though the babble of voices in the hall was still audible through it.

"Mr Semple, I am Inspector Allerdyce of the City of Edinburgh Police. I must ask you to accompany me to the Police Office for an interview."

Semple rushed for the door back to the stage. The sergeant grabbed him hard in a full-Nelson grip and Semple, his spine arched, grimaced. He strained to speak.

"What's this about?"

"The murder of the Duke of Dornoch."

"That's absurd!"

"Is it, Mr Semple?"

"I was in Ayrshire when he died." Semple spluttered with pain. "I can prove it."

"You can explain that at the Police Office. You have to come with us."

"And then what will you do to me? Damn you to hell for this."

Semple kicked out as the sergeant lifted him bodily from the floor, and a chair clattered to the bare floorboards. Allerdyce opened the back door and the sergeant thrust Semple into the chill outdoor darkness, still clasping him tightly by the arms.

Allerdyce was completely unprepared for what happened next.

The sergeant was barely through the door, Allerdyce right behind him, when a shot cracked out from the darkness.

Semple didn't scream. He only gave a short 'ugh' before his body went limp in the sergeant's grasp. McGillivray stumbled backwards before regaining his footing.

"I think it's got me too, sir."

Allerdyce pushed past him, drawing the revolver from his pocket. He could just make out a dark figure running into trees. He held his pistol out at arms length but the figure ducked and weaved between branches, making a clear shot impossible, disappearing into the utter darkness of the forest.

Before disappearing completely the figure stopped and seemed to turn. Allerdyce took aim, but before he pulled the trigger he saw a flash of light in the woods and reeled with a sharp pain in his left arm. He steadied himself and returned fire, but the man had started running again.

He dropped his revolver and put his right hand to his injured arm. He felt dampness through the serge of his jacket, then put his fingers to his mouth and tasted blood.

He turned round. By the light of the door he saw a warped *pieta*, the sergeant kneeling with the trade unionist in his arms, blood trickling from Semple's mouth as his sightless eyes looked heavenward.

"He's gone, sir."

"And you?"

"I think it maybe just clipped me. Can you run, sir?"

"Yes."

"Then head for the trees. The men are coming from the hall. They'll kill us."

Allerdyce knelt and felt on the ground for the revolver.

"For God's sake sir, just run! I'll follow!"

He gave up feeling for the gun and ran headlong for the trees, his arm pulsing fresh agony with every tortured pace. He heard a shout behind him.

"There they are! The bastards have shot Semple! After them, boys!"

The sergeant's voice was closer.

"I'm right behind you, sir. Run faster. They've seen us."

"Where's Jarvis?"

"God alone knows. Run!"

Allerdyce ran as fast as he could, clasping his shattered arm and feeling the blood pump with each stride. Branches grazed his face and hands and he pushed past them. Don't let me die, he thought, don't let me die tonight. He thought about the photograph in his wallet, the family he should have been at home with instead of careering around in the woods between a mob and an assassin.

He stumbled over a root, falling heavily onto his left arm. Everything before his eyes went red and he thought he would pass out with dizziness and nausea.

The sergeant stood above him in the darkness.

"Get up, sir."

"I don't know if I can."

"Get up, sir. You have to."

He felt the sergeant pull him roughly to his feet.

"Run."

The voices of the mob were only a few yards away.

"Run! I'll distract them! We'll take different directions. Run!"

He launched himself again into the wood, staggering without direction between the trees. He heard the sergeant shout to the mob.

"You'll never catch us!"

The branches brushed and crackled over to his right as the

mob followed the sergeant. After a few moments he heard an angry shout and what sounded like a hard punch and head being shoved against a tree before the running started again, becoming gradually more distant.

Allerdyce ran for as long as his strength could carry him. At last, when he thought he could go no further, the forest cleared and he found himself beside the canal. Beyond it the moonlight glinted on the silvered steel of the railway, but it was inconceivable that he could cross the canal. It might as well have been the Styx, for all his chance of reaching the other side alive. Men were still shouting in the forest and branches were cracking, some of them sounding as if they were getting nearer. But he couldn't run. He couldn't even stand. He lay down by the canalside hedge like an injured bird waiting for a predator. He knew he could resist unconsciousness no longer, whether he was going to live or die.

I'm sorry, Margaret, he thought. You don't deserve to be left alone. Do your best for the children. I'd come home if I could.

Chapter 16

For an uncertain period nothing in his mind had given him a solid purchase on where he was or on the passing of time. He'd felt himself floating through different, varyingly bizarre situations. His wounds had been washed down by Margaret while Antonia massaged him to arousal. He'd been carried across country by a giant McGillivray and laid gently under a hedge. He'd been floating away to a warm sensual heaven, called by a flame-haired Rosetti angel whose shimmering face never quite resolved itself into Helen's, until another angel had slapped him harshly on the cheek.

"Wake up, Mr Allerdyce! Wake up! You have a visitor!"

"Not possible. I don't even believe in heaven."

The angel slapped him again and he opened his eyes. The white-starched female leaning over him was out of focus, but his eyes fixed more clearly on the familiar bull-headed figure behind her.

"Burgess? Are you dead too?"

"Don't be daft, man. I'm as alive as you are."

"Oh. Is that good?"

"Better than it should have been. You could have bled to death."

The nurse left them. Allerdyce tried to prop himself up, felt an electric pain up his left arm and into the centre of his brain, and subsided back onto his pillows.

"Where am I?"

"The Royal Infirmary. You're lucky about that too. The helmsman of a barge spotted you and put you on board. He thought you were a vagrant and handed you over to the workhouse hospital in Linlithgow. They found your warrant card in your jacket when they sent it away to be fumigated and got in touch with us."

"What happened?"

"That's what I'd like you to help me understand, Allerdyce. I find that I've got two injured policemen and one dead suspect in circumstances which are not at all clear to me."

"What about McGillivray?"

"He'll live. He got a nasty graze on his chest from a bullet and some bruises from a beating. He's resting at home."

"Paid?"

"I've seen to that. But Allerdyce, what happened?"

Allerdyce told the Superintendent about the meeting and the chaos that followed. Burgess frowned.

"That's consistent with what Sergeant McGillivray told me. It's not entirely the same as what Jarvis said."

The mention of Jarvis caused a fresh flash of pain as Allerdyce lifted his head.

"Jarvis? Was he there? He was meant to meet us but we didn't see him."

"He says he was there, but that the disturbance made it impossible for him to meet you as arranged. Once the mob started chasing you he had no chance of escorting you away and had to look to his own safety."

"What a hero."

"What disturbs me, Allerdyce, is that Jarvis claims not to have seen anyone in the woods, and not to have seen any shots from there."

"I've told you everything I can, sir, and I swear it's the truth."

"So Jarvis is lying?"

"What do you think, sir?"

The Superintendent paused, frowning.

"I don't know, Allerdyce, I really don't know. If I was being charitable I'd say that in the confusion of the event it's unsurprising that different people should have seen different things. But if I had my own way I'd suspend all of you until the matter had been properly investigated. No offence to you, Allerdyce, but it's a serious matter when a suspect dies during a police operation, and all the more so when the policemen involved can't agree about the facts."

"So what are you going to do, sir?"

"Nothing. The Chief Constable has congratulated me on a successful outcome to the operation and told me that, as far as I'm concerned, that's an end of the matter."

"And do you really think that McGillivray or I wouldn't tell you the truth about what happened?"

Burgess drew closer to Allerdyce and spoke softly.

"No, Allerdyce, I don't. But I'm not so sure about Jarvis. I don't know what he's doing most of the time – he keeps getting orders directly from the Chief Constable – and I don't like it. But the man's become untouchable – the Chief thinks he can do no wrong."

"I see."

Allerdyce shifted position awkwardly before continuing.

"Sergeant McGillivray saved my life, sir. I'd like him to receive a commendation."

Burgess looked tired and old again.

"I'm sorry, that's not going to be possible."

"Why?"

"Because the Chief says that the operation never officially happened at all."

...

The nurse unwound the bandage, red-black with caked blood, from Allerdyce's arm before pulling the matted cotton wadding away from the wound.

"Ow! God! Please, Sister, that hurts!"

"It's for your own good, Mr Allerdyce. And besides, you want to be looking your best when your wife comes to visit, don't you?"

"Margaret is here?"

"She's just waiting outside the ward until visiting hour starts. The gentleman who came earlier was admitted specially."

He looked at the cauterised red-black of the open wound and shivered as, at its base, he saw a sliver of white bone.

"How bad is it, Sister?"

"The surgeon had to cut away some flesh because the bullet had drawn in some filthy fabric from your clothes which was starting to go septic. The bullet just chipped your bone slightly."

"It'll heal?"

"It'll take a while to become completely better, but thanks to this new carbolic spray it shouldn't become infected, so you'll be all right. Once you're fit to leave here we'll give your wife instructions about changing the dressings while it heals. Hold still while I put some more on."

The nurse pressed the plunger on a little brass can and sprayed antiseptic onto the wound. Allerdyce wasn't sure what was worse – the intense stinging or the chemical stench. She pressed fresh cotton wadding onto the wound and then bandaged it, briskly but neatly.

"All right then, Mr Allerdyce, slip your dressing gown on and we'll let the ladies in."

The nurse rang a handbell and a handful of ladies entered the ward, clutching baskets with fruit or flowers. Ahead of them ran little Alice in her blue bonnet and coat, a posy in her hands.

"Daddy! Daddy! Daddy!"

She ran up to the bed, jumped on and pressed the posy up to his nostrils.

"Oh Daddy, are you going to die? Please don't die, Daddy, I don't want you to die."

He put his good arm around her, trying not to wince as she accidentally pressed her elbow against his wound.

"No, darling, I'll be all right. I've just hurt my arm a little."

"Oh good. I love you, Daddy."

She nestled against him, her thumb in her mouth.

Margaret came up to the bed. She still looked thin-faced and drawn, but in the clear light from the ward windows he could see a certain beauty in the delicacy of the features.

"Alice, you'll have to get down from there," she said. "You're not allowed on the beds."

"I don't want to!"

The nurse came up.

"Get down right now, little girl. It's unhygienic."

Sulkily, Alice let her mother remove her from the bed. Margaret sat down beside the bed, Alice standing in front of her.

"Archibald, I've been so worried. The Superintendent called to see me earlier. He said you were still under the chloroform but he thought you'd wake up during the day."

"Did he tell you what happened?"

"He said you were shot at on a secret mission."

Margaret looked round the ward, where the sick and injured were doing their best to look cheerful for their visitors.

"I didn't want to bring Alice to this terrible place but she was insistent she wanted to come. Millie's looking after Bertie and the baby."

"I'm glad you both came."

She pulled her handkerchief out and wiped away a tear.

"Oh Archibald, your life shouldn't have been like this."

"Margaret, I'll be all right."

"I wish I could believe that, Archibald. But every time you've gone out at night I've worried that something will happen, and now it has. It could be worse next time."

"Margaret, I'll be careful. I always am."

"But that's not good enough is it? One night someone's going to get you, whether you're careful or not."

"Please, Margaret, don't upset yourself. It's not much more than a bad scratch."

"It's so unfair, Archie. You should have been a doctor. Or anything you wanted. If only your father hadn't lost all his money."

"It wasn't his fault. He was cheated. He wanted to believe the best of everyone. It broke his heart that he'd misplaced his trust in his business partner."

"I know, but if you'd been able to complete your degree you wouldn't have to put yourself in danger. You'd be a doctor, and you'd come home every night to a nice new home in the Grange. Other people got scholarships when their parents couldn't afford the fees."

"Yes, but they were the sons of clergy. No-one had endowed a scholarship for the sons of printworks owners. And my life would have been completely different. I might never have met you, Margaret."

Alice, getting bored, was pulling at the bedclothes.

"Don't do that, dear."

She pouted at her mother.

"I sometimes think that's the start of your silly prejudice against religion," said Margaret, sniffing back tears. "Do you know, I pray for you every day, morning and evening? That I pray that you'll come back safe to me? I suppose you think that's nonsense."

"No, I'm grateful, whether it does any good or not."

Margaret's tears were coming more strongly now.

"I love you, Archie. I need you to stay safe. Please, Archie, be careful. For me."

"I will."

"Now look what you've done. I'm crying in front of Alice as if I was a baby myself."

"That's all right."

"I'd better go now. I'll come back tomorrow. Alice, come on."

Alice looked up at her father.

"I'll say a prayer for you too, Daddy."

As they left, he put his hand over the posy which Alice had left on his chest. He though for a moment that he, too, was about to cry, thinking about Margaret and the children left alone if the bullet had found its target. He'd not loved her as well as he should, and she deserved better. Alice deserved a father who could give her all the love and attention she needed. But as he drifted off to sleep it was Antonia's face that he saw, her lips descending to meet his as she stroked her fingers gently down his body. He fought the image, struggling against what felt like a double infidelity against both Margaret and Helen, but the memory of Antonia's erotic genius overcame his will as he surrendered to oblivion.

Chapter 17

After three more days the wound had healed enough for him to be discharged. Allerdyce knew clearly what his first duty was.

McGillivray's home was a short walk down the hill from Cumberland Street, on some flat, flood-prone land beside the Water of Leith where rows of workmans' houses known as the Colonies had been newly built.

As Allerdyce walked past the rows of identical little two-storey terraces, with steps up to the upper flats, he realised that he knew nothing about the home life of the man who'd twice saved his life. Children were playing in the cobbled streets and washing gaily flapped in the breeze in the little front yards – might any of these children be the sergeant's? He felt a twinge as his heavy coat pressed on the dressing of his wound.

Finally he saw 'Rintoul Place' carved into the stonework of one of the corner houses. He pushed his way past a washing line of wet sheets and bandages to get to the front door of number 14. He rapped at the door and a plump, comely red-haired woman, probably no older than thirty, opened the door.

"Can I help you, sir?"

He instantly recognised a Gaelic accent.

"My name is Inspector Allerdyce. I've come to pay my compliments to Mr McGillivray."

"Oh sir, come in, come in. Hector will be so pleased to see you."

She showed him into the hall and disappeared into the room at the end. He could hear her calling the sergeant.

"Hector! Hector! Your Mr Allerdyce has come to see you!"

McGillivray came down the hall in his stocking soles. Allerdyce noticed a caked stain of blood on the right hand side of the chest of the sergeant's white shirt.

"By God, it's good to see you, sir. When we last parted I wasn't sure that either of us would meet again in this life."

The sergeant clasped his hand and shook it.

"Come through to the parlour, sir. Jeannie will put some tea on for us."

The sergeant led him through to the small parlour, where a fire was burning in the black-leaded range, a kettle already on the boil on the hob beside it. McGillivray's wife could be seen in the tiny scullery which opened off the parlour, fetching a tin out of a cupboard. Two little children, a boy and a girl with dark curly hair, looking about four and six years old and in patched clothes, were sitting on the rug in front of the fire playing with a little wooden dog on wheels.

"Children," said McGillivray, "This is Mr Allerdyce of the police force."

They stood up and shyly proffered their hands to be shaken. Allerdyce shook each child's hand.

"All right then, children," said the sergeant, "now go and entertain yourselves while Mr Allerdyce and I talk."

The girl opened curtains which Allerdyce hadn't noticed into a

171

bed-recess at the end of the room opposite the single window. She pulled her brother, still clutching the toy dog, up into the bed and shut the curtains behind them.

"Please, sir, take a seat."

There were easy chairs either side of the range and the men lowered themselves into them.

"The Superintendent told me you'd survived and were in the Infirmary, sir. I can't tell you how glad I was to hear that."

"I'm in your debt for it, Sergeant."

McGillivray's wife came through with a tray.

"Do have some fruitcake, Mr Allerdyce. I'll fill the teapot and then leave you men to talk."

"Thank you. I hope I'm not imposing."

"Not at all, sir. It's our privilege."

She pulled the curtain of the bed recess aside.

"Come on, children, no spying on our guests. Go and play outside."

She bustled out with the children and Allerdyce was left facing the sergeant. In the silence he was embarrassed that he had practically nothing social to say to the man he spent more waking time with than his own wife. After a few moments he tried to break the silence.

"That's a fine family you have, Sergeant."

"Aye, they are that, sir. They're a daily blessing to me."

Silence settled again as the two men supped their tea, then McGillivray spoke.

"It was a queer business, sir."

"It was certainly that."

"I mean Mr Jarvis not turning up, and that man shooting at us."

"The queerest business I've ever been mixed up in in over twenty years police service, Sergeant."

McGillivray paused.

"I don't think any of us was meant to come out of that alive, sir."

"You think so?"

"Doesn't look like it to me, sir. I think it suited someone that Mr Semple should be killed outright rather than questioned and tried. I don't think they wanted any witnesses to survive either. It was their bad luck that they didn't shoot well enough to kill us, but they probably reckoned the crowd would finish us off."

"As they might well have done, Sergeant."

"I'll tell you one peculiar thing too. The informer was ready to open the door from the stage and let the men through as soon as Mr Semple had been shot. I think he was in on it, sir."

"I wouldn't be surprised."

"So you see my point, sir."

"Yes. I'd been thinking along similar lines myself."

McGillivray leant back in his chair.

"Do you think Semple did it, sir? I mean, murder the Duke?"

"I don't know, Sergeant. I honestly don't know. He had plenty of reason to hate the Duke, and the telegram does ambiguously suggest him, but my guess is that he didn't need to resort to murder for his revenge. A general strike would have done the job more effectively for him."

"That's what I think, sir."

"So, in probability, the Duke-killer's still at large, and we're not meant to be alive. What do you suggest we do, Sergeant?"

"Do our duty and watch our backs, sir."

173

Chapter 18

Allerdyce was back at work on Thursday. His arm still hurt, and his wound was covered by a seeping scab which kept breaking and bleeding, but he couldn't justify to himself the idea of taking more time off when his investigative faculties were unimpaired. Besides, there was someone he needed to see.

He went straight into Jarvis's office without knocking. Jarvis looked up from his paperwork but remained seated.

"Ah, Allerdyce, the hero returns. I thought you might have decided to take a nice long break."

"Where the hell were you, Jarvis? You were meant to get us out of there, not let us get murdered."

"That's no way to speak to a <u>Chief</u> Inspector, Allerdyce."

"Chief Inspector?"

"The Chief Constable's promoted me. He seems to think the Winchburgh operation was rather a success, all things considered."

"A success? The suspect dead and McGillivray and me left for dead? Christ, Jarvis, that's the strangest success I've ever seen. And then the Holy Joe goes and promotes you even though I'm the one who's out there getting shot?"

"Come on, Allerdyce, you know that police work's more about brains than bravery. The operation was my idea, and with

Semple's death we've destroyed the union's capacity to organise a general strike. We've eliminated the man who killed the late Duke, at minimal cost to the taxpayer and at no embarrassment to the family. I'd call that a success, wouldn't you?"

"Justice, Jarvis? You mean you're actually admitting that Semple was meant to be shot?"

"Shut the door, Allerdyce."

"No."

"Shut the door, Allerdyce, please. I want to be able to be frank with you."

Allerdyce closed it but remained standing.

"Can I be frank with you then, Jarvis? I think you meant to kill me."

"Please, Archibald, have a seat."

"I prefer to stand, Jarvis."

"Very well then. But please do me the favour of listening to, and considering carefully what I say."

"No, Jarvis. You listen to me, you santimonious bastard. You put my life in danger. You put my sergeant's life in danger. A suspect is shot dead. I don't know what the hell you think you're doing Jarvis but you should be tried for murder." God, thought Allerdyce, it would be so satisfying just to punch and kick Jarvis till he bled.

Jarvis put his papers neatly to one side and leant his elbows on the desk.

"We're in a war, Allerdyce. Semple knew that, the Chief Constable knows it, and I know it."

"And people have to be killed because you think that?"

"Just hear me out, Allerdyce. It's not a war of the old sort, where your enemies declare themselves and fight you openly.

175

It's not a business of heroic charges and Victoria Crosses in the Crimea. It's something quieter, something insidiously undermining the freedoms and prosperity we enjoy, something like typhoid in the water or a poison creeping its way through our system. Not everyone can see it yet, but we're in as deadly a conflict as we've ever been. And one where the outcome is very finely balanced.

"Did Semple mention a certain Karl Marx at the meeting, Allerdyce?"

"Yes he did."

"Well, you have to know your enemy. The socialistic and communistic disciples of Marx are all around us, telling the workers that they're in a civil war against capital. Throughout Britain – throughout Europe – they're being stirred up for mutiny and revolution. Every trade union is a front for plotting the violent overthrow of our freedoms."

"I think the miners at the meeting just wanted to prevent their pay from being cut, Jarvis."

"That's how the seditionists work, Allerdyce. They're clever. They're like us – they can see that it's a war. They recruit their battalions of workers by latching into their grievances then using them as their infantry in a campaign of strikes and intimidation, with the false promise that it'll make things better for the workers. They don't care a damn what actually happens to the workers as long as the cause of revolution is advanced. They won't be content until they've achieved the complete destruction of our system of free enterprise."

"So where do I fit in, Jarvis? Why does this war mean that McGillivray and I have to be shot at? Are we the enemy, Jarvis? Are we on the wrong side?"

Jarvis's eyes narrowed and he smiled slightly.

"I don't know, Allerdyce. What do you think?"

"I think you're an evil, twisted bastard, Jarvis."

Jarvis's smile faded and he looked straight into Allerdyce's eyes.

"This is a modern war with modern weapons, Allerdyce. Look at America. What happened there? The South tried to play gallant, like the Light Brigade. All Stonewall Jackson and gentlemanly Robert E Lee. What did the North do? They fought a total war, of economic blockade and scorched earth. They sent Grant and Sherman to burn the South down, farm by farm and city by city. They didn't baulk from sending their own men into danger and difficulty. And they've got the South licked.

"We're soldiers, Allerdyce, soldiers of internal security in a modern war, and we take a soldier's risks. None of us is more important than victory."

"So what happens now, Jarvis? Do McGillivray and I get killed anyway in your dirty war? Does anyone get held accountable for the murder of James Semple?"

Jarvis's face relaxed.

"In answer to your last question, Allerdyce, not unless they have to be. I've been appointed as investigating officer. The Chief Constable would be content for the case to remain unsolved – after all there are conflicting accounts of what happened and perhaps nobody can get to the bottom of it. So it might just get filed as a cold case.

"But, Allerdyce, I'd like you to think carefully about what would happen if I chose to re-open the case. Burgess would have to testify that he sent you to Winchburgh. I'd have to testify that I gave you a gun. You were the only armed policeman known to be there. Lots of people saw you in the hall, and saw you go into the back room. The gun's been found and is in a safe place. It had clearly been fired, and the bullets are of the same type as the one that killed James Semple. No-one ordered you to shoot Mr Semple – we'd have to testify that you exceeded your authority. Murder, Allerdyce – a capital offence."

"Come on, Jarvis. Even you wouldn't stoop so low."

"Not unless I had to."

"You're a wretch. You're beneath contempt."

Jarvis shrugged.

"I'm a soldier in a total war."

...

Allerdyce called in next on the Superintendent.

"Very good to see you back, Allerdyce. But are you sure you're fit for it? I don't want you straining yourself before you're ready."

"I'm fit, sir. I want to get back to work. I've still got a live murder case on my hands."

Burgess glanced away from Allerdyce.

"Sorry, Allerdyce. The Chief's decided the Duke's case is closed."

"Jarvis suggested something along those lines when he was gloating to me about his promotion."

"Yes. The promotion. Not my doing, Allerdyce. I know you're the better policeman."

"Sir, I don't want to sound bitter, but I think Jarvis has gone mad. He's all but admitted that he arranged to have Semple shot. I think he wanted McGillivray and me out of the way too."

"Excuse me a second, will you, Allerdyce?"

The Superintendent got up, crossed the room and told the clerk in his outer office to run an errand. He shut the doors behind him and resumed his seat, leaning across the desk and speaking softly.

"Look, Allerdyce, I don't like what's going on here either. It gets worse every day. Jarvis is accountable only to the Chief Constable. He's choosing the most hardened men in the force to form his personal flying squad. He's running informers everywhere – even in the force itself. I can't even be sure my own thoughts aren't mysteriously known to him.

"I spoke to the Chief Constable and he just said it was modern policing. He practically told me to modernise or retire.

"I can't do it, Allerdyce. I can't get past the simple notion that evidence and trials are what catch criminals. I don't know how long I can last."

"I'm sorry sir."

"Look, Archibald, you've got to think about your career. You're a younger man than me. You're clever and versatile. Maybe you should learn the new methods. You could do well."

"I don't want to, sir. They're corrupting us."

"It's your choice, Allerdyce. But the Chief's clear that anyone who doesn't agree with his methods is an enemy of progress."

"So be it."

"If you stay on the force all you'll get to investigate is burglaries."

"I still want to solve this murder, sir. I've never left a murder investigation uncompleted in my life. I don't think James Semple did it. I at least want to find the other suspects who've been identified to us."

"I've told you, Allerdyce. The case is closed."

Allerdyce paused and looked out the window for inspiration. The far-off hills were still topped by snow, under a clear sky.

"Perhaps I should take a vacation to recuperate, sir."

"That's not like you, Allerdyce. But I think it would be a damned good idea."

"Somewhere northerly, with a fresh breeze from the sea. Dornoch, perhaps."

"I see your point. I certainly can't stop you."

"Thank you sir. I'll tell you if I find out anything interesting."

"Take your time, Allerdyce. Make a proper holiday of it. I wish I could promise still to be here when you get back.

"And be very careful."

Chapter 19

There was something about getting away that gave him room to think. At home, he'd always be subject to the childrens' joyful or tearful attentions. At work, Burgess would no doubt put some new cases in his way to distract him from the 'closed' murder case. And whatever he did he'd never be free from Jarvis and his informers.

Jarvis. Just thinking about the man made Allerdyce want to throw his glass against the wall. The evil, scheming, murderous bastard.

Even here, lying in his clothes on the bed in a single room in Dornoch's Eagle Hotel, he couldn't feel free from Jarvis's gaze. It was absurd. All the way up to Tain, a train journey of nearly eleven hours, he'd been scanning his fellow passengers in the compartment or on the platforms and wondering if any of them were in Jarvis's pay. On the short ferry from Tain to Dornoch he'd had to persuade himself that the man with the heavy black beard wasn't one of Jarvis's constables in disguise. And even in the hotel he'd imagined that the boy who'd carried his bag up to the room might be about to send a telegram to Jarvis to inform him where his rival was staying.

Allerdyce sighed. What was the point of giving yourself the time and privacy to think if all that came to mind was Jarvis?

Maybe Margaret was right that it was daft for him to want to get away on his own, that he wasn't well enough yet and that he'd just get ill. He felt his brow – it was a little hot but he couldn't say he had a fever. He'd already re-dressed his wounded arm and, thank heavens, the wound still looked clean though peeling the old dressing off had given him a pain as intense as if he'd been tearing off his own flesh. Maybe it was a simple dereliction of his duty at home to come up here.

No, he thought. This is my duty. I owe it to justice, I owe it to James Semple, and I owe it to myself to find out who killed the Duke of Dornoch. And only by finding out who really did it can I show the Chief Constable that Jarvis is wrong. It's the only thing that's going to stop Jarvis's insane secret war.

The fire crackled in the grate and Allerdyce breathed in the unfamiliar peat-smoke, so much mellower than the acid coal-smoke of Edinburgh. I don't know what I'll find here, he thought. At least I'll understand the Duke better by finding out how he's regarded here. Maybe I'll learn something more about Patrick Slater.

Thinking about Slater brought McGillivray's image to mind, standing in his blood-caked shirt. Whatever else, thought Allerdyce, I'm going to find out more about the wounds this good, strong man bears – his family cleared off the land of Sutherland, his father dead on the passage to Canada.

He lay back on the bed. He could hear nothing but the hissing of the burning peat, the gentle rattling of the windowpane in the chill North Sea breeze, and the muted murmur of conversation from the bar below. He shut his eyes and tried to enjoy the quietness. Somehow, though, he couldn't relax his mind or his body. He kept turning from side to side and his mind refused to slow down. It wasn't even the thought of Jarvis that was consciously bothering him any more, it was a more nameless discontent.

He sat up. The name for his discontent had suddenly come to mind.

I'm lonely, he thought. I'm away from all the noise and distraction of home. I thought I'd find peace but I'm lonely.

He had half a mind to get the first train back south in the morning and get back to Margaret and the children. He'd tell them how he'd missed them, and bring them back little souvenirs of the Highlands.

But before he could think of returning he had to do his duty here.

...

Only a handful of people were in the hotel's bar. Four men, dressed like shopkeepers thought Allerdyce, sat round a table playing cards. At another table a tweed-suited man a weather-beaten complexion – maybe a tenant farmer – was arguing with a dark-suited gentleman, some papers between them on the table. The barman stood polishing glasses, holding them up in turn to the bright paraffin light behind the bar before putting them away. Allerdyce listened carefully in case, in these far northern parts, anyone was speaking Gaelic but he only heard English. He ordered a beer.

"How are you, sir?" asked the barman. "Is the room to your liking?"

"Yes, fine thank you."

"You've made an excellent choice of a place to recuperate, sir. Fresh sea air. Healthy walks. Spot of golf on the links maybe."

"Yes. Perhaps."

The barman leant confidentially towards him.

"And, sir, if you feel the need for company that can be arranged. Comely Highland wench, fresh from the glens."

He was ashamed to feel a flush of temptation for an instant.

"No, thank you."

"Very well, sir."

He decided to turn the conversation back to duty.

"It's an attractive town. Who lives in the big house outside it?"

"Dornoch Palace? It's owned by the Duke of Dornoch."

"The carriage went past it on the way in from the ferry. I thought it looked French – round towers with conical roofs, formal garden at the front."

"That would make sense, sir. The 5th Duke built it because his French wife wanted one. Said she'd go back home if she didn't get it."

"Interesting. And does the Duke come to Dornoch often?"

"No, sir. Mainly just stayed in the south. Came up here for a few weeks each year for shooting. Died just a few weeks ago."

"I suppose that was a blow to people here."

The barman shrugged.

"Makes precious little difference as far as I can see, sir. The rents will still be collected. I suppose we'll see the new Duke soon enough."

The tweed-suited man came up to the bar to order a couple of glasses of porter. The barman addressed him.

"Our guest here was just asking about the late Duke, Mr Smith. You knew him a bit, didn't you?"

"Aye, that I did." Allerdyce was surprised to recognise a thick

Yorkshire accent. "A most efficient landlord."

"Efficient?" asked Allerdyce.

"Rightly so. I'm renting over ten thousand acres of sheepwalk from the Dornoch estate. The Duke saw to it that we had no nonsense from squatters. There's not a single man or woman on all the acres I manage except for my workers and their families."

"What happened to them?"

"That's not rightly my concern. All I know is that, if I can agree the right prices with the gentleman over there, I'll make the sort of profit I thought I'd have to emigrate to Australia for. Twenty thousand fattened lambs for delivery to Smithfield between April and July."

"Did you ever hear of a Patrick Slater?"

"Aye, he was hard done by. He did a grand job of getting the squatters off the land, but he was punished harshly for it."

"I heard he was transported," interjected the barman.

"Word is he's back. I heard tell that he's hiding out somewhere beyond Lairg. But they say he's gone mad and he's helping the natives to stay."

"Interesting."

"Anyway, if you'll pardon me gentlemen there's money to be made. I'll bid you a good evening."

. . .

Allerdyce set off the next morning for Lairg on the mail-coach, leaving most of his luggage behind at the hotel. After passing over rich pastures beside the sea, with sand-dunes and the grey-blue expanse of the North Sea behind them, the coach turned inland up a wide glen. Hills rose on either side, grass and birchwood giving way to high heather moorland. Every mile or so the coach would pass the roofless walls of abandoned houses, some of them tumbled almost into ruin, others with bare charred roof-timbers still standing or collapsed into the middle. Walls enclosing little fields round the houses had been knocked roughly to the ground, allowing the sheep to wander through the villages and eat the weeds and thistles which had colonised them.

It's like a war, thought Allerdyce. This must be what it's like in Georgia right now, with an army burning and murdering its way towards the sea.

The impression was re-inforced when, a few miles up the glen, the carriage passed a large village of white tents. It was navvies, not soldiers, who were queuing up at the cookhouse tent for their breakfast before heading up to work on the raw new scar of railway embankment which cut its way through the grass, rock and heather. Nonetheless, Allerdyce couldn't resist the impression of a hungry army working its way inexorably through the Highlands, the vanguard of harsh, commercial modernity.

The coach reached Lairg by lunchtime. Whatever the town had looked like before must have been changed utterly in the past months. The railway was practically complete here. Beyond the bright sandstone of the station-house, sidings reached out towards new corrugated-iron sheds and metal-fenced pens of various sizes. The commercial traveller sitting next to Allerdyce explained that they were looking at the new sheep and cattle mart which would draw in livestock from all over Sutherland for auction then pack them onto trains to the slaughterhouses of the cities. It seemed cruelly efficient, thought Allerdyce, a whole county that's dispensed with human beings as far as it can, to rely on the industrial-scale production of animals for transport and slaughter.

The coach halted outside a brand new hotel building from which hammering and sawing could be heard inside, opposite a wide, fast-flowing river. Allerdyce got down and looked up and down the main street. New stone-built shops with plate-glass windows and sizeable detached houses in various states of completion lined the street, facing the river. None of them would look out of place in one of the better suburbs of Edinburgh – there was obviously good money to be made out of livestock. At either end of the street, however, the grand new buildings gave way to low small-windowed cottages with a thatch of heather. Whoever's going to remember Patrick Slater is more likely to be found in one of them, he thought.

He walked along and looked into the open door of one of the cottages. An old man sat with a bottle of whisky in front of him in the smoky darkness. His straggling beard, toothless smile and patched hessian jacket marked him as someone the new economy had passed by. The floor was covered in rushes and a fire burned in a hearth in the centre of the room, its smoke rising into the chimneyless thatch. Dark joints of meat hung down from the thatch on iron hooks and a chicken pecked round the man's feet. Allerdyce felt as if he was looking back into darkness of a previous century.

The man waved at him to come in. Allerdyce took his hat off and stooped under the lintel of the door. The dense smokiness of the interior made him cough and brought tears to his eyes.

The old man motioned him to sit down and poured a whisky. He held a glass out to Allerdyce in his trembling hand.

"*Slainte*," he said.

"And your good health too, sir."

Allerdyce knocked back a mouthful of acrid, peaty whisky

which felt like it was stripping his oesophagus.

"*Cò às a tha sibh?*"

"I'm sorry? Do you speak English?"

"*Tha Gàidhlig agaibh?*"

"I beg your pardon?"

The old man smiled at him and shrugged. There clearly wasn't much possibility of learning anything about Patrick Slater from a man who couldn't even speak English. Allerdyce drank another mouthful of the whisky, smiled at the old man, and stood to leave. The man pointed towards the door, grinning, and he saw a thin dark-haired middle-aged woman, plainly dressed, coming in with a loaf of bread under her arm. She spoke sternly in Gaelic to the old man before addressing Allerdyce.

"I'm sorry, sir, you'll have to excuse my father. He doesn't have the English and his mind is a bit wandered. I have to come in and look after him."

"I apologise for intruding, madam. I was looking for someone who might be able to tell me something about a Patrick Slater."

The woman's eyes narrowed.

"Slater? Why do you want to know?"

Allerdyce had prepared his line.

"I heard that he had returned to the area to do good. I thought it might make an improving instructional story. I write books about modern Christian heroes."

Her face relaxed.

"That's a high calling, sir."

"It is. But I don't know yet if Mr Slater is truly a suitable subject."

"I used to think he was the very devil, sir, but a great change seems to have come over him."

Allerdyce sat back down. The woman pulled up a stool and sat to tell the story she knew. The earlier part of it was familiar from McGillivray – rents raised unaffordably high, eviction notices served, families burnt out of their houses in winter, the empty villages. The later part of the story was more extraordinary. Last autumn, fourteen years after he was transported, Slater had been seen disembarking from a ship at Cromarty. Thinner, ill-looking, but unmistakeably the same man who'd harried crofters from their homes all over Sutherland.

Since then there had been other fleeting sightings of him, usually on the open road at dusk or dawn. There had also been strange happenings in the few townships, on the very worst land or in pockets outside the Duke's ownership, which had so far survived the clearances. A hungry family would find a haunch of venison on their doorstep. A family about to be evicted for arrears would find gold sovereigns at their door. Where there was a sick child a doctor would arrive and say he'd been paid to attend. The story had got around that Slater was going round like a spirit, leaving a blessing behind him. No-one knew where Slater lived, how he knew where crofters were in distress, or how he had the money to do good. Many people thought he really was a spirit, forced to do a penance of good works to avoid the fires of hell.

Interesting, thought Allerdyce. Perhaps not the conduct of a murderer, but it must be worth meeting Mr Slater. If I can.

. . .

Allerdyce stayed overnight at the new hotel in Lairg, slightly dizzy from the fumes of fresh paint and varnish. He laid an Ordnance Survey map in front of him on the bed. From the handful of people he'd spoken to in Lairg he'd established at least some sort of pattern to Slater's appearances. They ranged from Altnaharra in the north to Strath Carron in the south, from Glen Einig to the west to Strath Brora in the east. Acts of charity had been done on the east side of Loch Shin but not the west.

Drawing a rough circle between these points Allerdyce reckoned that the centre of Slater's movements must rest somewhere north of Lairg, and to the east of Loch Shin. He searched the map for isolated houses where a man might be undisturbed for weeks on end.

There was one that seemed to be a possibility. Nearly at the centre of the circle, and completely inaccessible by road, a single building was marked at Dalnessie. It was on high moorland, near the headwaters of the River Brora, five miles off the track from Lairg to Strath Naver. That's where he would look first.

Chapter 20

It was a relief to step into the fresh air at dawn. The cool breeze from the heather moors was invigorating rather than chilling. The last stars were still shining through the brightening sky as Allerdyce walked northwards out of the village.

He covered the first few miles along the narrow gravel road easily, enjoying the exercise and listening to the wind through the rushes, the fast tumbling of the little burns which the road crossed, the far-off cry of the curlew and, everywhere, the bleating of sheep. Every now and then he stopped to check the map, seeing which ruined hamlet he had reached and how far he was from the place where he would need to leave the road and cut across the moors to Dalnessie.

It's a desert, he thought, it's a man-made desert but there's a certain beauty to it – the sheer space and silence of the place. He breathed deeply, tasting heather and grass in the clean air. It was a joy to be out of the stink of smoke and ordure which polluted the city. Perhaps a few days up here really would help him recuperate.

Finally, just where a wide peat-dark burn ran under the road, he saw a narrow path running off to the right, into the heather. He checked the map. This must be the place to turn off.

Looking around at the sheer wild emptiness it seemed

incredible that anyone had ever lived here, and more incredible that he'd find anyone living at Dalnessie now. He wondered what sort of existence McGillivray's family had managed before they were expelled from this barren land. The path, however, wound a narrow course through the heather which showed that somebody was still using it. Perhaps it was just used by shepherds or deer stalkers, or perhaps his guess was right and he'd find an inhabited house at the end of the path.

Walking was more difficult on the path. The tall heather snagged at his trousers and his boots kept sinking into peaty mud. The vastness of the landscape made his progress feel paralytically slow, with the dark ridges of the hills remaining steadfastly distant. The sky was clouding over and he felt a smir of rain on his cheek. The wound on his arm had started to sting again and he thought it must be seeping blood or pus into its bandage. After fording a burn, his trousers were soaked up to his knees and with each pace he felt like he was lifting lead weights out of the sticky mud. A stag looked curiously at him then bounded away across the moor.

After an hour and a half, with the rain blattering down properly now and his legs shaking with tired weakness, he finally saw a house beside a stream. 'House' was perhaps an exaggeration. Half of the roof of the low drystone cottage was missing, and the right hand gable had collapsed. Some smoke, though, rose from the chimney of the other gable before being dispersed into the whipping rain-soaked wind. Allerdyce pressed on, anxious for the heat and warmth promised by that chimney.

Whoever lived here had built a wall of peat between the ruined portion of the cottage and the end where the thatched-heather roof still survived. There was no door in the peat wall, merely a narrow opening across which crudely stitched deerskin had been hung. Allerdyce pushed the deerskin aside and stepped into the dark hovel.

Some light struggled in through a tiny window, and a dull glow came from the hearth. As his eyes adjusted Allerdyce could see the figure of a man knelt in prayer before a wooden cross on a simple table. The hovel was pathetically simple – a bed of heather along one wall, a cooking pot hanging over the hearth, a couple of dead grouse hanging from the thatch and a shotgun leant against the corner of the wall.

The man looked round. Allerdyce prepared to reach for the gun before he did, but the man just smiled at him.

"Peace be with you, stranger."

Allerdyce looked at his gaunt cheeks and dark-rimmed eyes under lank, greying hair. I've seen that look often enough in the slums and taverns of Edinburgh, he thought. That's a man who won't last another winter.

"Are you Mr Patrick Slater?"

"Yes I am."

"I am Inspector Allerdyce of the City of Edinburgh Police. I am required to ask you some questions."

Slater sighed.

"I'd been expecting something like this."

"Really?"

"You can't go around doing good to the poor without offending the rich. I suppose you want to arrest me for poaching."

"Poaching? No, Mr Slater. I want to ask you about a murder."

"Murder?" Slater laughed, though the noise of the air in his thin throat sounded like the rustle of dead leaves. "Me?"

"Your name has been mentioned to the police in connection with the death of the late Duke of Dornoch."

Slater laughed some more, rocking backwards and forwards as he wheezed. Allerdyce wondered if he was actually mad.

"Come now, Inspector. You can't be serious. Sit down on the bed. Let us share some stew while you dry off and we'll talk about this like rational men."

Allerdyce stooped down on the heather, reassured that he was between Slater and the shotgun. Slater poured some sloppy stew out of the cooking pot and brought it over. Allerdyce tasted the strong venison, feeling warmth return to his body. Slater sat opposite, crouched on a low stool with his own bowl.

"You're injured," said Slater, looking attentively at Allerdyce.

"How do you know?"

"The way you're holding your bowl. You've been injured in your upper arm."

"It's nothing to worry about, Mr Slater."

"I could tend to the wound. I collect lichen and berries. They have healing properties."

The pain in his arm was more intense now. Perhaps the rain soaking through his coat and into the dressings had made things worse, but he couldn't put himself at the mercy of an armed and possibly deranged suspect.

"No thank you, Mr Slater."

"As you please."

"I take it you're aware of the death of His Grace?" asked Allerdyce.

"Yes. I'm not a complete hermit. There's a handful of good people from the villages who I speak to at night sometimes. They tell me the news – who's ill, who's in trouble. They told me about the Duke's death. An accident, the newspapers said."

"Not a complete accident, Mr Slater. I can't imagine you were sorry to hear about it."

Slater smiled.

"To my shame, Inspector, no. When I made my peace with the Lord Jesus Christ I told myself that I had forgiven the Duke for his part in my transportation. My reaction when I heard he was dead showed me that my spiritual regeneration was woefully incomplete."

"And do you know where you were on the night of his death?"

He laughed again.

"I can't help you with that, Inspector. Living out here I do not keep a strict calendar. I remember days by whether it snowed, by whether I shot a deer, or whether I saw an eagle, not by dates printed in a diary."

"And so you would be unable to demonstrate that you were here at the time of his death?"

Slater put his bowl down and looked directly, still smiling, at Allerdyce. The Inspector felt unsettled by a look which spoke of sadness and compassion rather than anger.

"Inspector, you will have to believe what you choose to. Since my return from Australia I have never ventured more than twenty miles from this place. My entire mission has been to make some poor restitution, as far is it is within my powers, for the evils I did in Sutherland as a younger man. I have visited townships secretly to learn what troubles they face. I have made a small number of confidential friends who will bring me news, and to whom I entrust gifts of food or money to alleviate the sufferings of the poor. I seek only to sustain life, not to take it."

"I see."

"Tell me, Inspector, who suggested that I might have killed the Duke?"

"His brother. George Bothwell-Scott. The advocate."

Slater sighed.

"So the family still hate me for telling the truth about them. Well, Inspector, let me be honest. You deserve that after making the effort to find me. For ten years I did sincerely want to kill the Duke and would have done so if I hadn't been half the world away.

"He confined me to a barely-living hell, Inspector, by his refusal to testify that I was directly carrying out his instructions when I evicted people in the winter of '49. Each day in Tasmania I was scorched and parched under the sun, exhausted by hard labour clearing swamps and forests, bitten by disease-bearing insects, starved, and beaten whenever I faltered in my work. My heart had hardened into stone and the only force that kept me alive was anger and the burning desire for revenge. I thought I had been cast out entirely from men and God into a place where only devils lived.

"One day I collapsed while I was working in a quarry. I'd already drunk my pint of water and I lay on the ground too weak even to push my pickaxe from off my chest and stand up. I simply waited for a guard to find me and beat me.

"Another prisoner came up to me first. He offered me water from his bottle. I refused – I knew he'd be flogged for it and it didn't seem worth it. But he lifted my weak body and poured water on my face. I opened my mouth and drank.

"When I had drunk my fill I asked him why he had done so. He told me the words of Jesus that if you offer even a cup of water in His name you will be blessed. I asked him what he would do if he was flogged for his kindness, and he said he would sing praises to his Saviour for His continued presence with him even amidst the horror which surrounded us.

"I asked the Lord into my life at that moment, Inspector. I gave Him the rest of my life and promised that I would use it to make restitution for my sins."

"And you repented of wanting to kill the Duke?"

"Yes. I made some money when I was released on ticket-of-leave from the prison camp. I advised landowners on how to draw up contracts with gold prospecters. I did quite well. I brought nearly a thousand pounds back with me from Australia and I hope to spend every penny of it on helping the poor before I die here. I think that's a better restitution of their afflictions than murdering the Duke."

Allerdyce was silent. He knew that religion was mostly humbug and deception, and he still didn't quite trust Slater's sanity. Something had clearly happened though, whether madness or religious inspiration, to make him pour out the remainder of his life in the service of the weak.

Slater still fixed him in is gaze.

"So, Inspector? Do you think I did it? Do you think I killed the Duke? If you do, I suppose you ought to arrest me."

Allerdyce looked at the physically broken man who squatted before him, who only seemed to be held together by his force of will.

"No, Mr Slater. No, I don't think you killed him."

...

It was well after dark when the coach from Lairg rolled back

197

into Dornoch. Allerdyce went up to his room and lay on his bed, exhausted. He should probably stay up here for another couple of days and track down anyone who could corroborate Slater's whereabouts on the night of the murder, but in his heart he just couldn't see him as the killer. And for tonight, he should just relax and enjoy a drink and a meal.

He lay down on the bed and shut his eyes, but couldn't relax. It wasn't any question of Slater's possible guilt that was unsettling him. It was something undefined about the man himself. He couldn't believe in the religious side of Slater's conversion story but there was something in it – something about the need for a change of life – that troubled him. He felt as if Slater had looked into him and seen some nameless deficiency.

He'd only lain on the bed for a few minutes when he heard a knock on the door. He opened it to the hotel-keeper's boy.

"Telegram for you, Mr Allerdyce. It was handed in while you were away."

He opened the envelope and froze.

Dear God, he thought, not that. Please, anything but that. He read it again, willing the words to go away.

'ALICE GRAVELY ILL STOP

RETURN HOME URGENTLY STOP

ENDS'

Chapter 21

Every minute of the journey back felt like a leaden hour, even as the express train hurtled through the Highlands at up to fifty miles an hour. He tried to smoke to calm his nerves, but the tobacco tasted like bile in his mouth. When he closed his eyes he imagined little Alice tossing and turning in a feverish chill, then the image turned to Helen in her wild alternations between quiet delirium and fevered madness as she wrestled with typhoid for three weeks, her red hair spilling over the white pillow as she screamed and cursed in her final agonies before the infection finally conquered her. As the locomotive's whistle shrieked on entering a tunnel Allerdyce put his hands over his ears, but the shrieking continued in his mind.

At last, after nine o'clock at night, the train reached Waverley Station. He leapt onto the platform as the train slowed. He pushed his way to the head of the queue for cabs and told the driver to hasten to Cumberland Street.

He opened his front door, dropped his valise in the hall, and rushed up the stairs to Alice's room. As he entered he could see Margaret bent over the child's bed, sponging her with cold water. The stench of diarrhoea assaulted his nostrils.

He put his hand lightly on Margaret's shoulder. She turned, and he saw her eyes reddened by tears.

"How is she?"

"I'm so frightened, Archibald. I think we're going to lose her."

"What happened?"

"She was a little feverish the first night you were away. I called the doctor but he said it was nothing to worry about, and just to give her some gripe water with a dash of laudanum and put her to bed early.

"It was awful, Archie, when I came in to see her in the morning. She'd had watery diarrhoea in the bed and had been too weak and fevered to get up. Her brow felt like hot coals and she was alternately sleeping and mumbling nonsense. I sent for the doctor again."

"What did he say?"

"He said it was cholera. I thought I'd die when I heard that, Archie. He said to keep her cool and give her a few more drops of laudanum to make her comfortable, but that we'd just have to watch and pray. She's got quieter during the day, and she's had less diarrhoea since the middle of the afternoon, but she's so weak. Oh Archie, I think she's slipping away."

He knelt and looked at his daughter's pale face. Her eyes were darting from side to side and didn't seem to recognise him. Her mouth seemed to be forming, silently, the random syllables of a baby's babbling. He put his hand on her forehead and felt its heat.

"The doctor's an old fool, Margaret."

"What?"

"He doesn't know how to treat cholera. The police surgeon treated a prisoner with cholera last year with a new method. He survived long enough to be tried and hanged."

"What can we do?"

"She's not just lost a dangerous amount of water, she's lost a lot of energy and a lot of the chemicals her body needs. In every pint of water we give her we need to dissolve a teaspoon of salt and a tablespoon of sugar and the juice of half a lemon."

"I'll go and make that up. Are you sure it'll help?"

"I can't be sure of anything, Margaret, but it's the best thing we can do for her."

Margaret left the room and he took over from her at sponging Alice's fevered face. It felt like a useless thing to do, but he had to do something. He couldn't just sit powerlessly and watch death claim her.

Margaret came back with a jug of water and a glass.

"I mixed it up like you said."

"Thank you. Let's give it a try."

He lifted Alice gently from her pillows and held the full glass to her lips. At first the water simply ran down her chin, but as he tipped her head back, her eyes still darting madly from side to side, more of it entered her mouth and she started to swallow by reflex.

"More, Margaret, more. We don't know how much she's lost. Keep it coming."

After they'd made Alice drink four pints of the watery solution they settled down to a routine. They'd each take two hours vigil, and make her drink some more of the fluid, while the other tried to rest. Millie put a large pile of clean sheets in the room, in expectation of the diarrhoea starting again.

And start again it did. For each period of his vigil, as Millie brought up jugs of the special water, he had to change the sheets at least once. It felt like a race to make her body absorb the life-giving fluid faster than she was losing it. As he watched her rapid breathing he couldn't help praying for her to live through the night, though he didn't know why he should allow himself to pray to the cruel non-existence who'd brought his daughter to the margins of death.

At last some sunlight started to creep round the edges of the curtains of the sickroom. He couldn't honestly say that she looked a lot better, but she was sleeping more soundly and her eyes had stopped their crazy flickering. She was still hot, though, and her breathing was fast and shallow. He wanted to hope, but he knew her life still hung by a fragile thread.

He jumped when he heard the doorbell, followed by the maid's quick footsteps down the stairs. If that's the doctor, he thought, I'm going to kick his incompetent arse straight back onto the pavement.

Millie came back up.

"There's a soldier to see you, sir."

"A soldier? What in God's name for?"

"He says it's very urgent."

"More urgent than looking after my daughter? Tell him go away."

"He's very insistent, sir. Can you just come down for a minute, please?"

"Oh, very well then."

A young corporal in Highland dress was standing at the front door, his Glengarry bonnet under his arm.

"The ADC to the GOC presents his compliments, sir, and requests your immediate attendance at the Castle."

"Try and make sense, man. I hardly understood a word of that. And I'm not going anywhere. I have a sick daughter to look after."

"He says it's most important that you come, sir."

"I'm sorry. I can't. Why should I?"

The soldier paused and bit his lip before answering.

"There's been a murder."

...

Allerdyce was greeted at the Governor's House by the same officer who'd shown him into the Brigadier's office before, though this time his tunic was undone and he was pale and unshaven. He introduced himself as Major Edward Farquharson, the Brigadier's *aide-de-camp*.

"So, Major," asked Allerdyce, "what's happened?"

"Come through to the Brigadier's room, please, Inspector. You too, Corporal."

The Brigadier's office hardly looked changed from when he'd first seen it. The whisky decanter was still on the desk, though it was practically empty. Brigadier Sir Frederick Bothwell-Scott still stared cholerically from the portrait behind the desk. The only changes were that the Russian sword was missing from its stand and the wood-panelling door to the Brigadier's water-closet stood ajar.

"Through here, please, Inspector."

The corporal opened the door to the water closet and Allerdyce went in.

The Brigadier was sitting on the lavatory, leaning against the wall to one side, his trousers and long-johns round his ankles, his tunic unbuttoned and a sword stuck through his heart. He stared lifelessly at the Inspector, a trickle of dried blood running from his mouth to his chin. But what stood out most, literally as well as

203

figuratively, was the massively erect penis of the man who had, so briefly, been the 8th Duke of Dornoch.

"We thought maybe we should cover it up," said the Major. "Professional respect and everything. But then we thought you ought to see everything just as we found it."

"Thank you. Might just be a touch of *rigor mortis*," said Allerdyce. "Does strange things to a man's body." He wondered, however, what the Brigadier had been up to in the moments preceding his death.

Looking carefully at the scene, he noticed that a piece of paper had been folded and left on top of the Brigadier's crumpled long-johns. Allerdyce picked it up, his nose closed against the sweaty whiff of the victim's underwear, and opened it.

The message was spelt out in letters cut from a newspaper and pasted onto the paper.

'RELIEVED OF COMMAND.'

He showed it to the Major.

"We appear to be dealing with rather a droll murderer, Major."

"Indeed."

He folded the paper back up and put it in his pocket. He needed to get away from here, back to Alice's bedside, but he knew he had to ask the required questions.

"What were the circumstances of this discovery?"

The corporal answered.

"I'm the – was the – Brigadier's batman. I was meant to wake him up at seven o'clock with his shaving water and hot coffee. He wasn't there when I went to wake him, and his bed hadn't been slept in. I feared that he might have been taken ill – he was prone to fits of apoplexy, sir, and combined with the effects of strong liquor I feared he'd maybe had a stroke or a heart attack. It's been a constant worry to me, sir."

"I don't think you need to worry any more, corporal," said Allerdyce.

"No."

"So what did you do next?"

"I came down here to see if he was in his office. I'd half expected to find him asleep on his desk if he'd had too much whisky last night, but he wasn't there. Then I saw the door to his water closet open and thought he'd maybe been taken ill there."

"As indeed he was."

"I couldn't believe it, sir, seeing him staring at me from the privy, with that old Russian sword through his chest. I went immediately to wake Major Farquharson and he told me to fetch you, since you'd already had some dealings with the Brigadier."

"You did well, corporal."

"Thank you, sir."

Allerdyce looked at the polished wooden floor of the privy to see if the killer had left any other traces, but none was visible.

"Could anyone have got in here un-noticed, Major?"

"It's possible, Inspector. There's all sorts of tradespeople and visitors coming and going during the day. And at night there are the officers' invited guests, and the guards at the gatehouse also let the soldiers' bawds in."

The corporal appeared to blush slightly.

"I see, Major. And what about getting into this particular building? When I was last here I recall there were sentries at the door. They would surely be able to identify anyone who entered?"

"They're not on duty at night, Inspector, unless the Brigadier is hosting a dinner or some other event. It would be quite possible for a stranger to be admitted unobserved."

"Wouldn't the Brigadier expect you to open the door to a guest, Corporal? Or would he expect some other servant to do so?"

"I would be on duty if he was expecting visitors, sir. But last night he dismissed me after I had ensured that the whisky decanter was full and he had a sufficiency of cigars."

"And did you remain in the house? Could you have heard any disturbance?"

"No, sir. I retired to the barracks. I spent the evening in the Corporals' Mess."

"Thank you, Corporal. You've been most helpful. Might I prevail on you to pass a message to two of my colleagues, requesting their immediate presence?" He scribbled down the home addresses of Superintendent Burgess and Mackay, the police surgeon. "In the meantime I'll examine the Brigadier's room more closely for any signs his visitor may have left."

"Yes, sir. I'll be right back."

The corporal hesitated on his way out the room.

"Do you think he might have done it himself? Suicide?"

"No."

...

He rushed back to Cumberland Street after briefing Burgess and Mackay, praying that he'd find Alice still alive. Margaret greeted him at the front door, crying and clasping him tight.

"Oh, Archie," gasped Margaret, "she stopped breathing. My little angel, she stopped breathing."

Allerdyce thought he'd collapse against her. He felt the tears start at his eyes as he cursed the late Brigadier for tearing him away from his daughter's deathbed.

"She didn't breathe for a whole minute. Then she gave a little shake and I thought it was her spirit leaving her. Then she started again."

He shook himself loose from Margaret's grasp and ran up the stairs.

Alice was lying, pale as death, in her bed. He laid his hand on her brow and felt its coolness. He listened to her breathing, slow, deep and regular.

Instantly, he was sobbing over the girl's bed.

God willing, she would live. And if she did, his whole life's work would be to become the father and husband he ought to be.

Chapter 22

Alice was still desperately weak when Allerdyce left for work the next morning, but she'd been able to take some soup and to speak.

"Daddy, I was scared."

"Your mother and I were scared too."

"I thought I was going to go to heaven. I didn't want to go and meet Jesus. I wanted to stay here."

"You're going to be all right, Alice. You're a very brave girl."

"I love you, Daddy."

He walked to the Police Office feeling as if he'd just, himself, been through some grave illness. He desperately wanted just to stay at home, rest, and keep watch on Alice's recovery, but his duty was absolute. The investigation of another murder had fallen squarely on him.

Immediately, he was called into Burgess's office. The Superintendent sat, looking pale and ill. Jarvis was already sitting at the other side of the desk from Burgess. As Alledyce sat down he saw that, for once, Jarvis's self-satisfied smirk had been wiped off his face.

"Gentlemen," said Burgess, "This is the worst bloody mess we have ever been in since the establishment of the City of Edinburgh police."

Allerdyce felt the blood draining from his face. Burgess continued.

"Never, never before have we allowed two of Scotland's premier aristocrats to be murdered when they were the object of our special care and attention. The press have been told that the Brigadier died from a seizure but soon enough everyone in Scotland is going to have guessed that somebody is killing the Dukes of Dornoch while we look on in complete impotence."

Burgess gazed in silence at each of Allerdyce and Jarvis.

"Well, gentlemen, have you nothing to say? What do you suggest we do now?"

Jarvis spoke.

"The two deaths may not be connected, sir. Semple may well have been responsible for the first murder."

Burgess stood. His face flushed red. He pointed at Jarvis.

"For Christ's sake man, I'm not daft you know. If you hadn't been so bloody cocksure about Semple the Chief wouldn't have closed the investigation. Think about it, man, think about it seriously. Your prejudice about Semple may have cost the Brigadier his life. If the Chief Constable didn't think the sun shone out of your arse I'd have you up on a charge for obstructing justice."

Jarvis chose not to reply – neither apology nor explanation – but stared back at Burgess. Burgess is in more danger from Jarvis and the Chief, thought Allerdyce, than Jarvis will ever be from him.

The Superintendent sat down.

"All right, men, I'm sorry. The first murder happened before we could have anticipated it. It seemed reasonable at least to want to interview Semple. But we're still as deeply in the mire as we could be."

"I understand Inspector Allerdyce undertook informal investigations in Sutherland, sir," said Jarvis.

Damn, thought Allerdyce, how did he know that? Maybe he did have me followed.

Burgess look unsurprised at Jarvis's knowledge.

"Well at least one of you was doing something useful. Mr Allerdyce should have been on sick leave but he voluntarily searched for any information there. Perhaps you'd care to report, Allerdyce."

He recounted his investigations, including his conclusion that Patrick Slater was not a credible suspect.

"So," said Burgess, "where does that leave us, gentlemen? If we have two dead Dukes then my assumption, as a simple man, is that we are probably looking for a single killer with specific reasons for wanting each of them to die. What common reason might there be?"

"Inheritance, sir?" suggested Allerdyce.

"All right, that's one possibility, but rather remote I'd have thought. The titles and the properties will pass down the family, and I can't honestly imagine that the Bothwell-Scotts are murdering each other for money."

"Don't forget, sir, that the Reverend Bothwell-Scott suggested that his oldest brother had a daughter by a marriage which he had repudiated."

Burgess tapped his fingers against the desk.

"Yes. That's interesting, Allerdyce, very interesting indeed. We clearly need to speak to her. What else do we know?"

"The messages associated with each death seem to suggest a person of some wit and intelligence," observed Allerdyce.

"True enough. And what sort of person might bear a sufficient resentment against both of them to want to kill them, apart from this possible woman?"

"The list of people with reasons to resent William Bothwell-Scott is immense, sir. It could be anyone who'd suffered under his clearances of the Sutherland estates or under the management of his mines."

"All right, and what about the Brigadier?"

"Possibly rather a narrower field, sir. His oppressions have been principally military. The message left at the scene of his death – 'relieved of command' – may be an ironic reference to his removal from active command in the Crimea and his subsequent mismanagement of his duties in supplying the army there."

"Fine. So we're looking for someone who might share both those resentments. Can we think of anyone?"

Jarvis's reptilian smirk had crept back. That's a look of sheer malice, thought Allerdyce, as Jarvis turned to look at him.

"I can think of one person," said Jarvis.

"Really?" asked Burgess.

"Yes, sir. Mr Allerdyce's sergeant. McGillivray."

You poisonous bastard, thought Allerdyce. You'll do anything to destroy us.

Burgess sat bolt upright, shocked into pallor. He held tightly to the arms of his chair.

"Mr Jarvis, are you daring to accuse a fellow police officer?"

Jarvis sat back and crossed his legs.

"I'm not accusing anyone, sir. I just want to make sure we've considered every possibility."

"Damn you, Jarvis." Allerdyce turned on him. "What the hell do you think you're doing? You wrecked my last sergeant's career. Now you're telling us that Sergeant McGillivray may be a murderer? Are you mad?"

Superintendent Burgess trembled as he spoke.

"Mr Jarvis, I must say that I share Mr Allerdyce's astonishment. Justify yourself, Chief Inspector, if you can."

Jarvis flicked some lint off his trousers before answering.

"Sir, I'm only drawing a reasonable inference from things which Mr Allerdyce has told us in previous conversations. We know from him that McGillivray and his family suffered under the Duke's evictions. We know too that they suffered under the Brigadier's management of military affairs in the Crimea. I don't think Mr Allerdyce is in a position to give an alibi for his sergeant's whereabouts at the time of either of the murders. It does raise some interesting questions, doesn't it sir?"

Why are you doing this, thought Allerdyce? Are you trying to destroy the sergeant and me because we caught you fondling a boy in the Timberbush? Do you want rid of us because of our involvement in your Winchburgh conspiracy? Do you just hate us for trying to find the truth?

"Well," asked Burgess, "what do you say Allerdyce? Is there anything in this?"

"It's absurd, sir. McGillivray's a brave and honest man or I'm no judge of character."

"But," said Jarvis, "we're modern men. We have to put our emotions to one side, and we know how deceptive our impressions of character can be. Everyone thought Madeleine Smith was the soul of genteel respectability until she was tried for murdering her lover. All we can rely on is evidence. We know that Sergeant McGillivray is a trained and practised killer from his military service. We know from Mr Allerdyce that McGillivray has a sufficient motive of revenge – his father dead as a direct result of eviction from the Duke's land, his brother dead as a result of the Brigadier's alleged military shortcomings. We know that his presence at Mr Allerdyce's interview with the Brigadier gave him ample opportunity to reconnoitre the scene of the latest atrocity, and we can be sure that as an old comrade – holder of the VC no less – he would have had no difficulty securing admission to the Castle by night. I make no accusation, sir, I only wish to draw the evidence to your attention."

Allerdyce felt his blood pressure rising as Jarvis spoke. He could bear no more of Jarvis's calm, devious reasonableness and leapt to his feet, feeling his fists clench and his arm muscles tense in preparation for striking the man.

"You're a wretch, Jarvis. You know you're accusing an innocent man. Stand up and look me in the eye."

Burgess stood and roared at both of them.

"Men! Stop this! Sit down at once!" He sat and put his head in his hands. "Dear God, has it come to this, that we're tearing each other apart while a murderer is on the loose."

"I'm sorry, sir," said Allerdyce. "But I can't believe Jarvis's story."

"I don't like it either, Allerdyce."

Jarvis was obviously trying to look grave, but he couldn't entirely suppress his smirk.

"I don't think any of us takes pleasure in suspecting a comrade, sir. I wouldn't have raised the possibility if I didn't believe it was my duty. As it is, sir, I think the Chief Constable would be surprised if we didn't follow up any possible lead, however distasteful we may find it."

"Help me, Allerdyce," groaned Burgess. "Can you disprove Mr Jarvis's suggestion."

"I can't believe it, sir. Whatever Jarvis suggests, I can't conceive that Sergeant McGillivray is a murderer."

"That's not what I asked you, Allerdyce. I asked you whether you could disprove it. An alibi would be good. Can you disprove it? Yes or no?"

Allerdyce kept silent. There was only one truthful answer to the question as asked, but it was an answer which would throw a good man into hell. Burgess stared straight at him, his face ashen.

"I require your answer, Mr Allerdyce."

"I can't specifically disprove Jarvis's wild accusations, sir, but I don't believe them."

Burgess gave a deep sigh of unarticulated pain before speaking.

"So, gentlemen, what do we do now?"

"I'd suggest that Sergeant McGillivray is taken into protective custody while I question him," said Jarvis. "We may need to charge him as a formality if we're going to keep him for a while."

Burgess looked up. For the first time ever, thought Allerdyce, he seemed close to tears.

"I can't believe it. We're throwing one of our own men into the pit. They're our own family and we're turning on them."

"I'm sorry, sir. But do you agree it's necessary?"

Burgess looked distractedly over the policemen's heads.

"All right then. Do what you have to."

"Thank you sir."

"And just go now. I need some time to think."

Chapter 23

How many chains and bolts would it take to keep death out of the house?

For the second time this year, before spring had even started, Arthur had had to bury a brother.

Frederick had been a worse, more ignorant, bully than William and it was hard to mourn the loss of someone who'd brought him only contempt and misery, and who'd brought poverty and humiliation to Josephine. The congregation of the great and good had been slightly smaller, the walk from the church to the mausoleum had been even colder, and Arthur had known himself to be one coffin closer to his own place in the family mausoleum.

The Inspector had told him not to worry unnecessarily, that there was no definite reason to suppose that any further members of the family were under threat, but to take sensible precautions for his own safety until the case was solved. Arthur had found it hard, though, to accept even the partial reassurance which the Inspector had offered. The person who had murdered two of his brothers might still think the job was only half-done.

Arthur had made Wilson ensure that the doors were locked

and chained, the windows locked and the shutters of every room bolted, and that no-one was admitted to the house without his express permission.

Death might, however, already be in the house. Maybe, as if in a melodrama, the murderer had been living as a servant under his roof for years, eating Arthur's food and accepting his pay until the opportune moment to strike. Maybe Wilson himself, underneath his bland servility, was incubating some secret, murderous intention.

Arthur drew closer to the fire. He'd locked the parlour door from the inside, so not even Wilson or the maid could get in without forcing the door. Even so, it was a comfort to be in easy reach of the poker to defend himself if necessary.

He tried to distract himself by concentrating on the book which Josephine had given him. *The Essence of Christianity* by Ludwig Feuerbach, in a translation by Mr George Eliot.

Josephine had no doubt intended to be kind when she gave him the book. She'd written an inscription in her beautiful, tiny, feminine handwriting, inside the front cover. 'To my dearest Arthur, my beacon and my rock, may this book bring you consolation at this difficult time. Your loving cousin and sister in Christ, Josephine.' He'd read the inscription again and again before he'd even started the book, lying back in his chair and feeling the warmth stir in his veins as he thanked God for the privilege of offering guidance and support to his hurt, beautiful cousin. And she'd explicitly written of loving him, though the reference to Christian sisterhood was a barb to his sensitive soul as well as a necessary modesty.

The book, however, had signally failed to offer the consolation it promised. It was so unlike the improving certainties of home-grown church literature, with their emphasis on manly faith and building a citadel of godliness to repel the legions of evil and unbelief. The book, with its German subtlety, was like an enemy agent, entering the citadel in the uniform of an ally then slowly dismantling the defences from within. Every block it removed from the walls of faith was taken away gently and irresistibly by reason and persuasion, appealing to him to recognise things he felt he'd always known but dared not say, and each logical step he took with the author felt like a compliment to his intelligence, until suddenly the book was finished and he was left looking across a dark wind-swept waste-land which he had always suspected was there, but which he'd been sheltered from by thick walls of illusion.

The argument, beneath the references to Herr Hegel or Doctor Leibniz, was simple enough. God existed only as the projection of human qualities. Whatever qualities we saw in God – love, wrath, jealousy, retribution – were only the qualities which we valued most highly in ourselves, and deified. There was no heaven, no hell, no blessings or curses, only the lives we chose to lead in our brief interval under the indifferent sun.

He'd tried to remember the proofs of Christianity which had been drummed into him at University, and to pray. When he thought back to the proofs it seemed to him that he had always known that they were dusty myths which could be blown away by the chill wind from the darkness, or stories which people had comforted themselves with as they huddled round the fire against that icy breeze. When he tried to pray he heard only the noisy babble of his own mind talking to itself, above the crackle of the flames in the hearth.

He sat back and stared beyond the pool of light from his reading-lamp and into the dark corners of the room, where the firelight cast only shadows. What God would have allowed the torments he'd faced at his brothers' hands? What God would have let a woman of unblemished virtue like Josephine be despised and rejected by the men who should have been her protectors?

And, every Sunday for his whole professional life, had he only been telling comforting fairy-stories to his sparse congregation?

There was only one piece of wreckage he could cling to in the oceanic waste. Even Feuerbach admitted that the best of men were those who had created a loving Christ as their God, and built a God of love itself. So, he would love. His reason for being would be love, to love Josephine and see her re-established in the dignity and wealth she deserved. He would love her with a force beyond reason, and damn the consequences.

And, in a world without divine retribution, where he was only a heartbeat away from inheriting the wealth which he so yearned to share with her, surely any action was permissible in the cause of love?

...

As Allerdyce passed through the orderly-room on his way out of the Police Office the constables stopped talking and the silence was broken only by the tapping of his heels on the polished floorboards. I'm sorry, he thought. I'd have saved McGillivray from arrest if I could. He struggled to maintain a dignified pace rather than running headlong out of the office.

He emerged into the overcast daylight and turned his steps towards the Calton Jail. Walking over the North Bridge he looked at the jail's dark back walls, soot-stained by two decades of smoke from the station below, rising from the raw rock. The fortified sheerness was broken only by rows of tiny slots of windows, and he wondered which window McGillivray might even now be struggling to see out of.

The head warder took Allerdyce up to McGillivray's cell, leading the Inspector past rows of locked iron doors. Each one enclosed a silent prisoner in a cell, except for one from which the shootings and ravings of a deranged man could be heard. Every fifty paces the warder opened a barred door across the gas-lit corridor, let Allerdyce through, and locked it behind them.

"We don't get many policemen on murder charges here," observed the warder as he let Allerdyce through another gate. "It does add a bit of interest to the job, wondering what's going to happen to a prisoner."

At last they reached McGillivray's cell. The warder opened the iron door, creaking on its hinges. Allerdyce paused. Should he really go in? Why subject himself to the sergeant's contempt and hatred? And if McGillivray had really killed two men for revenge, what would he want to do to his accuser? But it would be an act of cowardice not to visit this man on whom he'd relied for his life. He entered.

McGillivray stood with his back to the door, his arms stretched to push against the whitewashed brick of either wall of the narrow cell. His head was bowed, and the pale light from the barred window above him shone down on the muscled back of his neck. Even through the heavy serge of the prison outfit Allerdyce could see the sergeant's broad, powerful back and a stain of blood where the wound in his side must have re-opened.

Samson Agonistes, thought Allerdyce, as the door clanged behind him and the lock clattered shut.

"Just give us a shout if there's any trouble, or when you want out," said the warder through the peephole in the door.

Dear God, thought Allerdyce as he looked at the sergeant, what have I done? If this strong, brave man is condemned unfairly, may the stones of this prison come crashing down on me.

McGillivray turned slowly. His face was blemished by a large bruise and he stood stooped, as if he'd been punched in the stomach.

"It's you, sir."

"Yes."

"When Inspector Jarvis arrested me he said that you'd accused me."

That's low of him, thought Allerdyce.

"Actually it was Jarvis's suggestion."

"But you agreed?"

"I don't believe you killed the Duke or the Brigadier. I had to agree, though, that every possibility that couldn't be disproved had to be investigated, even if I personally found them distasteful of incredible."

"Did you, sir?"

"You'd have done the same, Sergeant. It was my duty."

And, he thought, it's the betrayal of a friend.

McGillivray stood straighter, his fists clenched by his side.

"We knew what our duty was in the army, sir. It was to stand by our comrades, whatever happened."

Allerdyce couldn't meet the sergeant's eyes. He glanced aside, towards the chipped water pitcher which stood on a little wooden table.

"It's only a precaution, Sergeant. We can't allow you to serve while you're under any possible suspicion. We just need to keep you here until you're eliminated from our enquiries."

"Couldn't you just have sent me home, sir? Why did you have

to have me locked up? Do you think I might murder someone else, sir?"

"It's partly for your own protection, Sergeant. If anything else happens to the Bothwell-Scotts, no-one can blame you since your whereabouts is known."

"Protection, sir? Do you know what happens to policemen in prison? That I've already been assaulted in the exercise yard with the full knowledge of the warders? Don't you realise that I could hang for this? If you can't find the real murderer do you think there's anything to stop that happening? Or maybe you really do think I killed them. Jarvis sounds like he thinks I did it. Do you, sir?"

Allerdyce paused. Jarvis's accusations had sounded incredible, but they'd left a faint tidemark of suspicion in his mind.

"I find it highly unlikely, Sergeant. I promise that everything will be done to find out who did it."

McGillivray's look couldn't conceal his contempt.

"As thorough an investigation as was carried out before James Semple was killed, sir?"

"I promise, Sergeant. I'll do everything I can to help you."

McGillivray sighed. He didn't seem to have the strength to stand straight anymore, and he stooped and looked at the floor.

"I don't know what hurts me more, sir. The thought that I might be hanged, and leave Jeannie and the bairns unprovided for, or the thought that a man I honoured as a comrade and a friend thinks I may be a murderer." He raised his head and looked at Allerdyce, his face twisted with pain. "How could you, sir? Don't you know me well enough to know that I've seen enough pain and death already, after ten years in the army? Don't you know I'd rather save a life than take one?"

"I'm sorry. I did what I had to." And, he thought, may I never have to do as hard a duty again.

"All right sir. I can only pray that you'll realise soon enough that you're mistaken. May I still ask two favours of you?"

"Of course, Sergeant."

"Sir, I appreciate what you did for Sergeant Baird and his family. May I presume to ask that you'll give Jeannie and the family whatever assistance you're able to?"

"I will."

"And sir, for the sake of our former friendship, may I ask that you don't visit this cell again."

. . .

As the door of the cell clanged shut behind him, Allerdyce wondered whether he'd see McGillivray again. He shuddered as he realised that the only future occasion might be as a police witness at McGillivray's trial, telling the court what the sergeant had confided to him about the deaths of his father and brother from the actions of the Bothwell-Scotts. Or worse, perhaps Jarvis would arrange some 'accident' in prison so that another suspect disappeared, quickly and cheaply, without the inconvenience of a trial. Again, he felt himself drawn deep into the same rushing tide of inevitability that had led the boy to be hanged for murdering the father who'd daily abused him. McGillivray's words about comradeship tore at him. The sergeant was right – there was a duty to other people which pulled at the heart more strongly than a duty to the law. It didn't make it right to choose duty to a friend instead of justice, but by God it made the choice a hard one.

I can't save him until I've found William Bothwell-Scott's

daughter, he thought, and may I have the strength and skill to do that.

In the meantime, he knew what he had to do. Leaving the prison, he walked down to the Union Bank in George Street. He withdrew ten gold sovereigns and walked down Dundas Street to the artisans' houses where McGillivray's family lived.

Turning into McGillivray's narrow street he saw, again, children playing on the cobbles. A ragged boy looked up from his marbles.

"It's him!" he heard the boy shout. The children dispersed, some of the running indoors, others standing sullenly on the doorsteps of their houses.

He walked on, feeling the absurdity of his fear of running the gauntlet of a handful of children. He felt a sharp pain in the back of his neck, between his collar and his hat, and turned round. None of the children looked as if they'd moved but, putting his hand to his neck and feeling hot blood, he knew one of them had thrown a stone. Wiping the blood off his fingers into the lining of his coat pocket he went on towards McGillivray's house.

He pushed his way up the front path, brushing away the damp sheets which hung heavily from the washing lines, and rapped on the door. After a moment McGillivray's wife opened the door, wearing a clean white apron.

"What do you want?" she asked.

"I want to help you and your family while Sergeant McGillivray's suspended from the force."

"You? You want to help after you've had Hector put in prison? You'd have him hanged but you want to help?" She gave a dry laugh.

"I'm sure everything will be sorted out soon, but I expect you could do with some assistance in the meantime."

She put her hands on her hips.

"You're beneath contempt, Mr Allerdyce. You shove my man into jail after all he's done for you then you want to feel less guilty so you come down here and say you want to help. You're worse than Inspector Jarvis. You can go to the Devil."

"I thought maybe you could do with some money to tide you over."

He held out the little velvet bag in which the bank clerk had put the sovereigns. She appeared to hesitate, looking first at his face and then at the bag, before snatching it from him. She felt its weight in her hand, opened the bag, and looked inside. She turned it upside down, let the coins pour out onto the path, and spat in his face.

"We'll only accept help from our friends. Now go away!"

"Please, I want Sergeant McGillivray be cleared as much as you do. Please let me help you."

"Judas!" she hissed. She pushed him back and slammed the door in his face.

He stood, dazed, feeling the glob of spit run down his cheek. Looking down at the golden coins in the dirt, he wondered whether he should pick the coins up and stick them through the letterbox.

McGillivray's woman opened the door a chink.

"Go away!" she shouted. "Rot in hell!" She slammed the door shut again.

He turned and walked back down the path, wiping his cheek with his handkerchief.

The children were still watching, silently, from the front yards of their houses. He walked past, looking neither to left nor right. As he reached the end of the little street he felt another sharp blow on his neck, but didn't turn. I don't blame them, he thought, but I know who I do blame. It's Jarvis who wants to destroy us, and I won't rest until I've confounded him by finding out who really did kill the Dukes of Dornoch.

Chapter 24

Waking up next to Margaret, Allerdyce felt terribly alone.

He looked, in the feeble light that struggled through the curtains, at her sandy-gold hair falling in tangles on the pillow and her thin shoulder, turned against him, rising and falling under the white lace of her night-dress with the rhythm of her breathing.

They'd each been up twice in the night to check on Alice. He'd only slept shallowly, troubled by images of McGillivray in his cell and imagining himself taunted by a gang of children chanting 'Traitor! Traitor!' at him.

Margaret sighed gently and shifted her body slightly, pulling the bedclothes around her.

Have I made myself a stranger to her, he thought? I'm lying here in an inner agony that I can't tell her about. It's not fair on her to make her bear my troubles when she's still not as strong as she should be and when she's been wracked with worry about Alice.

He thought about Antonia. Just a few weeks ago he could have confided in her, as he had for years since Helen's death, but something had changed. It wasn't just Antonia's coldness when he'd last seen her. Something more profound had happened over that night and day when he and Margaret had nursed Alice back from the margins of death. Where previously he'd justified his continuing to see Antonia by telling himself that it was all right since it was no longer carnal, he now felt that the relationship was wrong. He belonged here, in his marriage to Margaret. His friendship with Antonia was wrong because it took his attention away from Margaret and because he could never tell her about it. It was an adultery of the mind, if not of the body.

And yet, and indeed because of that relationship, Margaret felt like such a distant creature. She lay there in her restless sleep dreaming dreams he couldn't even guess at. He didn't know her thoughts, and he knew his own were utterly alien to her.

Perhaps I'd feel closer to her if we still made love, he thought, but she's been too weak since Stephen was born. Or maybe that's just an excuse covering up my own distance from her. Margaret sighed again and turned around. Her face was now only a couple of inches from his, and he could feel her soft breath and see, in the three-quarters darkness, the pale outline of her cheeks. She stretched an arm out from under the bedclothes and laid it over him.

He wondered whether it would be wrong to make love to her now, whether she was too fragile still, whether he'd simply be taking advantage of her to satisfy a need. He reached over and embraced her, pulling her gently towards him.

He was surprised that she responded by pressing her body closely to his. He could feel her ribs under his hands, her small breasts pressing against his chest. She put her face to his and kissed him. As he responded, she turned over on her back.

"Please, Archie," she whispered, "I've waited too long for you to come back."

As they made love she kissed him and ran her hands down her back. He thrust gently, imagining her body to be made of some fine porcelain. As he came, he realised that for the first time in years he had made love to her without either Helen or Antonia's image coming into his mind once.

Perhaps there was a part of his life where, at last, he could act without betrayal.

...

For the first time, Allerdyce mounted the front steps of Dalcorn House alone. The Ducal flag drooped at half-mast in the damp chill of the day. The drizzling coldness seemed to seep its way through the seams of his coat and he shivered as he thought of McGillivray facing the lottery of justice. With no solid alibi, and every good reason for revenge, it was practically certain that a jury would convict him, if he had to face a trial.

The Brigadier's erect, dead penis stuck in Allerdyce's memory, though. If it was simply the result of rigor mortis – and the police surgeon had suggested that was possible – it didn't do anything to change the case against McGillivray. If, however, it had been engorged at the moment of death – and Mackay had said this was possible too – it seemed inconceivable that McGillivray had been engaged in some unnatural act with the Brigadier. It suggested a woman, and God willing this interview would help him to find her.

A footman showed Allerdyce into the large sitting-room where he'd met the Duke's valet twice before. He stood in front of a little table with a gilded snuffbox and a silver cigarette box. There was no fire in the grate, and the room was nearly as chill as the damp outdoors. They must have turned the radiators off between Dukes, he thought. As if they needed to save a few pounds.

After a few minutes Warner came in, dressed immaculately in

his dark suit and winged collar. He stood in front of Allerdyce.

"What do you want now, Inspector?"

"Sit down Warner."

"I said, what do you want? I've told you everything I can."

"Don't play the fool with me. Sit down and tell me the truth."

The valet hesitated then sat down at the other side of the table from Allerdyce. The Inspector stood, looking down on him.

"Unfortunate isn't it, Mr Warner, to lose two Dukes so quickly."

"What are you suggesting, Inspector, do you think I did it? After all the help I gave you? I didn't and I can prove it."

"I'm not sure that I believe you Warner."

"Come on, Inspector. I'm no murderer."

Allerdyce looked around the opulent room, with its profusion of paintings and ornaments.

"You must be a little bit underemployed, Mr Warner. No Duke in residence and no-one to keep an eye on what you're up to."

"What are you insinuating, Inspector?"

"Nothing. Only trying to imagine what you might be doing to fill your time and earn some money."

"Just stop there, Inspector. I'm not up to anything. I'm still getting paid since no-one's dismissed me yet, and I'm hoping that if the new Duke decides to move here he'll keep me on. The mad photographer bloke."

"You mean The Honourable George Bothwell-Scott QC."

"Yeah, him. So don't go getting any notions that I'm up to something. I'm earning an honest living."

"Is that right, Warner? So let me ask you one simple question. Does the name Augusta Mitchell mean anything to you?"

"Shit." Warner fiddled with his fingers and looked away,

towards a portrait of a former Duchess.

"Well? Is that a yes, Warner?"

"I can't say anything, Inspector. The family would kill me."

Allerdyce looked down at the valet, who avoided his gaze. I'll beat it out of you if I have to, he thought.

"Somebody's killing them, Mr Warner, and I need to find Miss Mitchell. I think she may know something that would help us. You surely don't want to obstruct a police enquiry?"

"I'm sorry, Inspector. I swore I wouldn't say anything. They'd stop at nothing if I did."

Allerdyce picked the snuffbox off the table and slid it into his pocket.

"You know, Mr Warner, a suspicious man would wonder what the servants get up to when there's no master around. Maybe picking up some money he might have left lying around? Maybe stealing some valuable trinkets that they think nobody will notice? I think they'd be particularly suspicious of a servant who'd done time in prison if, say, a valuable snuffbox with the Duke's arms on it appeared in a pawn shop."

"You bastard."

"So tell what you know about Augusta Mitchell. It's five years in prison for theft if you don't."

Warner sighed. He took a cigarette from the silver case, lit it, inhaled deeply and coughed.

"What do you want to know?"

"Everything. Was William Bothwell-Scott married to Miss Mitchell?"

Warner drew again on the cigarette and exhaled before answering.

"The Duke never told me so, but I'd heard the stories below

stairs. Some of the older servants remembered when the Duke had been a student he'd been sweet on the new governess. They'd liked it well enough at the time – it made him a bit better-tempered for a while. There was a story that he'd run away with her and maybe got married, but no-one could prove it."

"No stories about a child?"

"No."

"So you want me to believe that all you know is servants' rumours?" Allerdyce took the snuffbox out of his pocket and examined it. "You're going to have to do better than that, Warner."

"Not quite." Warner's eyes darted as if he thought someone was observing them, and he leant closer. Allerdyce smelt the tobacco staleness of his breath. The valet continued.

"I once had to run an errand for the Duke, about ten years ago. Before he got married.

"I'd been working for him for nearly two years, and he seemed to trust me as much as he trusted anyone.

"He'd withdrawn a large amount of cash, in notes, from the bank. He gave the money to me with an instruction to take it to a house some miles out of Edinburgh, up in the Pentland Hills. He said it was something he couldn't be seen to do himself."

"Where was the house?"

"Bavelaw Lodge. Up beyond Balerno. Anyway, I went into Edinburgh and hired a cab to take me out from there. That way nobody could know I'd come from Dalcorn.

"I'll admit, Inspector, that I was curious to see how much money was in the leather doctor's bag that the Duke had given me. Not to take any, you understand, just curiosity."

"I'll try to believe you."

231

"He'd taken it all out in relatively small notes – nothing bigger than a fiver. I supposed it would attract attention if the person he was giving the money to tried to cash a hundred pound note. So it took me ages, sitting in the back of the cab, to count it all out."

"And?"

"There were five thousand pounds there, Inspector. A lifetime's income for an ordinary man. I was staggered, and I did wonder briefly what my own life could be like with that sort of money in my hands. I'm an honest man, though, and I wouldn't have touched it."

"Of course not, Mr Warner. Especially with your police record."

"Ungenerous of you to mention it, Inspector. I reckoned that sort of money must be a pay-off to someone dangerous and I started to worry about what sort of men I was going to meet at Bavelaw."

"And who were they?"

"I'm getting to that, Inspector. The cab went up this long road into the hills – nothing around us but heather, bog and the odd clump of trees. I couldn't help thinking how easy it would be to dispose of a body up there – just dump it in a bog and no-one need find it for thousands of years. At last the cab turned into a driveway which led between thick conifers for fifty yards or so before coming to a white house, hidden from everything by the trees.

"I can't tell you how surprised I was when the door opened. The girl must have been about twenty years old. It's an image that'll stay with me for life, Inspector, that beautiful blonde woman, dressed all in white like a bride or a saint. I can see her slim white hands now, her waist gathered-in with a white ribbon, and her perfect bosom. Her skin looked warm and soft to the touch, her rosebud lips were slightly parted, and she looked passionate and angry."

"Most attractive, Mr Warner."

"Don't mock, Inspector. If you'd seen her you'd never have forgotten her."

"So what happened?"

"She said I was expected. She said that her mother was too unwell to see anyone, but that she had what my master wanted in exchange for the agreed payment. She handed me an envelope, took the bag with the money, and said that that concluded her mother's entire dealings with my master. She told me to tell the Duke that he was released from all obligations towards her mother except for the obligations of decency and morality, and that she prayed that the hounds of conscience would chase him mercilessly until he found his special place in hell. She bade me good day and shut the door.

"The envelope wasn't sealed. Maybe she wanted someone to know what was inside, before it was destroyed. Anyway, I felt I was owed some sort of explanation of what I'd just seen, so I opened it and unfolded the single sheet of paper inside.

"It was in French, but I could make out well enough what it said. It was a marriage certificate, issued under the authority of the Mayor of Paris, confirming the marriage of William Bothwell-Scott and Augusta Mitchell on the 17th of July 1832.

"I gave the envelope to the Duke as soon as I returned. He opened it, checked the contents, and put both the envelope and the certificate into the fire. That's where my involvement ended."

"You should have told me this before, Mr Warner." Allerdyce felt his hand tighten on the sharp corners of the snuffbox. "I should still have you arrested for obstruction."

"I've told you now, Inspector. And if the family ever find out I'm finished. I can't do any more for you."

"What about the telegrams, Mr Warner? Didn't it occur to you that maybe the peculiar telegrams the Duke used to receive, up to the one which immediately preceded his death, may have been sent by Augusta Mitchell or her daughter? Mightn't they have been trying to extort more money from him?"

Warner sighed and sat back in his chair.

"I don't know, Inspector. I honestly don't know. Please, I've told more than I should have. Just leave me alone."

Allerdyce stood up, his hand still clenched on the little box.

"I'm taking this with me, Warner. If I ever doubt that you've told me the full truth you'll be spending the next five years breaking rocks."

Chapter 25

Allerdyce felt a sense of progress as the cab wound its way up the long road from Balerno. The sun was breaking through the cloud in occasional bright shafts, bringing out the sedge in a vivid green where the light hit the ground. A curlew paced the moor and, far off, a falcon swooped on some unsuspecting prey. It was like finding a pocket of Sutherland a few miles from Edinburgh.

Every rotation of the cab's wheels was bringing him closer to finding Augusta Mitchell and her daughter, and to finding answers that might release McGillivray from suspicion. He thought again about the telegram – 'Mine all Mine' – could it refer to the husband who'd abandoned Augusta Mitchell, not to the shaft the Duke had been dumped down? He pictured the fiery daughter Warner had described, cut off from her legitimate inheritance, murdering her way through the family that had disowned her.

As the dark trees of the driveway closed around the cab he felt his optimism starting to drain away. Surely it was fanciful to imagine some woman he'd never met had premeditatedly murdered two Dukes? Was he clutching at straws to avoid having to confront the sergeant's possible guilt? And if Augusta Mitchell or her daughter really had anything to do with the deaths, why would they stop now? Would they keep on killing until the family was extinct?

He stepped down from the cab into the shadowed chill of the little courtyard in front of the house. A plump slack-jawed girl in a grey hessian dress and bonnet stood staring at him. He reckoned she must be about fourteen, and graceless with it – obviously not the blonde heroine Warner had met.

"Hello," he said. "My name is Inspector Allerdyce of the City of Edinburgh Police. Does Miss Augusta Mitchell live here?"

The girl stared at him vacantly. He advanced a little closer.

"Augusta Mitchell? Or her daughter? Do they live here?"

The girl backed away slightly.

"Awmmummum. Hnmumum."

He moved a step closer.

"Please, can you speak more clearly? I represent the police and I require an answer."

The girl gave an animal grunt and ran away round the back of the building. Bloody hell, he thought, why does everything have to be so difficult?

The door into the vestibule of the house was open, but the inner door was shut. He pulled the doorbell and heard a loud clanging inside the house. Pressing his face against the pane of frosted glass in the door he could see a shadowy movement across the hall. He pulled the bell again but saw no more movement. After thirty seconds, impatiently tapping his foot on the tiled floor of the vestibule, he gave a more powerful pull and the bell clanged so loud and so long that he thought it would surely wake the dead.

For a full minute there was nothing visible inside, then he saw a squat, dark figure come up the hall and disappear into a room. A moment later a taller figure emerged into the hall and came towards him.

The woman who opened the door must have been in her fifties, thin-faced but handsome, with hair which was still dark under her white lace bonnet. Her black silk dress covered a strong figure. If this was Augusta Mitchell he could see how, thirty years ago, she could have captivated the young aristocrat. The idiot girl was a mystery, though, unless William Bothwell-Scott had fathered another child with Miss Mitchell that no-one had yet told him about.

He took his hat off.

"Good afternoon, I wonder if you can help me. My name is Inspector Allerdyce. I'm looking for Miss Augusta Mitchell."

The woman pointed at her ears and then her mouth and shook her head.

"Augusta Mitchell, madam? Do you not know her?"

The woman shook her head again.

God, thought Allerdyce, what sort of house of idiots is this?

The woman picked up a little schoolroom slate which was hanging from a hook inside the door. She wrote on it, the stylus screeching against the surface, and held it out to him.

'Deaf and dumb,' he read.

He took the slate, rubbed her words out with his fingers and scratched out his own message.

'Can anyone here speak?'

The woman took the slate from him. As she rubbed out his message and scratched her own a younger child, a boy, appeared in the hall, staring towards him with open-mouthed fascination before giving a loud groan. Allerdyce glanced back to check that the cab was still waiting to take him away from this mad place. She held the slate out to him again.

'No. Deaf and dumb school.'

His heart sank. The prospects of finding Augusta Mitchell

were fast receding. He wrote again on the slate.

'Augusta Mitchell?'

'No,' wrote the woman. 'Gone away.'

'When?'

'Long time.'

'Daughter?'

'Gone too.'

'Where? Either.'

The woman gestured to him to wait. She turned round and went down the hall. The boy in the hall stood staring silently at him, and the idiot girl appeared from a side room, looked at him briefly, then ran back.

The woman came back, smiling politely. She took the slate, wrote on it, then held it out towards him.

Dear God, thought Allerdyce as he read the address she'd written, not that. In the name of all that's sacred, please not that.

...

Arthur jumped in his seat as he heard the doorbell ring. He reprimanded himself for a foolish timidity. Surely his killer wouldn't turn up in the middle of the afternoon and ring the doorbell to request admission?

He wasn't expecting a visitor, though, and he wondered who it might be. Probably a parishioner wanting him to hold a funeral or visit some dying peasant. He'd have to go, even if leaving the house meant exposing himself to unnecessary danger.

Or maybe someone was bringing news.

He thought about the news he'd most fear. Had someone come to tell him that the killer had struck again, and that his brother

George was dead?

Poor George. Arthur supposed that if George died he might, quite apart from concern for his own welfare, actually be sorry. George hadn't been a bad brother. He'd never beaten Arthur, he hadn't locked Arthur in a cupboard and left him overnight like Frederick had done, and he'd spared Arthur the daily humiliation and ridicule which he'd suffered from Frederick and William. George's death would make Arthur the Duke of Dornoch, with the staggering fortune which went with that, but Arthur would miss the brother who'd even shown some signs of spiritual regeneration since he'd lost his wife, even if Arthur couldn't share his delusions about the spirit world.

Wilson opened the parlour door, interrupting his thoughts.

"The Dowager Duchess to see you sir."

"Very well, Wilson. Show her in."

Arthur was shocked when Josephine came in. Her eyes were red as if she'd been crying, and there were dark lines under them which he'd never seen before. She wore no hat and her hair, normally so neatly tressed, straggled randomly over her shoulders. Her pale complexion had turned ashen.

"Josephine!" He stood to greet her. "What's wrong? What's happened?"

She hung her head.

"I'm sorry, Arthur. I've done something so awful that I have no right to be received under your roof."

"Josephine! Surely not? You know I could forgive you anything."

He led her over to an armchair at the opposite side of the fireplace from his. She sat, her head still bowed, with her hands in her lap.

"Would you like some tea, Josephine? Perhaps a sherry?"

"No thank you, Arthur. I don't feel strong enough for either."

He sat.

"What happened?"

Josephine sat in silence for a few moments, her fingers fiddling with the dark bombazine of her dress. Arthur felt the tension mounting in him unbearably. At last she spoke.

"It's your brother George, Arthur."

"What about him?" Arthur felt a surge of anger and incomprehension. Had all his faith in Josephine been an illusion? Had Josephine come to tell him that she had given herself to George? Were all his hopes doomed to turn to ash? Josephine continued.

"George came round to my cottage just now. I know that, strictly, I probably ought not to have admitted an unmarried gentleman, but he is family after all, and a widower, so I didn't think it was any great impropriety.

"At first he was solicitous. He said that, now that he had succeeded to the Dukedom, he wanted to see that I was established more appropriately."

"What did he mean by that?"

"I assumed he meant that he'd allow me to inhabit my old apartment in Dalcorn House. I asked him if that was what he meant and he said no, he wanted to establish me in Rock House. Was he going to move to Dalcorn House, I asked? He said no, he couldn't because his late wife's spirit was at Rock House and he couldn't leave it."

She paused and took a lace handkerchief out of her sleeve to dab her eyes. Arthur's mind raced, imagining Josephine being taken away from him and forced to live in his brother's sick spirit-world. She went on.

"I thanked him, but said that there was no possibility of my sharing Rock House with him, that even for a brother-and-sister-in-law to live in such close proximity would be unthinkable.

"He said that there was no question of us living together in that way. He said he could only share Rock House with me as man and wife."

Arthur felt a sudden faintness. Had she consented to marry George? Was he going to have to officiate at the wedding of the only woman he'd truly loved? The room was swimming before his eyes and he thought he'd fall off his chair.

Josephine was weeping now. He leant forward to touch her on the knee. There was something steadying about still being able to touch her.

"What did you say?" He dreaded hearing the answer.

She looked up at him with her tear-stained eyes.

"I said no, of course, Arthur."

Arthur's relief was mixed with perplexity.

"You spoke well, Josephine, and I can understand why such inappropriate behaviour by George should upset you. But why do you torment yourself with the thought that you have done something wrong?"

Josephine put her head in her hands. Her narrow shoulders heaved with a great sob. She spoke without looking up.

"Something so awful happened after that, Arthur, that I dare not mention it."

He touched her shivering arm.

"For God's sake, Josephine, tell me! Tell me anything! I cannot bear to see you suffer. Please, tell me and let me offer whatever help I can!"

She glanced up at him then spoke, her voice stronger and clearer now. Her face was utterly grim and her fingers pulled at the handkerchief in her lap.

"George didn't accept my answer, Arthur. He spoke rashly, saying that he'd known we were kindred spirits from the moment he'd seen me, that our souls were conjoined in the spirit world and that our bodies must follow. He said his late wife had been speaking to him from the other side, telling him that it was time for him to stop his mourning. His wife had said it was his soul's destiny to be with me. He was so vehement, Arthur, that I started to fear both for his sanity and for my own safety.

"I asked him to leave. I told him that it was very wrong of him to speak to me in this way. He refused.

"There are no bellcords in the cottage, Arthur. It's so simply built that there's no provision for summoning a servant. I stood up, and hoped that George would accept that as a signal that he should leave, and that if he didn't I would leave the room and ask my maid to show him out. Then..."

She seemed to be looking into the distance behind him, her lips pursed so tightly he could hardly see them. He looked intently at her but she didn't speak. Her arm was shaking and he could hear her slight, rapid breathing. He leant in close, and felt the warmth of her breath on his face.

"Go on, Josephine, please go on."

"I'm sorry, Arthur, I don't think I can."

"Please."

She hesitated an instant then continued, looking down at the floor.

"What happened next was horrible beyond my power to describe it, Arthur. Your brother took my standing up as an opportunity to pounce and catch me off balance. He pushed me against the wall and pressed himself against me. I tried to beat at him with my feeble strength but he pressed his face against me and tried to kiss me. I kept struggling and turning my face away but he grabbed my chin in his vice-like hand and held it while he kissed me and told me that he loved me, his other hand roving over my body and even over my bosom.

"I tried to cry out to the maid but he stifled my scream with his hand and then with another forced kiss. Arthur, I felt utterly soiled and violated.

"That wasn't all. As he was kissing me he started to undo the buttons on his trousers. I felt paralysed, Arthur, rigid with fear. The assault and degradation I feared from him was so inconceivably awful that my mind was overwhelmed and I doubted my power even to scream, even if I could release myself sufficiently for that.

"I believe God gave me words to save myself at that moment when I feared the very worst. George stopped kissing me for an instant, and I whispered the words that came into my mind from Providence. 'Too soon,' I said. 'Too soon. Your wife's spirit is here and says it is too soon.'

"Those words seemed to calm him. He let go of me and said he was sorry he had been so rash, that our souls were rushing to join themselves before our minds were ready. He left, with a promise to return before long."

Arthur felt as if he had, himself, been assaulted. He had been plunged into a horror blacker than he had known possible. The last of his brothers had proved to be the worst, in his unspeakable evil against the best of women. He wanted to get up and go straight to his wretch of a brother and punch him, as hard and repeatedly as his strength would allow, until he lay broken on the floor. But, for now, he had to steel himself to be calm and pastoral to his wretchedly abused cousin. He spoke words which he prayed would help her.

"You did no wrong, Josephine. I can offer no apology for my brother, though. He has behaved with a wickedness I had not thought possible."

Josephine was weeping again.

"I feel so soiled, Arthur. I acted so weakly. I should have had the moral strength to dissuade him. The guilt is mine too."

"No, no, Josephine, the guilt is all his."

"Do you not think me contemptible?"

"No, Josephine. I love you. I love you with all my heart as the best and bravest of women."

He was shocked to hear himself speak the words he had, till now, only dared to think. He shivered with a fear that, like his brother, he was assaulting her with an unwelcome love.

She reached out and laid her hand on his.

"I love you too, Arthur, as my strength and guide and comforter."

At any other moment, he would have been overwhelmed by a rush of joy at hearing her speak frankly of love. But, now, the spark of joy was extinguished instantly by a stronger, darker force.

Hate.

What George had done went beyond forgiveness. Forgiveness was too cheap. It would be a moral failure if Arthur didn't accept his duty as a man, and make sure that George was punished. He deserved to be shot like vermin.

He felt his soul hardening into steel as, in his mind, he buckled on the armour of retribution.

Chapter 26

Allerdyce kept looking round to see whether he was being followed. Perhaps one of Jarvis's men was tailing him, as he led them towards another suspect. To his relief, there didn't seem to be anyone on his tail. He'd taken precautions – coming back from Bavelaw he'd taken the cab to Ravelrig Station and then got off the train at Haymarket, where he was less likely than at Waverley to meet anyone he knew. He'd not gone back into the Police Office before setting off to walk circuitously to Stockbridge. To avoid a chance encounter with any beat constables he'd taken the shadowed path in the deep gorge of the Water of Leith, which emerged back into the light barely a hundred yards from his destination.

Danube Street.

He'd promised himself, as Alice struggled for life, that he'd never come here again, but fate had dragged him back within days. As he pulled the doorbell he felt a heavy sickness in anticipation of another betrayal.

Antonia's maid opened the door.

"Oh, Mr Allerdyce, we weren't expecting you. I'm sorry, Miss Antonia is engaged."

He took out his warrant card and showed it to her.

"Police business. It can't wait."

"I'll let her know. Come in."

He sat down, as so often before, to wait in Antonia's parlour. He tried to ignore a shout of male anger and the running of heavy steps down the stairs, and the slamming of the front door.

Antonia entered in her dressing gown, her blonde hair streaming down on her shoulders. She smiled weakly at Allerdyce.

"Not a social call, I gather, Archibald."

"No. I'm sorry. Police matters."

"Well then, we'd better speak here. More suitable for this sort of business than the boudoir, I think."

Antonia stood by the window, the light streaming through her hair. As he looked at her, and at the parlour with its upright piano, its potted palm, the dark silk wallpaper with its pattern of vines and grapes, and the canary in its cage, he was irresistibly reminded of Holman Hunt's *The Awakening Conscience*. Antonia, though, looked like a stronger, more difficult, person than the kept woman, with her core of innocence, in the painting. Antonia's posture was erect, and her gaze firm. The floral scent of her perfume couldn't fully mask a musky, more carnal smell. In the unforgiving daylight the fine lines radiating from her eyes and mouth spoke of fixity of purpose rather than laughter.

The image of McGillivray's bare, whitewashed cell came into his mind as he looked at the over-decorated parlour and he wondered what the sergeant was doing at this moment – picking oakum in silence in his cell, trudging drearily round the circle of the exercise yard, or, perhaps, being beaten discreetly by some inmates in a quiet corner of the prison while the warders turned a blind eye. He felt ill. It isn't Antonia's conscience that's the problem, he thought. It's mine.

"So, Archibald," said Antonia. "To what do I owe the privilege of this unusual visit?"

"I'm looking for a lady by the name of Augusta Mitchell. I was directed to enquire after her at this address."

"Well, you won't find her here, Archibald."

"The name clearly means something to you, though." He hated himself for having to adopt his assertive, investigatory tone with Antonia.

"Of course it does. It's my mother's name."

"Your mother?" He felt a dizziness as inevitability closed round him. "And where is she?"

"Gone, Archibald."

"Gone where?"

"Dead."

"I'm sorry."

Antonia sat down. As she sat he couldn't avoid a glance at the beautiful curve of her pale breasts. She pulled her dressing gown tighter around her and he looked away, cursing his weakness.

"You'll appreciate, Archibald," she said, "that mention of my mother causes me some upset. She died in quite distressing circumstances. Do you have a particular reason for your enquiry?"

Allerdyce paused.

"It's in connection with a murder investigation."

Antonia laughed, mockingly he thought.

"Well, I don't think my mother can honestly be a suspect, Archibald. I buried her ten years ago."

"I still need to know some details of her life and relations. I'm sorry."

"An unhappy subject, Archibald. May I know the subject of your investigation?"

"The murder of William Bothwell-Scott, Duke of Dornoch. And also of his brother, Brigadier Sir Frederick Bothwell-Scott."

"I should have known."

"I recall that you said, last time we met, that the Duke's name had some unhappy associations for you. "

Antonia paused before answering, looking Allerdyce directly in the eye.

"Yes. William Bothwell-Scott was my father."

Damn, thought Allerdyce. He felt like he'd been hit with a hammer. It's true. Like it or not, she's at the centre of all this. And if she is, so am I.

"Did you know him?"

"He used to visit from time to time. He'd rented a secluded house for my mother out in the Pentlands where he could visit her secretly."

I know, he thought, but I'm not going to tell you that I know.

Antonia continued.

"Of course, he didn't say he was my father. I was told to call him Uncle Bill. My mother made up a story that my father had gone to India as a missionary and got sick and died, and that Uncle Bill was his brother who was helping to look after us.

"I suppose I probably believed that when I was little, though as soon as I started noticing things I thought it was strange that, after he'd asked me how I was and given me a shilling, he'd go away to mother's bedroom with her. And as I got a little older I thought it was strange that mother hadn't displayed any mementoes of my father's life – no photograph, no locket with his hair, nothing. Though frankly I was so seldom out in the world that I was poorly-equipped to know what was normal."

"So when did you learn that Uncle Bill was your father?"

"Only shortly before mother died. She'd been quite animated for a while, talking about how we might be able to go to Europe with Uncle Bill, how we might even be able to live sometimes as a family together. I'd heard it before, so I wasn't expecting anything. Then there was a visit when they shouted and swore and I heard things being thrown in mother's bedroom. He stormed out ignoring me and slammed the front door behind him.

"I went into her bedroom and saw her sitting on the floor, holding a handkerchief to a cut in her forehead. She was crying. I asked her what had happened. That's when she told me – she'd been secretly married to Uncle Bill, I was his child, and for over two decades she'd lived for his visits and for the hope that, at last, they might be able to share more of their lives together. Now, he'd told her that he wanted to cast her utterly aside, and that he would cut her off without a penny unless she surrendered her marriage certificate to him. Her poor, shrunken life had been ripped apart."

God, thought Allerdyce, that's a harsh story. He felt wretched for re-opening Antonia's pain, but his duty – to the law and to McGillivray – meant that he had to press on with his questions.

"Were you sorry when you learnt that William Bothwell-Scott was dead?"

She laughed again.

"Sorry? Sorry, Archibald? If you knew even a fraction of how he'd blighted my mother's life and my own you'd have held a party to celebrate his death."

A voice in Allerdyce's mind said, stop her now. Stop her from incriminating herself. You've already allowed one friend's candour to place himself in mortal danger – don't let Antonia follow him. But a stronger voice said that this was evidence and needed to be heard. He held his tongue and Antonia continued.

"Do you know how my mother died, Archibald? Do you? She didn't want to live after the Duke had discarded her, but she didn't know how to die. At first she just seemed to be wasting away through depression and not eating. Then she asked me to go to a pharmacist and obtain prussic acid. She said it was to poison the mice that infested the house, but I suspected her true purpose and said I wouldn't go. So do you know what she did, Archibald? She drank a cup of neat bleach.

"I found her on the kitchen floor, still alive. Her lips were burnt as if someone had held a red-hot iron to them. Blood was frothing out of her mouth. She might have been screaming or she might have been trying to speak – I couldn't tell because the bleach had burnt-out her voice box. Her eyes were rolling around like a lunatic and her legs were kicking out in mad spasms.

"I tried to make her drink water but she only choked. I knew it would take me at least half an hour to ride to the doctor's house in Balerno, and another half hour to come back with him even if he was in, and that that would be too late. So I held her in my arms, trying again and again to get her to drink some water or some milk to put out her inner flames, with no success. She died in sheer terror, Archibald, and I hope that I never have to see such suffering again. So, frankly, it gave me nothing but joy to hear about his death. I only pray that it was painful."

"And when did you last see the Duke?" Please, he thought, don't let her answer incriminate her further. "Was it when he last saw your mother?"

"No. I was cursed with seeing him once more. As a client."

Allerdyce swallowed, feeling nauseous. Could the Duke have been such a degenerate that he even lay with his own daughter?

"I'm sorry."

"This business isn't what I'd ideally have chosen, Archibald, but I'm good at it. In fact, I like to think that I'm at the top of my profession, and my fees reflect that. My mother was an intelligent woman and she gave me as good an education as she was able. I could have made my living as a governess or a schoolmistress, if anyone would have given a job to an orphan girl with no references. But frankly, that didn't appeal. And no-one was going to marry a fatherless girl whose mother was a suicide.

"My mother, days before she died, said something that stuck with me. She said she'd thought for many years that she was a wife, but only now realised that she was a whore. She'd just been a sexual outlet for William, for which he'd paid by renting the house and giving her a small allowance.

"I was determined my life wasn't going to be like hers. I was going to take control. I would use men on my terms, and for my profit. So if men routinely used woman as whores, I would make sure I profited handsomely from it.

"Have you ever thought about how I set myself up here? About the expense of buying this house? William gave my mother enough money in exchange for the marriage certificate for me to buy this house after her death, but not enough to maintain me in the comfort I thought I deserved for the rest of my life. So, I set out to earn an income that would give me complete independence from any individual man."

"You were going to tell me how you last saw the late Duke," prompted Allerdyce.

"I was coming to that, Archibald. I'm a quick learner, and I soon learnt the tricks, both conversational and sexual, that keep a man interested. I flatter myself that some of my clients quickly came to think of me as a friend as well as a whore – a quality of relationship which my father had denied to my mother. My reputation spread quickly and new clients arrived daily.

"I was horrified when, a few months after starting the business, my maid showed William Bothwell-Scott into my bedroom.

"I could have killed him right there and then. If I'd had a pistol in my room I could cheerfully have shot him in the stomach and watched him die.

"Fortunately for him, I didn't. He recognised me instantly. He stared at me for a second of disbelief and horror then turned round and left.

"So that's it, Archibald. I haven't seen him since and I'm glad he's dead."

Or was it, thought Allerdyce. Could you have blackmailed him? Could you have found a means to do what you thought was right and kill him?

He took out his notebook and flicked back a few pages.

"I'd like to be able to eliminate you completely from the investigation, Antonia. It would help me if you could confirm where you were, and with whom, on the nights when William Bothwell-Scott and the Brigadier met their deaths."

Antonia stood up, clasping her dressing-gown tightly around her.

"You swine, Archibald. I confide in you as a friend, and you make me a suspect. I had genuinely thought you were my friend, and is this the loyalty I receive? To be identified as a murderer?"

Allerdyce felt the black despair welling up inside him. He pressed on.

"It's purely a matter of routine, Antonia. A matter of elimination."

"Elimination of who, Archibald? Whoever visited me as a client on those nights would deny it in court, if they had a wife to think of or if they wanted to keep their position as a judge or a minister of the church. Plenty of them give me false names anyway. I can't give you a reliable alibi for any night when I've entertained clients." She put a slim hand against her neck. "I could hang, Archibald, if you choose to make me a suspect. Is that what you want?"

He visualised the rough hempen rope around her pale neck. He thought about the other friend whose life was already in jeopardy as a result of his suspicions.

Had McGillivray killed the victims? Maybe – he'd had the means and the motivation. Had Antonia killed them? She'd had the motivation in abundance to murder William Bothwell-Scott. The means? Perhaps – if she'd been meeting him to blackmail him. And the Brigadier? The motivation was less clear, unless she was working her way through the family until she was sole heir, but the circumstances of his death suggested a woman, and the droll messages which had accompanied both deaths suggested someone of Antonia's intelligence.

It could be either, it could be neither. In his heart he would like to be able to tell them both that they were free from suspicion, but that would be in defiance of reason and evidence. In the absence of other clear suspects he appeared to have a stark, dreadful choice.

Who goes on trial and takes their risks in the bearpit of the High Court?

Is it the man who saved my life? Is it the woman I have come to regard as a lover and a friend?

Antonia stood waiting for his answer. The canary fluttered and twittered in its cage. Her dressing gown fell open, revealing the golden, rounded figure to which her silk undergarment clung, and the magnificent décolletage which rose from it. He thought of the horrors which Antonia had suffered because of the Duke, her mother dying in agony on the floor after being cast off by him.

Whatever choice he made would be an appalling breach of loyalty. He wished the decision could be taken away from him. There was no way that was going to happen, but he could at least defer it until he had reported to Burgess.

"I won't be taking things any further for the moment, Antonia. But don't leave town – you may be required as a witness. And thank you for your candour."

Chapter 27

Parish business meant that Arthur couldn't get away from Dalcorn until the afternoon following Josephine's distressing visit. First he was called out to see a servant at Dalcorn House who complained that the Devil was tempting her to steal. A clear case of underemployment making space for evil, he thought, reflecting on his brother's refusal to take up residence at Dalcorn House and give the idle army of servants something to do. Then he had to conduct the funeral for a shale miner who'd been killed in a small underground explosion. The man hadn't been a member of the church, and hadn't even gone to the Free Church chapel, but the law said that he had to be buried by the Church of Scotland, so that was that. Arthur rushed through both occasions, imagining all the while that his brother might be perpetrating fresh outrages against Josephine.

At last he was able to get away. He discreetly slipped the little pistol which he'd withdrawn from the gun room at Dalcorn House into his pocket. Since Frederick's death, with its clear implication that the brothers were being murdered in turn, he'd carried the gun every time he had to leave the manse. He'd never fired a weapon in his life, but he assumed that if he just pointed it and pulled the trigger he might wound his assailant. And, if necessary, he could use it to reinforce his arguments to George.

Of course, he'd be reasonable, as befitted a Christian. His first aim must be to make George appreciate the gross error of his ways and repent, opening his heart to regenerating grace. The best outcome would be that George realised that he had committed a grave wrong against Josephine and resolved voluntarily to seek amendment of life. The arguments of reason, faith and decency might suffice.

But what would he do if George showed no sign of penitence? That was altogether more difficult. He could threaten George with the fires of a Hell that neither of them believed in any more. He could plead to George's sense of the honour of the family, if George had retained some sense of that through his fog of spiritualism and lust. But, ultimately, the pistol represented the final possibility, the threatened or actual use of force.

Arthur was resolute as the servant admitted him to Rock House. His success in preventing his brother from committing any further evil against Josephine, and his determination to punish George tenfold for any sin against her, were his tests as a man. At last he'd been presented with a truly chivalric challenge, and he would not fail.

He did pause, though, when he saw a Paisley-patterned shawl hanging on a coathook in the lobby. It looked remarkably like a shawl he'd seen Josephine wear when she went out driving in the Ducal open carriage, before she had adopted mourning dress. Could it mean that Josephine was here? Or, more likely, had his blackguard brother stolen it from Josephine's house as some perverted lover's token? Or was he allowing his imagination to run too far ahead of himself about what was, after all, a relatively common pattern of shawl or scarf which had probably belonged to

George's late wife? That must surely be it – George's sick conviction that his late wife was still spiritually resident in the house must have made him reluctant to discard or put away this remnant of her physical presence.

There was no sign of another visitor when Arthur was shown into George's studio, bright with the early spring sunlight which streamed through the skylight and the French windows. His brother was in a chaotic state of semi-undress – shirt-sleeves rolled up and waistcoat undone – and the wooden boxes, lenses, and glass plates of various cameras were strewn over the table along with a claret bottle and a teapot, but he knew this to be nothing unusual. If only, thought Arthur, George had a lens to look into his own soul.

George looked up.

"Hello there, Arthur. Nice of you to drop by."

Arthur stood just inside the door, his hat in his hands, grateful that his clerical collar gave his neck an imposing stiffness, keeping his chin erect even if he felt an inner fear at confronting his brother.

"George," he said, "I have come on the gravest business."

"Dearie me, Arthur, you do look a bit serious. Come and sit down. Tea? A glass of claret?"

"George, I prefer to stand."

"A bit odd, Arthur, if you don't mind me saying so. What's on your mind?"

"I need to speak to you very seriously about Josephine."

George looked dreamily towards the skylight.

"Ah, dear sweet Josephine. You know, when Matilda passed over I thought I might never love a woman again, except in the purely spiritual realm. Now I find that Josephine is giving me reason to hope that I might love again in this earthly, physical existence."

Arthur felt he could strangle his brother there and then. Earthly, physical love with Josephine? How could this monster who had caused her so much grief even dare to mention his brutal desire for physical love with her? He struggled to maintain his composure, but as he spoke he was aware that his voice sounded shrill.

"George, you have done a great wrong to Josephine. I have come here to ask you to repent, and to promise before me and Our Lord that you will offer no further offence to her."

George simply looked perplexed. The meeting wasn't following the script which Arthur had crafted so carefully in his head.

"Offence? Steady on, Arthur. I can't say that I follow you."

"Do you need me to spell it out? To speak of the unspeakable?"

"Well, I suppose you'd better, old chap, or else I won't have the slightest idea what you're talking about."

"George, please, at least have the decency to yourself and to me to speak the truth. Did you visit Josephine at the dower-cottage yesterday afternoon?"

"Well, yes, actually, I did, though I can't see that that's any concern of yours."

"And what happened when you were there?"

"We conversed, Arthur. Oh, and we took tea. I really can't see that you could be offended by that."

Arthur tried to steel his voice, and pitch it half-an-octave lower, but it only sounded as if it was breaking.

"George, as we stand in the awful presence of the Almighty I urge you, for the sake of your eternal soul, to tell the truth. What happened between you and Josephine?"

George stood up.

"Look, Arthur, it's been a terrible strain on everyone. First William and then Frederick. I can't say it's been good for my nerves either. But do try and pull yourself together. Sit down. Have a drink."

"No, George, I insist you tell me the truth. Did you, with gross indecency, assault Josephine in the dower-cottage yesterday afternoon?"

George's perplexity was hardened with an edge of anger.

"No, of course not."

What do I do, thought Arthur. What possible influence can I have on a man who flatly denies the truth?

"You're saying that you laid no hand on her?"

"That's right, Arthur. I honestly don't know what's got into you today."

"And you said nothing to her about marriage, or about her coming to live with you at Rock House?"

George stood closer and touched Arthur on the arm.

"I really do think you'd better sit down. There's something I want to tell you."

"No, George. I choose to stand."

"All right then. But please just listen for a moment. I'm sorry that I'm going to have to say something which may upset you."

The truth, or at least part of it, at last, thought Arthur. George continued.

"I have an understanding with Josephine, Arthur. She's been rather adrift since William died, and I'm afraid Frederick was a tad beastly to her. I've also been feeling rather lost – I know Matilda is still with me in spirit but I've been feeling that it's time for me to move on too. The fear that death is stalking the family has spurred things on somewhat for me. I don't need to tell you that Josephine is a damned attractive woman, and still of childbearing age, given the right sire.

"We've grown close over the past couple of months. There's a sort of comfort that perhaps only two widowed people can give to each other. The long and the short of it is, Arthur, that we've decided to get married once Josephine's out of mourning. If we're spared."

"No!" Arthur felt tears welling up, and a constriction at the back of his throat.

"I'm sorry, Arthur. I'd hoped to be able to tell you at a more opportune time. I know you're rather sweet on Josephine – it's been plain for everyone to see. But we think this is the right thing for us, and for the family."

"No! You're lying!"

"I know it's a disappointment to you, Arthur, but you've always been a generous soul and I'm sure you'll be the first to wish us well, once you're used to the idea." He grasped Arthur in a loose embrace. "Friends?"

In the split second before his inhibitions could engage Arthur shoved his brother, hard, away from him. George stumbled, looking back over his shoulder, and then there was a sharp crack as his head struck the edge of the table. He fell inert on the floor.

Arthur knelt down. His brother was still breathing and his eyes were still open, though they didn't appear to be focussing. George gave a low groan with every breath.

Get help, said a voice in Arthur's head. Call the servants and get help. But a subtler voice spoke too – leave him. Whether he or Josephine spoke truly, your brother tried to steal her from you.

If Josephine spoke truly, he is justly punished for his evil to her. If George spoke truly, he has confessed that he wants to take her from you. Run away, and leave his fate to the wise judgement of God.

Arthur stood up, opened the French windows, and ran.

Chapter 28

The beefsteak and Burgundy at Professor Boyd's house tasted like hard-tack and brackish water in Allerdyce's mouth. The Speculative Society was to be treated tonight to an exhibition of spiritualism by one of Boyd's latest finds – the 'Seer of Brora', Mrs Flora MacIver. There's a spirit here right enough, thought Allerdyce. It's Sergeant Hector McGillivray standing behind me in his prison chains, as real as Banquo's ghost.

He tried to get through dinner with as little conversation a possible. Normally he'd have been a leading spokesman for rational scepticism, but tonight he didn't feel he had either the energy or the certainty to argue about anything. It was a relief when dinner was over and they were led through to Boyd's drawing room, where Mrs MacIver's spirit cabinet had been set up.

The room was lit feebly for the occasion by a single red-shaded paraffin lamp on a stand by the door. Chairs had been set out in a circle, and in the middle of the circle was a table on which Allerdyce could dimly discern a book, a candlestick, and a handbell. At the far side of the circle he could see the old woman's pale and crinkled face, the shadowed light etching the lines deeper into her face so that she looked like Death personified. The rest of her was invisible – black clothing against a background of temporarily erected black curtains, the standard equipment of the music-hall supernaturalist.

He took his seat and Professor Boyd turned the light down to allow the séance to proceed in darkness. Allerdyce blessed the darkness which allowed him to endure the unobserved privacy of his inner agony while the unconvincing rattles, bangs, and appearances of phosphorescent objects proclaimed the alleged presence of the spirits summoned by the old Highland charlatan. He felt the air disturbed by what might have been a spirit, but was more likely the medium's accomplice appearing from behind the curtains.

He was sorry when Boyd stood up after the 'spirits' had been quiet for a few minutes and ignited a bright lamp with a clear shade.

"The next experiment," announced Professor Boyd, "is not dependent on the whims of spirits who may be shy of the light. It is a simple controlled experiment into the power of thought transference. Mrs MacIver, do you consent to be blindfolded."

"Aye."

"And to turn your chair so that your back is to the table and there is no prospect of your being able to see any image or object placed on the table?"

"As you please, sir."

"Thank you. Now, Mr Allerdyce will you consent to examine this piece of black cloth, which has been folded over three times? I'd be obliged if you could hold it against the lamplight and confirm to me that no discernible light or image is able to pass through the cloth."

Allerdyce got up and reluctantly held the cloth to the light.

"It's as you say, Boyd. Practically impenetrable."

"Thank you, Allerdyce. Now would you tie the blindfold round Mrs MacIver's head, to exclude all possibility of her seeing anything."

"Very well."

He felt his hands shaking as he tied the cloth behind the old woman's black headscarf, imagining himself tying it round McGillivray's head before his execution. He fumbled the knot twice before getting it right and sitting down with relief.

"Right," said Boyd. "I have in my hand a set of cards. Not common playing cards, but a series of distinct shapes designed precisely for experiments of this nature. To avoid any suspicion that they are in a pre-arranged sequence known to Mrs MacIver may I ask Professor McIntyre to shuffle them, if that is within his pledge as a minister of religion not to conspire with the powers of darkness. Professor McIntyre?"

"All right then."

McIntyre shuffled the cards three times then handed them back to Boyd.

"Now," said Boyd, "I will lay out ten cards, one at a time, on the table in front of us. As I place each card on the table I want all of you to hold that image strongly in your mind, as far as possible to the exclusion of all other thought. I will lay the first card now."

He placed the card down. Allerdyce tried hard to hold the image in his mind – trying to think of nothing more complex than a black printed shape on a white card kept other, more painful, thoughts at bay.

The seer paused for nearly two minutes before speaking.

"A circle."

"Correct, Mrs MacIver. I will place the second card now."

The answer was quicker this time.

"A star."

"How many points?"

"Five, sir."

"Correct again, Mrs MacIver. Now for the third card."

Allerdyce tried, again, to focus on the card but his thoughts refused to be held at bay. It was Antonia he saw this time, with her dressing gown falling alluringly open. Could she have done it? Could she have taken what, in common justice, appeared to be a richly deserved revenge on William Bothwell-Scott? Should he have arrested her already? Was he protecting her because of love, friendship or cowardice?

The medium appeared to be flustered, her head moving from side to side as if she was looking into the blackness of her veil for an answer.

"Mrs MacIver? Do you have an answer? Mrs MacIver?"

"I cannae see, sir. I don't see it clearly. It comes into view and then out again. Is it a square?"

"No, I'm sorry Mrs MacIver, it isn't. Would you like another attempt?"

The medium continued to look around for an answer, her body now rocking backwards and forwards in her chair.

"Mrs MacIver? Are you all right? Should we stop? Do you want a glass of water?"

"I cannae see, sir. There's too much confusion of energy coming from a gentleman in the room."

"All right, we'll stop this now."

"No, wait." The medium sat bolt upright and appeared to be staring straight ahead of her through the thick blindfold.

"I have a clear message come into my mind, sir. It is addressed to a gentleman of uneasy conscience. It says 'You will see a good man hanged and a wronged woman's revenge. This <u>will</u> be.'"

No! thought Allerdyce. Not that! Please let me not believe that that message is for me. It's all nonsense, isn't it?

But a chill sweat had already broken out on his back and his pulse was racing. He felt sick to his core. Without thinking he found himself praying to whatever unseen presence or vacuity permeated the universe.

Save my friends. Don't let them die. And for God's sake save me too.

Chapter 29

Allerdyce had just arrived in the Police Office the next morning when he was summoned to Burgess's office.

The Superintendent was pacing distractedly in front of the window, then turned round and saw Allerdyce.

"Ah. There you are."

"Sir."

"Take a seat, for Heaven's sake."

"Thank you sir."

They sat, and Burgess tapped his pen against the desk for a moment, looking at a spot somewhere over Allerdyce's left shoulder, before speaking.

"We've lost another Duke, Allerdyce."

Allerdyce felt as if the floor was disappearing beneath him. Burgess continued.

"George Bothwell-Scott was found yesterday evening by his butler, dead in his photographic studio."

"Murdered?"

"Without a doubt. Face down in a tray of silver nitrate in his darkroom, with a bullet through his head."

"Why wasn't I called out? Margaret could have told you where to find me."

"We didn't need to. The butler told us who did it, and we've brought the suspect in. He's yours to question when you're ready. And the crime scene has been sealed and guarded – nothing moved except the body, and Dr Mackay can tell you all about that."

"Who's the suspect?"

"I can hardly believe it, Allerdyce. The press are going to love it.

"The Reverend the Honourable Arthur Bothwell-Scott."

...

First of all Allerdyce went to Rock House with Mackay, the Police Surgeon. He needed to see the location of the crime, speak to the butler, and understand the mechanics of how it had been committed before he questioned the suspect.

He should, he supposed, feel some sense of relief. This was one murder, at least, which couldn't be blamed on McGillivray.

Any relief he felt was, though, overwhelmed by a dark fear of what might happen next. There would be the inevitable tide of blame, from the newspapers and from the Chief Constable, that three Dukes had died before the police had found their man. Unless the evidence showed this latest killing to be the work of the same hand as the previous deaths, the sword of justice still hung over the sergeant. And was it really possible that the mild clergyman could have murdered his way systematically through his own family?

And Antonia? Could she be involved? Had he left her at liberty to commit a further atrocity?

Anything is possible, he told himself. Just keep an open mind until you've examined the evidence.

The butler's account, after Allerdyce and Dr Mackay had been admitted to Rock House, was simple. Arthur Bothwell-Scott had turned up mid-afternoon yesterday and said he needed to see his brother on a matter of urgent family business. The butler had shown Arthur into the studio and left them in privacy. He'd heard raised voices briefly, but not felt he ought to intrude on a private family conversation. His master in any case very much disliked being disturbed unnecessarily while at work in his studio, so the butler had decided it was best to let them be.

It wasn't until six o'clock, when he usually served a drink to his master, that he felt licensed to intrude. The studio itself was empty, with no sign of George Bothwell-Scott or his guest. The only peculiarity was that the French window was slightly ajar. The butler called out to attract his master's attention in case he was in the darkroom which opened from the studio, but heard no answer. Becoming suspicious, he opened the door to the darkroom, pushed the shade-curtain aside and saw his employer, evidently taken ill since he had collapsed into a bath of developing fluid. He tried to rouse his master, before discerning that he was lifeless and rushing out to attract the attention of the nearest policeman. The butler was adamant that, unless the master had privately admitted anyone by himself, Arthur Bothwell-Scott was the only person to have visited his employer on the day of his death.

A constable standing guard at the door of the studio broke the seal and let Allerdyce and Mackay in. Allerdyce checked round the room but nothing looked suspicious or out of place – even the jumble of photographic equipment on the table had some semblance of order. Nothing indicated that there had been a mortal struggle, though the nap of the carpet was slightly disturbed at the near edge of the table as if someone had dug their heels in. He opened the French windows, hoping that there might be soil outside which had absorbed the footprint of whoever had left the doors ajar, but they opened onto a gravel path where only the faintest indentations were visible.

They went through to the darkroom, pushing the heavy curtains aside to stand in the laboratory, lit by a single red-shaded gas flare, where George Bothwell-Scott had been found dead. Allerdyce had the odd feeling that he had walked into an actual spirit-cabinet, and that he was at the heart of whatever trickery or spirit-workings went on there.

The gas-light hissed. The dark-room, with its chemical baths, clothes-lines with drying photographic prints on them, and the upright concertina apparatus of the enlarging equipment, was oppressively stuffy. The bottles of chemicals on shelves above the developing bench, and the red glow of the light on brass, wood and glass, gave the place something of the air of an alchemist's workshop.

Some of the images hanging from the lines were clear, even in the ruby light. The dead man had taken a variety of landscape pictures, and Allerdyce recognised images of Arthur's Seat and Berwick Law. He'd also taken some still-lives of flowers and fruit, and some other pictures showed void spaces where presumably the deluded photographer had believed he saw the spirits of the deceased. There were also a handful of what Allerdyce supposed would be called 'artistic' images, clearly taken in the studio itself. They all appeared to show the same young woman, with dark hair and a delicate figure, in progressive stages of teasing undress culminating in complete nakedness as she sat sideways on the chair under the skylight. In all the images her face was turned away from the camera – either an attempt to increase the sense of erotic beguilement or to protect her identity.

One of the hanging pieces of card had no image on it, just

a message in what Allerdyce would guess was masculine handwriting.

'**An interesting development.**'

So, our droll Duke-killer strikes again.

"Has anything been moved, Mackay?" he asked.

"Just the body."

"You examined it when it was still here?"

"Yes. And in the mortuary."

"I should have been called as soon as the body was found. Anything – what he was wearing, the precise way he was lying, even the expression on his face – could have been significant evidence."

"I'm sorry, Allerdyce. Burgess specifically didn't want you to be the first person to examine the scene. He asked Sergeant Henderson to come down here with me and make notes."

"Why?"

"I shouldn't say, Allerdyce. I think he maybe feels you've been on the Bothwell-Scott case a bit too long, and maybe you've become a bit set in your views. He wants to see the case through other peoples' eyes as well – perhaps they'll notice something fresh."

It stung that Burgess, normally such a straightforward man, wasn't giving him his full trust.

"What about the body, then, Mackay? What did you notice?"

"Well, you know the basics already. He was shot in the head and we found him, still sitting on his stool, face down in that tray of developing fluid. It's normally as clear as water: the cloudiness which you see is the victim's blood."

"Anything else?"

"A couple of interesting things. He'd sustained a bruise to his left temple shortly before his death – certainly the same day, possibly

271

within an hour or two. Rather nasty, looked like he'd fallen against a blunt edge. Could have caused him some concussion."

"But presumably he was conscious at the time of his death?" asked Allerdyce. "He wouldn't be sitting here otherwise."

"True enough, but it was a nasty blow and he'd still have been feeling it. The other interesting thing is where the bullet entered his head. We wouldn't have been able to see any bruising if it had been on his other temple, because of the bullet's entry hole and the scorching round it."

Allerdyce looked past the spot where George had died, towards the curtains and the door.

"You mean whoever shot him was standing here."

"Yes."

"With the victim between them and the door?"

"Precisely, Allerdyce."

"That's interesting, Mackay. Very interesting indeed."

...

Allerdyce interviewed Arthur in a holding cell in the basement of the Police Office. Arthur was sitting on the fold-down bed in his dark suit and clerical collar, unshaven and with dark lines under his eyes. He had the cell's police-issue Bible in his hands but threw it aside when he saw the Inspector.

"Ah, Mr Allerdyce. How ironic. Last time we met you urged me to take precautions for my safety in case the family murderer struck again. Now you meet me when I'm accused of being that murderer."

"Unfortunate circumstances indeed, sir. Or should I say, Your Grace."

Arthur gave the hint of a smile.

"It's almost comical, isn't it Inspector? I find out when two constables turn up at my doorstep at seven o'clock in the evening that my brother is dead. So, at some stage between then and when I left George's house I'd become the 10th Duke of Dornoch without my knowing it, and inherited the entire wealth of the estates and mines. And look at where I've spent my first night as a peer of the Realm."

Better reassure the suspect, thought Allerdyce. Put him at ease and you'll get the most out of him.

"I just need to ask you a few questions, sir. Hopefully we can get all this sorted out and needn't detain you very long."

"Thank you, Inspector. I'll help you as far as I can."

"I appreciate that, sir. First of all, do you confirm that you visited your brother at Rock House yesterday afternoon?"

"Yes I did."

"At approximately what time, sir?"

"I arrived at about three o'clock. After attending to various items of parish business."

"And what was the purpose of your visit, sir?"

"A private family matter."

"I'm sorry, Your Grace, I must ask you to be explicit. It's important that I know the full circumstances surrounding the time of your brother's death. Otherwise we will be unable to eliminate you quickly from the enquiry."

Arthur glanced towards the barred window high in the cell wall, as if seeing the inescapability of the truth. He hesitated, as a door further down the corridor shut with a heavy clang, and looked up at Allerdyce.

"Do you think I murdered my brother, Inspector?"

Keep him calm, thought Allerdyce.

"We just want to reconstruct the pattern of events that afternoon, sir. Then everyone can get back to their business."

"Very well. I will be completely candid with you. I visited my brother because my sister-in-law, the dowager Duchess Josephine, had complained to me that George had been pressing unwelcome attentions on her."

"Rape, sir?"

"Thank the Lord, nothing quite as grave. But serious enough."

"And why would the Duchess choose to confide in you, sir?"

"I suppose, barring George, I'm her closest living family on this side of the Atlantic. And she's come to rely on me somewhat, in her widowhood, for spiritual consolation."

Spiritual consolation's a nice word for whatever you're up to with her, thought Allerdyce.

"So you wanted to confront your brother?"

"I wanted to reason with him. I wanted to help him to realise, for himself, that he'd treated Josephine wrongly and to repent."

"And were you successful?"

"No. He refused to acknowledge that his attentions were unwelcome."

"That must have been very vexing for you, sir."

"Yes, Inspector, it was."

"So what did you do?"

Arthur hesitated again before asking a question of his own.

"If there had been an accident, where maybe somebody had slipped and banged their head because the way someone else had touched them had made them lose their balance, that couldn't be construed as murder, could it?"

It might, thought Allerdyce, depending on the force used and the degree of intention. But the suspect doesn't need to know that right now.

"No, sir. I find it extremely unlikely that such an action would be considered as murder – and entirely impossible if it was a purely accidental action."

"Well, that's what happened and I'm bitterly sorry for it. George, God bless him, tried to reconcile us. He reached out to me and I pushed him away. He lost his balance and fell against the side of the big table. I hadn't meant that to happen – it was completely an accident – but maybe God was punishing me for rejecting his embrace of reconciliation."

Not as much as he was punishing George, thought Allerdyce.

"And then what happened?"

"He appeared to be unconscious. I satisfied myself that he was still breathing, and that he was lying in a comfortable position, and then left."

"How did you leave?"

"By the French windows."

"You didn't seek assistance? Or at least let the servants know what had happened?"

"It didn't seem necessary, Inspector. And, I confess, I was momentarily struck by confusion. I may not have acted entirely rationally."

Allerdyce let Arthur sit in silence for a moment, re-living his confusion, before continuing.

"Did you carry a firearm with you to Rock House, sir?"

Arthur looked up, quizzically.

"Yes. In accordance with your own advice, Inspector, that I should take precautions for my safety. I had a small pistol – a

Derringer I think is the correct term – in my pocket."

Interesting, thought Allerdyce. Either he genuinely doesn't know that his brother was shot, or he's lying and making out that he only gave him a little shove.

"Did you enter the photographic darkroom at any stage in the course of your visit, sir?"

"No. The entire conversation happened in the studio."

Allerdyce pulled out a piece of photographic paper from the inside pocket of his jacket and handed it to Arthur.

"Do you recognise the handwriting on this piece of paper, sir?"

Arthur squinted at it, his brows furrowed.

"That's very peculiar, Inspector."

"What is?"

"It looks like a facsimile of my own handwriting."

"You mean it _is_ your handwriting, sir?"

"It looks very like it. But it can't be. I never wrote these words, Inspector."

"I see."

"Please, Inspector, I've told you all I can. Do you think I might be allowed to go home soon?"

"Not just yet, sir. I think you should make yourself as comfortable as you can here."

...

"So," asked Burgess after Allerdyce had reported the interview, "what do you think of the good Reverend?"

"It doesn't look too good for him, sir. Admitting that he went there with a gun. Admitting that he got into a fight with the victim.

The message in the darkroom apparently in his handwriting."

"But you don't sound entirely convinced?"

"He says he left the studio immediately after the altercation which bruised the deceased's head. That's possible, sir."

"It's possible, Allerdyce. But he's an intelligent man. If I'd just shot someone I'd come up with a story like that, if I couldn't deny having been at the murder scene. Anything else?"

Allerdyce thought about Antonia. It would be easy just to keep silent. It would be easy but it wouldn't be right.

"I found the Duke's daughter, sir."

"And?"

Allerdyce told the Superintendent Antonia's story, without disclosing his prior acquaintance with her.

"So what's your estimation, Allerdyce? Think she did it?"

He paused, trying to find words which would accommodate the truth without unnecessarily condemning her.

"She had some cause, sir, particularly in relation to the first death. But I spoke to her shortly before the latest murder and it would have been remarkably incautious of her to have done anything when she knew she was already under some suspicion."

"Well," said Burgess, "that's it, then."

"Sir?"

"The messages at the crime scenes suggest a common killer. The Reverend was defintely at the last crime scene, armed. Frankly, Allerdyce, it would be criminally negligent not to charge him at least with the murder of George Bothwell-Scott and put him on trial."

"You're sure, sir?"

"I don't need to be sure that he did it. That's for a jury to decide. But I'm sure I want a jury to have that opportunity."

"And what about McGillivray, sir? Can we let him go now?"

"Best keep him where he is for the moment – just a precaution until we try the Reverend. But if we're right about the Reverend then Sergeant McGillivray will be free soon enough. Oh, and have the beat constable keep an eye on your prostitute friend in case we need to speak to her in future – can't have her absconding."

"Yes, sir."

Burgess stood.

"Christ, Allerdyce, I don't relish having to tell the Chief that we're charging a Duke with murder. But we're creatures of disinterested duty, aren't we Allerdyce?"

"Yes, sir."

"Good."

Chapter 30

Arthur couldn't complain about being uncomfortable. He'd been allowed – as befitting his newly-exalted station in life – the use of a bedroom and parlour in the Governor's house of the Calton jail. As far as comfort was concerned, he was being treated practically as a guest. He had newspapers delivered every morning, the Governor's manservant was at his disposal, the estate factor and the mining manager had been allowed to come in and discuss business matters with him, and he'd been invited to dine with the Governor and his wife. He'd experienced nothing but courtesy during his three nights of imprisonment.

He'd been woken uncomfortably early this morning, though. A bell had started to toll before it was fully light. He'd tried to ignore it, but finally got up and looked out the window. He'd seen the dawn rising above the horizon and, as the bell's last ring faded, a black flag run up the flagpole on the east tower. When the servant had arrived with his breakfast and newspapers he'd asked what it meant.

"A hanging, sir," answered the servant. "They run the flag up when the job's done."

Arthur hadn't touched his breakfast. For minutes on end he hadn't been able to tear his eyes away from the slow flapping of the black flag in the breeze. However comfortable he was now, his next destination could be the gallows. His clerical collar felt like a poor protection against the rope.

He'd tried to distract himself by reading the newspapers. It was a relief not to see himself mentioned. When he'd been charged with his brother's murder the papers had made it a sensation for a day – a Duke and clergyman arraigned for murdering his own brother. 'The Scotsman' had made what he thought was a facile comparison between him and the Satanically-possessed minister in Hogg's *Confessions of a Justified Sinner*. All the newspapers implied – as clearly as they could without actual libel – that he'd murdered his way through his entire family, rather than just giving his brother an innocent push with tragic consequences.

Today, though, in the fallow period between charge and trial, there was no mention of him. Instead, the papers were full of the news of General Lee's surrender and the end of all Confederate hopes. Arthur wondered whether he should draw a lesson from the news. On the one hand, it felt like an old order – an aristocratic order like his own where men understood their place of honour or humility in God's hierarchy – was being swept away by the brutal force of raw democratic materialism. On the other hand, maybe it was a sign that, after all the current horror of murder and accusation was over, it was a time to move on to a new beginning.

America. Why not just leave this tired country, where he'd laboured fruitlessly for the Lord for all his adult life and where he'd been brought down to the condition of an accused felon, and start a new life in the New World? He was heir now to the American estates which Josephine had brought back to the family, and what nobler task could there be than rebuilding them after the ravages of war? He could picture himself sitting in the gentle sunshine on the veranda of a great plantation house listening to the cheerful songs of the negroes in the fields – free, but bound by ties of loyalty – while Josephine rocked the cradle in the blissful shade of the house.

Josephine? Wasn't that a fantasy too far? She'd spoken of her love for him, but always in terms which were appropriate to her status as a sister in Christ, reliant on his moral support and guidance. It would be foolish to expect her, still in the depths of mourning, to do otherwise, but was there even the slightest prospect that she might love him as a man and a husband? And could there have been any truth in George's assertion, so shortly before his death, that he had an understanding with Josephine?

Reason said, Give up your fantasies. Josephine will never share your marriage bed, if you live that long. You don't even know the truth of what happened between her and George. You've built a castle of wishes on a cloud of deception. But when he remembered her beautiful, distressed face when she'd told him of George's atrocity towards her, and the soft touch of her troubled hand, he knew that she was a wounded creature of goodness and love, and longed to hold her in the tender healing embrace of husband and wife.

His thoughts were interrupted by a rap on the door.

"Come in."

The Governor's manservant opened the door.

"Visitor for you, Your Grace."

"Who is it? My solicitor?"

"No, sir. A lady. Says she's the Dowager Duchess of Dornoch."

"Thank you. Show her in."

Josephine swept in with a rustle of black taffeta, the waft of air from the door carrying the sweet floral fragrance of her perfume. She walked over and embraced his hands in hers.

"Oh Arthur, I came as soon as I could."

"Josephine! It's a great joy to see you."

"I'd have come before, had it not been for George's funeral." She smiled wanly. "It's peculiar, isn't it? I was the only family member left to arrange his burial, after your arrest."

"I suppose so." Arthur had read his brother's funeral record in yesterday's newspaper – the usual troop of dignitaries had turned up, and the minister of the High Church of St Giles had given a eulogy. "My involvement would hardly have been appropriate in the circumstances, even had I been free to attend."

"It was loathsome, Arthur. Having to listen to a stranger stand in your pulpit and say warm things about the man who'd tried to force my virtue. And then having to entertain all these ghastly people at the funeral breakfast in Dalcorn House and hearing them speak ill of you. How dare they?"

"I'm sorry, Josephine. It must have been terrible for you."

"It was." She glanced around the simple, comfortable parlour. "But not as terrible as seeing you incarcerated here for an action of which you're innocent."

"Please, Josephine, sit down. I would very much like to talk about that with you."

He poured her a cup of coffee before continuing. She took it, stirring in cream and sugar as he spoke.

"I may not be entirely innocent, Josephine. At least, not in my conscience."

"Why, Arthur? I know you are the best of men."

"I wish that were so, Josephine, but I must honestly confess to you that I have let a taint of sin into my heart, which is what has led here."

She stopped stirring and looked straight at him.

"Arthur, I believe you to be simply incapable of evil."

He continued.

"The last time I saw you was when you told me of the horrible assault which George had perpetrated on you. Had I been a true Christian I would have known that reason and forgiveness were the only arms which I could bear against my brother's sins, but I found that my heart was hardened. I confronted him in anger."

"It was good and bold of you, Arthur, to take my part."

"I went to Rock House to challenge him to repent. Instead of recognising his sin he denied all wrongdoing. He even claimed that he had been accepted as your suitor."

He paused, to watch Josephine's reaction. Surely, by look and word, she would prove George's assertion false?

She put down her coffee cup on the little table between them. She clasped her hands together, and looked at him with a thin-lipped anger which frightened him.

"That, Arthur, is the wickedest lie I have ever heard." He sat upright, feeling his hands shake in fear. Is she calling me a liar? She went on. "If George said that I had given him any encouragement at all to believe I would welcome his attentions then his wickedness is nearly as great as his punishment."

Arthur's body flooded with relief.

"So my brother was telling a flagrant untruth?"

"He was."

He glanced down at the floor.

"It still doesn't justify what I did."

"You said you confronted him. What possible sin is there in that, Arthur?"

"Our conversation became rather tense and confused. I pushed him at one point and he fell against the table, hitting his head."

"Is that what killed him?"

"No. I've been told by the police that he was shot. But it could have killed him. I cannot honestly say before God and man that I am innocent of George's death."

Josephine smiled.

"Arthur, no court in heaven or earth could convict you of an accidental crime which you didn't actually commit."

Arthur wished he felt like smiling.

"That's what my solicitor says too. I know I should believe it. But it's excruciating to sit here wrestling with an uneasy conscience and know that I could be dead within weeks if everything goes wrong."

"Arthur, it can't go wrong. It's absurd that you've even been charged. I'll do everything I can to make sure this whole stupid business gets dropped. There's some man out there who's guilty of your brothers' deaths and I'll hound the Chief Constable until the police find him."

A bell rang from the main prison. Arthur stood and went back to the window. Prisoners were slouching into the exercise yard, in dark shadow from the East tower. The black flag had, thank heavens, been taken down.

Josephine stood up. She came over to him and held his hand.

"Arthur, don't worry. No-one can touch an innocent man. I won't rest until you're free."

He squeezed her hand gently.

"Thank you. You're a better friend than I deserve."

"And Arthur, try to think of the future. I won't be in mourning for ever, you know."

His heart jumped. He looked at her, smiling up at him, and felt the gentle pressure and warmth of her palm on his. The April sunlight was streaming in the window and, looking out again, he was able to see beyond the dark towers and battlements of the jail to the coast and the sea beyond.

Maybe the Easter story was going to be the pattern of his life. Maybe this was the time of trial from which he'd rise again to a new, better life.

God willing. If there is a God.

Chapter 31

Allerdyce was astonished when the Superintendent walked into his room and closed the door behind him. Burgess looked surprisingly cheerful.

"Sir?"

"I've just come from the Chief Constable's office, Allerdyce. I've got news."

"What's happened?"

"Jarvis has been suspended."

Allerdyce restrained himself from cheering out loud.

"Why, sir?"

"Beating up a potential witness."

"In the cells?"

"No. In her home."

Allerdyce felt his elation tempered by anticipation of what he would hear next.

"Where was that sir?"

"Danube Street. Where you'd told me the possible suspect lived."

"Why was Jarvis there?"

"The Chief wasn't happy about charging Arthur Bothwell-Scott. Quite apart from his natural reluctance to alienate his aristocratic patrons, he'd been lobbied rather hard by the Duchess of Dornoch. She'd tried to persuade him that the Reverend was innocent, though she did admit he was rather impassioned against his brother when she last saw him."

"So the Chief sent Jarvis to interview the Danube Street prostitute?"

"Yes, Allerdyce. I'd had to admit to the Chief that there was another, more distant, suspect as well as the Duke. He chose to send Jarvis to see her."

"And?"

"She didn't tell him anything except her alibis for the nights of the first two murders. Quite amusing really. Her Majesty's Secretary for Scotland and Lord McLaren of the High Court."

"Nothing about the Bothwell-Scotts?"

"No. That's what got Jarvis riled. The prostitute was apparently a lady of some strength of character who absolutely refused to tell him anything more. Jarvis tried to beat the story out of her – so badly that she needed stitches. She managed to get away from him for an instant to her window and attract the attention of the beat constable who'd been watching the house. When the constable came in Jarvis asked him to help him restrain the whore, but the constable took one look at what had been going on and decided to arrest Jarvis for assault. I think he rather enjoyed subduing Jarvis with his truncheon and bringing him in."

"And the Chief's reaction?"

"He absolutely detests violence against the weaker sex. He called Jarvis up to his office as soon as he heard – Jarvis was still staunching a bleeding nose from his arrest – and told him he was a disgrace and that he was suspended pending a full investigation."

Allerdyce couldn't help imagining Antonia, kicked and bruised by Jarvis's frenzied anger. It wouldn't have happened if I'd just kept quiet, he thought. What a bloody awful thing to bring down on a friend. Another betrayal in the name of duty.

"Cheer up, Allerdyce," said Burgess, "I thought you'd have been pleased."

"Yes. Yes of course. So what happens now?"

"The Chief's accepted that the charge against Arthur Bothwell-Scott has to stand. The trial goes ahead without delay."

Chapter 32

This must be how aristocrats felt during the French Revolution, thought Arthur. Taunted by the mob on their way to condemnation.

He'd been spared the humiliation of being transported from the jail to the High Court of Justiciary in the Black Maria along with the common criminals. Instead, he sat in the Governor's closed carriage, with a prison warder sitting either side of him and the Governor sitting opposite. Two mounted policemen rode ahead in anticipation of trouble.

That morning's newspaper had mentioned that his trial was about to begin. It had brought out a crowd of the worst sort of people, ready to jostle and jeer at a Duke who had been brought so low. Going up the North Bridge there had been rough-looking workmen, and rougher-looking women, who'd shouted abuse as the carriage went by. Turning into the High Street the crowd thickened. Instantly, the coach was surrounded by grinning, leering faces. He started as an egg was thrown against the window and as he looked back he saw a criminal-looking vagrant, with practically no teeth in his grimacing mouth and one scarred eyelid stitched crudely shut, trying to pull the carriage door open. A warder held the door firmly closed from the inside. They'd come to a complete halt and, as if by the co-ordination of some demonic organiser, the crowd started to rock the body of the carriage from side to side.

"Hang the bastard!" shouted a woman in the crowd.

"Let him eat shit!" shouted a man.

"Sentence him to poverty!" cried a woman further back. "Let him live like the rest of us!"

As the carriage rocked crazily, throwing him against the bodies of the warders, he thought he might die there and then, torn limb-from-limb by the rabid, envious mob. A tumbrel that never even got as far as the guillotine, he thought. But the mounted police rode round the sides of the carriage and were lashing into the crowd with their truncheons, cracking the heads of men and women alike. He saw the leering one-eyed man struck down by a policeman, falling under the scrabbling hooves of the frightened horse. At last the carriage moved forward, cutting through the dispersing crowd to reach the sanity of the cobbled courtyard between St Giles and the law courts.

His legs were still shaking as he was led into the ante-room – with barred windows in case he took a notion to escape – where he'd meet his solicitor and the counsel who'd defend him. They weren't there yet, so as he heard the locking behind him he sat down to try and compose himself. Josephine had given him a sealed envelope with, she said, some words of comfort for him to read when his trial started. He pulled the lightly-scented envelope out of his pocket, opened it, and unfolded the heavy cream-coloured paper.

Josephine had copied out in a Bible verse in her neat, feminine hand.

'*But when they shall lead you, and deliver you up, take no thought beforehand what ye shall speak, neither do ye premeditate: but whatsoever shall be given you in that hour, that speak ye: for it is not ye that speak, but the Holy Ghost.*

Mark, Chapter 13, verse 12

May God deliver you safely through this time of trial, to the happier times that are surely promised us. I shall pray for you without ceasing.

Your most loving friend and sister in Christ,

Josephine'

He checked that no-one was watching before lifting the paper to his face. It had the soft, jasmine scent that he associated so strongly with her physical presence in a room. It was almost like having her here, speaking these words of comfort to him. He kissed the paper, before folding it and placing it in the inside pocket of his jacket, next to his heart.

He took his little Bible out of his pocket. The books Josephine had given him had shattered his faith in its literal truth, but he still clung to it as a talisman. Maybe there was more comfort to be drawn from the chapter that Josephine had copied her verse from. He turned to the thirteenth chapter of the Gospel according to Mark, and read the next verse.

'*Now the brother shall betray the brother to death, and the father the son: and children shall rise up against their parents, and shall cause them to be put to death.*'

He shut the book and put it away again. If that was the word of God it was saying things he didn't want to hear.

...

Allerdyce had never ceased to be impressed by the solemn pomp of the High Court of Justiciary. It had always struck him that the law showed a proper sense of the awfulness of the deliberate taking of a human life – whether by some poor murderous wretch or by the inexorable judgement of the Court – by ensuring that the events were conducted with such a grave theatricality. Every element – the procession of the mace-bearer, the call to all present to rise and be silent, the entry of Scotland's most senior judge Lord Justice General Forbes of Moulin whose heavy white wig disguised any weakness or humanity he might possess, the solemn swearing-in of witnesses on the great black Bible – spoke of the dispassionate and relentless progress of Justice. Even the crowd in the public gallery – packed out in anticipation of a good day's entertainment – were quieted by the dignity of proceedings.

What was more difficult to bear, though, was the ability of this solemn assembly to reach cruel and perverse decisions, from which there was no prospect of appeal. He thought again of the boy who'd struck the father who'd beaten and buggered him, and who within a week had been kicking and choking at the end of a rope in the Lawnmarket.

At least Arthur Bothwell-Scott didn't have to fear the public humiliation of a hanging in the Lawnmarket. If he was found guilty he'd be hanged in the modern scientific way, with precise calculations of how long a rope was appropriate to his height and weight, in the privacy of the Calton Jail.

Allerdyce had already given his own evidence as a witness for the prosecution. He'd kept it utterly straightforward, telling the court about the evidence that the victim had been shot in the photographic darkroom, about the message found in handwriting which the accused had admitted was similar to his own, and about the accused's admission that he had gone, armed, to Rock House to confront the victim and that he had struck the victim and then run away. He'd refrained from any speculation about the events in the darkroom.

Ronald Cullen QC, counsel for the prosecution, had probed further.

"Am I to understand that certain cryptic messages were also associated with each of the previous deaths?"

How did he know that, thought Allerdyce?

"Yes."

"Would you be so good as to tell the court the content of the messages?"

The judge interrupted.

"Is this course of questioning strictly relevant, Mr Cullen? His Grace is on trial only over the matter of the death of George Bothwell-Scott QC."

"With your indulgence, my lord, I believe my question may elucidate evidence relevant to this case."

"Very well, then."

"Inspector Allerdyce? What was the content of the messages?"

"The first was a telegram saying 'Mine all mine: meet at the well at midnight'. It was delivered shortly before the death of William Bothwell-Scott and the discovery of his body in an ornamental well – formerly a mineshaft – at Dalcorn House. The second, a note assembled from newsprint, said 'Relieved of command'. It was found at the scene of Brigadier Sir Frederick Bothwell-Scott's death."

"And what was that scene of crime, Inspector?"

"The Brigadier's private lavatory."

A laugh went up from the public gallery, and Allerdyce noticed that even some of the jurors were smiling.

"So, taken with the note to which we have already alluded – 'An interesting development' – would it be reasonable to assume that the same person committed all three murders?"

"That would be a matter of pure speculation. I am unable to make any such assumption."

"Very well, Inspector, no further questions."

Arthur's counsel had then competently set out the defence arguments that the accused, a man of good character and peaceful habits, and that the sole reason for his having carried a firearm was the advice of the police that, following the recent suspicious deaths of two of his brothers, he should take due precautions for his own safety. The defence had argued that the identification of Arthur's handwriting was inconclusive, that the messages associated with the previous deaths were an irrelevant distraction, and it was not credible that, after the altercation which the accused had admitted, he would have been able to entice George Bothwell-Scott to enter the darkroom after him to be shot. Arthur was called as a witness in his own defence and set out the series of events which he'd described when Allerdyce had interviewed him.

Allerdyce looked across at the jury. A couple of them were taking notes. One was scratching his chin. If they were asked to make up their minds now, thought Allerdyce, it could go either way.

Cullen, though, looked undaunted as he rose to cross-examine Arthur.

"Your Grace, Reverend, it pains me to have to ask you some difficult and intimate questions, but I must do so. How would you characterise your relations with the dowager Duchess of Dornoch."

Arthur's face appeared to flush as he paused before answering.

"I hold a respectful admiration for her."

"And would it be fair to say that she has come to rely on you for comfort and support in her widowhood?"

"Yes. I pride myself that I have been of some assistance to her."

"Most gracious. Would it be fair to say, in fact, that you were intimate with the Duchess?"

The judge intervened.

"Mr Cullen, again you stretch my patience. I believe you are trying to make an irrelevant insinuation against His Grace."

"My apologies, my lord, if I have given that impression. I do believe that the state of relations between the accused and the Duchess is of some relevance, to the extent that we might expect a man whose relations were in some way intimate or passionate with the Duchess would be moved to extreme jealousy by the victim's alleged misconduct towards her. However, I shall move on.

"Your Grace, the death of your brothers has made you the inheritor of their entire wealth, has it not?"

"Yes."

"A situation dramatically different from your modest living at the beginning of this year?"

"Yes."

"Where were you on the night of the 29th of January?"

"I don't recall."

"The night of your brother William's death? Surely you are able to recall that?"

"I remember now. I received a message that a parishioner was sick. I rushed out to visit them but when I reached the house there was no-one there."

"What time was this?"

"I received the message as I was preparing to go to bed. Probably about 11pm."

"So no-one can testify to your whereabouts at the time of the first murder. And, Your Grace, would I be correct in supposing that you are similarly unable to provide a witness for your whereabouts on the might of Sir Frederick's death?"

"That's enough, Mr Cullen," said the judge. "I hope I don't have to warn you again."

Allerdyce looked towards the jury. They appeared to be paying rapt attention. It was starting to feel as if Arthur was standing on thin ice – or perhaps on a thin trapdoor.

Cullen continued.

"Your Grace, should I say Reverend, let me ask you a simple question. Do you believe in the Bible as God's perfect Word for man?"

What's he getting at, thought Allerdyce. Arthur shifted uneasily in the witness stand.

"That's quite a complicated…"

Cullen interrupted him.

"It's a simple question. Yes or no?"

"I don't think…"

"Yes or no?"

"No."

The judge banged his gavel.

"Mr Cullen, you are in serious danger of being held to be in contempt of this court for your persistence in troubling His Grace with irrelevant and inadmissible questions."

"With respect, my lord, it is a well established principle that the religious opinions of an ordained minister are the legitimate concern of the civil courts. My lord is no doubt well aware of the ruling of the judicial committee of the Privy Council on 20 March this very year in the matter of Bishop Colenso versus the Archbishop of Cape Town."

"Oh, very well then."

Cullen continued.

"So, Your Grace, you do not believe the word of God in the book of Genesis that the world was created in six days?"

"No."

"Nor that the world was deluged for its sins in the time of Noah?"

"No."

"And I will not presume to ask what you think of the redeeming work of Our Lord lest your answer corrupt the simple believers here."

The judge sighed audibly but let Cullen go on.

"Your Grace, let me express myself plainly. You have admitted to this court the heat of your admiration for the dowager Duchess. You have admitted to this court the very great advantages which have come to you as a result of your brothers' deaths, both materially and in terms of your opportunity to build a relationship of intimacy with your eldest brother's widow. You have admitted that nobody is able to account for your whereabouts on the nights of your elder brothers' deaths. You have taken an oath on a Bible you profess not to believe in. Your Grace, if we cannot believe your oath what can we believe?"

Arthur opened his mouth to speak.

"But..."

"No further questions, my Lord. The witness may stand down."

Allerdyce looked across at Cullen, who had turned, smilingly, to receive the congratulations of his junior counsel. There was a murmur from the public gallery, as if they were pronouncing their verdict. He looked across to the jury box where 15 men of varying intelligence and impressionability were conferring seriously among themselves. He looked at Arthur, now sitting pale and shaken in the dock.

That's it, thought Allerdyce. He's going to hang.

Chapter 33

Everything seemed so terrible and unbelievable.

Arthur had felt like a spectator as the foreman of the jury pronounced the single word 'Guilty' and the judge donned his black tricorn hat to pronounce the inevitable sentence '…and be taken from here to a place of lawful execution, where you shall be hanged by the neck until you be dead…' It surely couldn't be him that they meant? Was he just watching some bizarre theatrical enactment in his own mind? Surely the court couldn't honestly believe that he was a murderer?

Reality had started to engage as soon as the judge had uttered his final fatal words – 'Take him down'. Instantly, the warders who'd been guarding him in the dock seized his arms and pushed him ahead of them down the dark, chill staircase that led to the cells in the vaults of the building.

He'd waited there for hours as the light in the tiny barred window faded into night. At last he'd been taken out and thrust into the Black Maria. He'd breathed a mouthful of the damp, smoky air of Edinburgh in the few feet between the courthouse door and the wagon, thinking it might be his last ever chance to smell and breathe the outdoors.

The crowd had gone and his short journey to the Calton Jail was undisturbed by anything other then the torment of his own thoughts. It's pathetic, he thought, my life's being taken away but it's not even enough of an event to anyone else to keep them hanging around for a few hours to shout abuse at me.

Now, he sat in a whitewashed cell in the east tower of the jail, the heavy serge of the prison clothes chafing the skin of his neck. The condemned cell, as the warder had said before locking the heavy iron door.

Other prisoners had sat here before on this thin, stained mattress and carved messages into the wall, their scratchings peeling the whitewash away to reveal the damp blackness of the stone. 'Barney Armstrong: remember me to Aggie'. 'Joe Johnson, innocent, 17 January 1865'. 'Hamish Macilwaine: My Trust Is In The Lord'.

Arthur sat on the edge of the bed, unwilling to lie down on the stains which spoke more eloquently of previous inmates' fears. His own bowels felt like jelly too, and he prayed that he might at least be able to keep his dignity if not his life.

What would I write? he thought, as much to distract his mind from his cramping body as anything else. He wished he could think of something faithful and comforting, but it was some lines from a poem which Josephine had given him that stuck in his mind as he looked towards the great grey abyss of non-being:

> *Wandering between two worlds, one dead,*
> *The other powerless to be born,*
> *With nowhere yet to rest my head.*

One last message caught his attention, scratched in a wavering hand.

'Hope springs eternal. John Anderson, 24 April 1865'.

Arthur looked again at the date. By God, he thought, that's the man who was being hanged when I was having my coffee in the

Governor's parlour a week ago. He felt a sudden sweat leaching into his prison suit. So much for hope.

He looked up as keys jangled in the cell door. Surely not yet, he thought. It's too soon. You're surely meant to be warned before they take you away?

"Visitor for you," said the warder.

"Thank you. Who is it?"

"A lady."

He caught a breath of fragrance before Josephine entered. That's the sweetest thing I've ever smelt, he thought. It means I'm not going to die alone.

As she entered she glanced around, evidently looking for somewhere to sit, but there was no seat and she remained standing. She turned to the warder and smiled sweetly at him.

"Would you be so kind as to leave us alone for a few minutes, please?"

"Can't do that madam. He's a dangerous criminal. It's not safe."

She reached into her black silk purse and took out a sovereign.

"I'd be very much obliged, warder. I'll alert you if I need to."

He took the coin and saluted.

"Very well, madam, but I must remove you if the prisoner shows any sign of trouble."

The door was closed but not locked. Josephine stood in front of it. Arthur looked her up and down, marvelling at how mourning dress could be cut so elegantly to cleave to her wonderful womanly figure.

"Arthur," she said softly. "I'm so sorry. How are you?"

"All right." He felt he had to tell an edifying lie lest he disturb the comfort of her simple faith. "I have great joy in knowing I will soon behold my Saviour's face."

"Oh Arthur, you're so brave."

"There's nothing else for it, is there?"

"Please, Arthur. Don't give up hope yet. I've written to Her Majesty's Secretary for Scotland – Jamie Dunsyre. He knows you – he's bound to see that there's been a ghastly mistake and get the case re-opened. He could even get you a Royal Pardon."

Arthur sighed. He'd like to clutch at this frail straw of hope, but feared it would be no more effective than her promised intervention with the Chief Constable.

"I'm grateful, Josephine. Truly. But I don't think I can escape my fate."

"Arthur, for my sake, please try to hope."

She looked round at the door and glanced into the eyehole before kneeling, with a rustling of jet-black taffeta, in front of him. She took his hands in hers and looked up at him, her eyes filling with tears.

"Arthur, my heart is breaking at the prospect of life without you. You <u>must</u> let me hope."

As the warmth of her small hands permeated his own he felt as if his entire body was being embraced by her. He felt his own eyes moisten as he thought of the loneliness this beautiful, wounded creature would face without him. He wished devoutly that he could live, as much for her as for himself.

Josephine continued.

"Would you forgive me if I spoke improperly?"

"Of course."

She hesitated, swallowing back her tears.

"Arthur, it isn't my place to say this, but in these ghastly circumstances I must throw aside all constraints."

"What is it, Josephine?"

"Will you marry me?"

He felt himself plunged back into the bizarre unreality in which he had heard his sentence pronounced.

"What?"

"I know, Arthur, it's positively indecent of me, a woman in mourning, to propose. But I've realised over these terrible weeks how insupportable my life would be without you. If – when – this awful business is over we must be each others' partners in our journey through life. And should, God forbidding, the worst happen, it would be a great comfort to me. If Our Lord is right, we would surely be re-united in another, better, life."

"But how…?"

"The prison chaplain can marry us. He only needs our word."

"But Josephine, are you sure?"

"As certain as I am of God's truth. Please, Arthur, you still have the power to give me this greatest happiness."

He looked at her gentle face, in which tears and a sad, slight smile combined. It felt so strange that the moment he'd thought would never come, the event he'd thought was a mere fantasy, had arrived at last, and that it had come by Josephine's decision and in this chill cell as he waited to die. But there was only one answer to her proposal of the one thing he had most wanted in his entire life. He steadied his rapid breathing before replying.

"Yes. Yes, Josephine, it will me my joy and privilege to marry you."

"Oh, thank you Arthur, you cannot know how happy that makes me."

She stood, and leant over him. He was conscious of glancing at her magnificently-corseted bosom before looking up at her face.

She leant her face towards him and touched his lips with hers. She pressed them more firmly, and he was astonished to feel her tongue moistly parting his lips. He felt instincts which had for so long been dormant rush through his body as he put his arms around her, pulled her more tightly towards him, and let his own tongue do sweet battle with hers to taste the warm sweetness of her mouth.

Truly, he thought, hope does spring eternal after all.

Chapter 34

Six. Allerdyce had heard every tinny chime of the clock of St Stephen's church, barely quarter of a mile away, since midnight. Margaret groaned gently and turned over in her sleep while the baby, in the cot at the end of the bed, gave a little chirruping cry then fell silent again.

Surely he had no good reason for sleeplessness. Arthur Bothwell-Scott would be hanged soon after dawn, but he'd been convicted by the due process of the law and it was daft to feel guilty about that. The Chief Constable had decided that there would be no further charges over the deaths of Arthur's elder brothers William and Frederick since the trial had all but established Arthur's guilt and he was going to be hanged anyway. Sergeant McGillivray had been released and reinstated to duty, and the taint of suspicion had been lifted from Antonia . By all rational calculations, Allerdyce thought, he should be sleeping the deep sleep of the saved, justice done and his friends safe.

So why was it that every time he shut his eyes he saw Arthur kicking and choking at the end of his rope, or imagined Antonia's mother writhing and dying, blood frothing at her lips, on the kitchen floor at Bavelaw?

As he lay there, the sheets damp with sweat despite the coolness of the room, he tried to batter the images away. He must have slept slightly for a few minutes, because he remembered pushing Antonia, her face raging and her eyes red, away from him and waking, gasping for breath, to find his fists striking the air in front of him.

Take them away, he shouted silently to the darkness. Take these horrors away and for God's sake let me sleep.

He stared towards the curtains. Maybe it was his imagination, or maybe there was the faintest hint of light starting to seep past the edges. The birds would be singing soon, and by then he might as well just abandon all thought of sleep.

What would Arthur Bothwell-Scott be doing? Would he be able to see the darkness turn to indigo and then turquoise as his last sunrise crept above the horizon? No – he'd be sitting in the glaring gaslight of the condemned cell waiting for his final moments. Poor bastard.

Margaret turned over again, then he felt the bedclothes pulled away from him as she sat up.

"Archie!" Her voice had a shrill edge.

"Yes, dear?"

"I just had a horrible dream."

"I'm sorry. What was it?"

"That minister you were investigating. The one who killed his brothers. I saw him in front of me, as if he was right here in this room. He was shining like an angel and reached out towards me, then he was jerked backwards into the darkness and I couldn't see him any more."

"Don't worry, Margaret. Try and go back to sleep."

"I'll try. But Archie, it felt as if he was trying to tell me he was innocent."

"It's just your imagination, Margaret. It's probably because of the newspaper articles about him."

"Do you think he did it, Archie?"

Allerdyce paused. The lightening around the curtains was slight but unmistakeable now.

"I don't know, Margaret."

And I've got about an hour to find out.

...

Night and day were indistinguishable here. He'd been moved to a different cell to wait for morning. A warder sat beside him, and another sat opposite at the far side of the plain wooden table. The harsh gaslight reflected against the bright whitewashed walls – there were no messages carved here, and presumably no prisoner had ever sat here without the supervision of the deathwatch warders.

There was no clock in the cell, and his watch had been taken away when he was given his prison clothes. He'd gone through the motions of prayer with the prison chaplain just before he'd been moved here. No-one had told him what would happen next – he imagined that the chaplain and the governor would come when it was time. The warders refused to tell him anything, even what time it was, or to engage him in conversation. All he could do was keep drinking from the pitcher of rough gin in front of him and try pray to the God who had abandoned him.

As he drank more, though, it wasn't prayer that came to mind. I'm a married man, he thought. The ten minutes of muttered responses which Josephine and I were allowed has made us husband and wife. One flesh. It's my right – it's my duty – to lie with her and make her truly mine. He found his right hand creeping into his inner thigh. Normally he'd have fought against the secret vice, but there seemed no point now. He was a married man and he shouldn't have to deny himself.

As he touched his stiffening member through the serge the warder opposite caught his eye. He pulled his hand away and quickly reached for the pitcher of gin, re-filling his tin mug.

Damn them, he thought. Damn them all. I'm going to die a virgin and it's a crime.

...

Allerdyce ran up the gaslit hill of Dundas Street, sweating and panting from the exertion. A night-soil cart rumbled past him, down the cobbled slope.

I have to get to Rock House, he thought. I have to get there before the sun comes up. I have to know what happened.

I should have remembered it before. The spirit camera.

George Bothwell-Scott had mentioned it when Allerdyce and the sergeant had first visited him. The camera that sat in the darkroom, its lens always open but its photographic plate unmarked by the dim red light in which the dead advocate had developed his photographs. George had said he'd set it up to capture the phosphorescence of the spirits which visited him. Allerdyce had seen it as further evidence of the man's madness, but maybe the camera had captured something more fatal than the appearance of a ghost.

As he rushed up the steps to Rock House the birds were in full song to greet the approaching dawn, though the dark bulk of the Calton Jail blocked his view towards the eastern horizon. The crisp crunch of his heels on the garden gravel was almost drowned by the chorus of songthrush, blackbird and chaffinch.

The windows of the house were all dark. He didn't know whether any of the dead man's servants were still living there or whether it was completely vacant, but in any case if he was careful no-one would hear him.

He worked his way round the building to the French windows of the studio. He tried the handle, fearing to rattle the door too hard in case of discovery, but it was locked. He took his penknife out of his pocket and prised its four-inch blade between the doors. Years spent among the housebreakers of Edinburgh gave him confidence and as he levered backwards and forwards he heard the brittle wood start to crack. With a final twist of the wrist and a crack no louder than a snapping twig the lock broke away from the door and he was in the studio.

Enough light was now permeating the studio by the windows and the skylight that he could see that some busybody of a servant had tidied all the cameras and lenses away from the table and put them back on their shelves, as if George Bothwell-Scott could return at any time and berate whatever butler or maid had failed to keep the place in good order. He prayed that, whatever they'd done, they hadn't decided to flood the darkroom with light and tidy it up.

He opened the door of the darkroom and saw, thank heavens, that the black curtain in front of the developing bench was drawn closed. Closing the door behind him, he lit the feeble red-shaded lamp before opening the curtain to reveal the bench, developing basins and shelves of bottled chemicals. The clotheslines still hung there with the developed images, now dry and curled, of views, still lives, and the unidentified woman who had posed, back towards the camera, for the dead photographer. Only the incriminating image of Arthur Bothwell-Scott's handwriting, taken and used in evidence, was missing.

He looked up to a shelf above the hanging photographs. A brass lens gleamed in the red glow. He reached up and took the heavy camera off its shelf and placed it beside the developing trays. He looked up at the row of glass bottles and read the labels. He'd never developed a photograph before in his life, but he remembered the dead owner of the house telling him that the plate had to be placed in a bath of silver nitrate to bring out an image. Looking up, the bottle in front was labelled as silver nitrate, and he poured the clear liquid into the tray. I don't even know, he thought, whether I'm meant to develop the picture in this fluid as it comes out of the bottle, or whether I'm meant to dilute it.

He unhooked the back of the camera and carefully lifted the glass plate out. Sliding it into the developing fluid he wondered whether he was making some elementary mistake which would destroy whatever image had burnt itself onto the plate. It was probably stupid even to think that there might be some image which would disclose anything about the moment of George Bothwell-Scott's death. Nonetheless, his hands were shaking and he felt a nausea which he knew he couldn't blame on the photographic chemicals.

He watched as the plate lay under the developing fluid. Nothing was happening. All he could see was the clear glass underneath the stillness of the transparent liquid.

I might as well leave, he thought. There's nothing here. Even if there was any evidence here before it's been destroyed by whoever tidied up the scene of the crime, or by my own ineptitude in developing this plate. There's nothing more I can do to know whether Arthur Bothwell-Scott killed his brother. Guilty or not, he won't see much more of this new day.

He turned to leave. As he pulled the darkroom curtain aside, though, he knew he needed one last look. If there was no image on the plate now he'd go, but he couldn't do that until he'd made a final check.

He looked back into the developing tray, the red light making the clear fluid look like dilute blood. As he looked, a faint darkening seemed to creep over the glass plate. He blinked, thinking it must just be the strain on his eyes in the semi-darkness, but the change consolidated and grew. He held his breath, watching the painfully slow appearance of the image as he thought of Arthur's life entering its final minutes. Come on, he thought, come on.

Finally, in the bizarre reversal of a photographic negative, he could distinguish an image. What should have been light was dark, what should have been dark was light. The flash of the gunshot which had killed George Bothwell-Scott spilt a thick blackness over the centre of the picture. But behind it – indistinct but unmistakable – was the image of the person who had stood behind the gun.

Allerdyce peered closer. The face was blurred but the overall figure was clear.

It was a woman.

...

Even without a watch or a window Arthur could detect signs that his time was coming. The warders, each of whom had dropped off briefly at various stages of the night, were more alert now, and the one opposite kept glancing towards the cell door. There were distant sounds of the life of the prison re-awakening – the far-off clanging of doors and shouting of orders. Even his own mind seemed fresher, as if readying itself for a day's work.

What a waste. Arthur ran his hand round his neck and felt the blood pulsing and his rapid breaths. How bizarre it was that everything in his body was continuing to function as if, at the deep level of blood, nerve and sinew, it had no idea of its own imminent extinction.

As he tried to picture what might happen next, though, he felt a sudden hot fever. He imagined these warders seizing him and dragging him away towards the scaffold. He felt the abrasion of the rope's knot being tightened round his neck and the rough pinioning of his arms behind his back. He imagined a pause, then a searing burn and a jerk as his body fell through the trapdoor followed by a last struggle for breath, his eyes popping and his tongue swelling. As he thought about it he felt his bowels liquefying.

And then what? Still part of his mind – habit, he supposed – was praying for God's forgiveness of his sins (pathetic and few though they seemed in balance with his fate) and his reception into a kingdom where all would be just and compassionate and where, soon enough, Josephine would join him for an eternity of joy. But a stronger voice was telling him that the brutal, industrial efficiency of execution would render him as dead as the animals despatched in their hundreds every day in the city's abattoir. All that would be left of him would be a carcass dissolving in its quicklime grave.

He was clutching his cramping stomach. Breathe deeply, he thought. Breathe slowly. Don't give these wretches the satisfaction of seeing you crumble.

And remember hope. Hope in this life if not the next. There's still time for a last-minute reprieve if Josephine has persuaded the Secretary for Scotland to review the case.

He reached out towards the gin then stayed his hand. No, he thought, I'm not going to stagger drunkenly towards my fate. His hand clutched instead round the envelope which Josephine had given, which she said had words which would give him strength and comfort if all other hope was lost. I'm either going to walk out of here a free man, or these pitiful men are going to have to drag me, in dignified non-co-operation, to the gallows. I refuse to co-operate in my own murder.

He looked at each of the warders' pale, poor complexions. Why should they be allowed to go home untroubled to wives and families after their complicity in putting an innocent man to death.

"You are the murderers here," said Arthur, looking directly at each of them in turn. "My blood will be on your hands."

The warder opposite leaned back in his chair and pulled out a fob-watch he'd concealed until now. He glanced at it and looked across at Arthur, his face as compassionless as stone.

"You want to be careful what you're saying, Reverend. Less than five minutes now before you'll have to account for it to your Maker."

He put the watch away. Arthur swallowed and took Josephine's envelope from his pocket.

...

Allerdyce ran from the darkroom. He couldn't waste time making a print from the plate – the image would have to sit there in its chemical bath until he'd stopped the execution. There would

313

be plenty of time after that to make it permanent and deal with the consequences.

It was nearly perfectly light now in the studio. The main gate of the prison was barely three minutes run away, but he wished there was some instant way the message could be transmitted through the ether like lightning. His own paces, bursting though the French windows and leaping down the steps to the street seemed painfully slow compared to the fatal revolution of the earth, nearly a thousand miles an hour, as the sun rose behind the prison.

Dear God, he thought, for once I know clearly what is right and what I must do. I don't know who the woman is – I don't want to think that it's Antonia – but help me to do what's right and save this innocent man. If you could just stop the sun from rising further and halt the clocks for an instant. I must save this man.

. . .

Arthur opened the envelope and unfolded the fragrant paper. He saw four words, written in what appeared to be his own handwriting.

'The Leap of Faith.'

"No!" he shouted. "Not that! Not her!"

He tried to rush for the door. The warders grabbed him. He kicked out against them and against the table and the walls but their grip tightened.

The cell door opened. The Governor and the chaplain stood there. The Governor nodded at the warders. They turned him round, lifting him so that he was kicking into empty space. He was facing a cupboard which he'd barely noticed, having sat with his back to it for the whole deathwatch. A warder pushed it with his foot and it slid easily aside on rails to reveal an open door.

And beyond it the gallows.

...

Allerdyce shouted as he ran, hearing the tolling bell resonate with the pounding of his blood.

"Stop the execution! Open the door! For God's sake stop the execution!"

He reached the metal-studded wooden gate of the jail and beat at it.

"Police! Let me in! I have new evidence!"

He pounded with his fists till he saw his own blood on the door.

"Open Up! Now!"

A grille opened in the door at eye level and a warder looked at him suspiciously.

"Who are you, sir?"

"Police. Inspector Allerdyce. Just let me in."

He heard a rattle of keys. As the warder worked the lock he turned to look at the east tower. Please, let there be time.

The bell sounded its last toll and a black flag ran swiftly up the flagpole.

He knelt, his face in his hands, and wept.

Chapter 35

The warder led Allerdyce through clanging gates down twisting and narrowing corridors, and up a whitewashed staircase. As they marched briskly towards the condemned cell Allerdyce felt as if he was hastening towards his own execution.

The warder showed him into the cell from which Arthur had just been thrust into eternity. The door from the cell to the scaffold was open and the rope hung limply from the gallows.

The Governor was standing at far side of the door, looking down into the trapdoor through which Arthur had fallen to his death. He turned to face Allerdyce, his grey-bearded face looking heavy and old.

"Who's this?" asked the Governor.

"Inspector Allerdyce of the police, sir," said the warder. "Says he wanted to stop the execution."

"Bit late now."

Allerdyce heard a heavy sliding noise in the other room. Dear God, he thought, they're dragging Arthur's body into his shroud.

"Are you sure he's dead?" Allerdyce asked.

"The surgeon has already satisfied me that the prisoner died almost instantly," said the Governor. "A highly scientific and efficient execution."

Allerdyce felt his whole body shivering and sweating and felt sick.

"He was innocent," he said.

"What?"

"I found new evidence in the past few minutes. I ran here as fast as I could. He's innocent."

"Are you sure?"

"Absolutely."

The Governor sat down at the table. He rested his head in his hands for a moment before, slowly, looking up at Allerdyce.

"You're telling me that we've just hanged Scotland's premier Duke because the bloody police can't find evidence until the moment before his execution?"

"It's something that didn't come to light until now."

The Governor poured himself a mug of gin from the pitcher on the table.

"What's this evidence, then?"

"A photograph. We've just found a photograph taken which shows a woman in the act of firing a gun at the scene of the crime."

"By God, you mean the murder was even photographed and yet no-one thought to mention that before now?"

"I'm sorry. We had no idea until a few minutes ago."

"And where is this photograph? Can I see it?"

"I don't have it. It's still sitting in the developing bath."   The Governor stood, his hands resting on the table. His voice trembled as he spoke.

"Mr Allerdyce, words cannot convey my horror at the inefficiency of a police service which consigns a peer of the realm to the ultimate punishment of the law, belatedly asserts that it is in fact mistaken, and even now is unable to produce evidence to establish its case. I will protest to the Chief Constable in the strongest possible terms about the conduct of this case. In the meantime, Inspector, I suggest that you retrieve the evidence which may yet save His Grace from the final ignominy of burial in a murderer's quicklime grave."

...

Allerdyce stood outside the open French windows of the studio. He drew on the bitter smoke of his pipe. He'd thought a moment of smoking and contemplation would steady his mind before he went back in to look again at the image in the chemical bath, but it wasn't working. The tobacco tasted like ash and whatever way his mind turned it saw horror.

Poor Arthur, the warmth still leaving his scientifically-murdered body at this very moment. Antonia dragged through the courts whether she was guilty or not. And Margaret. She'd be horrified and humilated if she found out that her husband had been close friends with a prostitute for all the years of their marriage. And if Allerdyce was suspended or dismissed because of the company he'd kept they'd be destitute.

McGillivray would be here in a few minutes to corroborate the photograph. Allerdyce had sent a cab from the prison to McGillivray's house to collect him. No doubt the sergeant would treat him with a hostility and recrimination which he deserved.

If he'd been religious he'd have described his thoughts as prayer. But he knew they were just the anguished cry of a mind which wanted to save itself and the people it loved from the horrors which would follow with the inevitability of an algebraic sequence. If only the past hour could be reversed, the photographic plate destroyed, and the case left closed.

For an instant, he wondered about going into the darkroom before McGillivray arrived and destroying the negative. But both duty and prudence told him not to. He'd already admitted the existence of the photograph. There was no escape.

He knocked the ash out of his pipe against the brickwork surround of the French window. As he did, he looked at the door. It was only slightly ajar.

Strange, he thought. I'm sure I left it wide open when I ran out.

He opened the French window and stepped into the studio. It looked entirely undisturbed. He stopped and listened, but there was no sound above the birdsong which flowed in through the open window.

As he stood and listened again, though, he thought he heard a slight noise, no louder than the gurgling of a drink from bottle to glass, in the darkroom.

He paced as lightly as he could across the carpet, conscious even of the slight swishing of his soles across the pile. He reached the darkroom door and placed his ear to it, his hand on the doorknob.

The sound was more distinct this time, like a stopper being squeezed back into a bottle. He turned the doorknob, wishing as he did so that he was armed against whoever was in there.

He opened the door and stood for a second as his eyes adjusted to the dim red light. As the clouds of colour faded from his retinas he saw a figure standing beside the developing tray, his hand on a bottle.

Warner.

He saw Warner pick up the bottle. He dodged aside as Warner threw it and heard it smash against the wall beside him. He rushed at Warner and pushed him against the back wall of the darkroom.

"What the hell do you think you're doing, Warner? You're destroying police evidence. You're under arrest."

"No I'm fucking not." Warner pushed back against him.

Allerdyce grabbed Warner's throat and pinned him back against the wall.

"Who are you doing this for? Who's the woman in the photograph? Is it the Duchess?"

"You'll never bloody know," gasped the valet, a fine haze of spittle hitting Allerdyces's face.

"Why did she send you? Why are you helping her?"

Warner's right arm was flailing towards the workbench as he tried to draw breath. I don't care about your pain, thought Allerdyce. I just need you to answer.

Allerdyce didn't see Warner's hand close round a bottle on the bench, but he screamed as he felt the acid burn into his eyeballs and skin.

"Help! I can't see!"

He struck out blindly but his fist hit the wall. He felt Warner punch him on the chest and trip him behind the ankle and fell to the floor, landing heavily on his half-healed arm. He recoiled from two sharp kicks to the stomach then heard the valet's retreating footsteps.

His face felt as if it was on fire. He grasped towards it with his fingers as if he could pull the heat and pain away, but the slightest touch redoubled the searing pain. He felt hot tears in burning rivulets down his cheeks and thought they were his melting eyes.

Only coolness could bring relief. He would crawl towards the open door.

He turned onto his hands and knees. Even in the pitch darkness of his blindness he could sense his directions from the garden-scented breeze.

As he found his way across the linoleum floor of the darkroom his right hand was stabbed by glass from the broken bottle, cutting deep into the flesh of his palm. He lifted his hand to his mouth and tasted blood mingled with an acid tang that stung like vinegar.

Pressing on, he felt his shoulder brush against the heavy black curtain before he reached the softness of the studio carpet. His burning eyes were closed but there was a kaleidoscope of colour and pain in his brain. The breeze was stronger here and he set his direction.

His forehead struck something hard. He reached up and felt the polished edge of the big wooden table in the centre of the studio. Lowering his head he carried on, praying that he could just leap into some chill vat of water and let the agony dissolve. At last a coolness blew over his face as the gravel of the path outside the French windows bit into his palms. He lay down on his side, hearing his rasping breaths and groans.

Jesus, he thought. What use am I going to be to Margaret if I'm blind?

He couldn't measure time. All he knew was that each beat of his heart brought a fresh pulse of pain. The stream of birdsong around him seemed to mock his agony. He had no idea how long it was before a gentle hand shook his shoulder.

"Sir?"

"Sergeant?"

"Are you all right, sir?"

"I can't see."

"What happened?"

"It was Warner. He threw acid in my face and ran away."

He felt himself being lifted.

"Come on, sir, we'll get you to a doctor."

"No!" He struggled in the sergeant's arms.

"You need help, sir." McGillivray grasped him more firmly.

"Not yet. You must go into the darkroom. There's a photograph in the developing tray. It shows who shot Arthur Bothwell-Scott."

"Can't it wait, sir?"

"No. I think Warner poured something in to destroy it. The image could be fading as we speak."

He felt McGillivray hesitate for a moment then lower him back to the ground. The door of the French window rattled as the sergeant barged past. He counted seventy of his laboured breaths before the sergeant came back.

"Well?"

"Nothing, sir. There's a glass plate in the bottom of the tray but it's completely clear."

He lay his head down on the gravel. He was completely defeated. Warner had wrecked the evidence. Without the photograph he could never make a case against the murderess. He couldn't even corroborate the fact that Warner had destroyed it. He'd let an innocent man hang while his murderer inherited a wealth beyond belief.

The Duchess of Dornoch. There couldn't be any doubt that she'd sent Warner. The woman he hadn't been allowed to interview, because of the Chief Constable's delicacy about her female sensitivity. The woman who must have murdered her way through an entire family to get what she wanted.

Allerdyce was surprised to feel a smile starting to spread across his face. Every now and then in a police career you found someone so far above the usual banality and chaos of the criminal mind that you had to admire them. If he could, he'd like to get up right now and ask her how she had managed to murder four Dukes without detection. It was a crime, but it was also genius.

And he'd done the right thing. He'd risked everything – his marriage, his family, his career – to follow his conscience and find out this morning who'd shot Arthur. He'd even, in the darkroom, risked his life. And by some strange providence he'd survived.

He opened one eyelid slightly. It felt like the tearing of delicate flesh, and it was too painful to open the chink for more than a second. But in that second he could at least see light, and vague forms of what could be bushes.

"I'll help you up, sir. You really must see a doctor right now." The sergeant's voice was close – he must be kneeling.

He let himself be lifted, and as he stood he held onto the sergeant's arm. He was amazed at the gentleness and strength of this man he'd wronged so badly. Grace – it was the only word for it, the power to do the right thing even to those who wronged you. And, he thought, may I have that grace too.

"I'm sorry, Sergeant."

"Sorry, sir?"

"I'm sorry I suspected you. It was very wrong of me."

"You did what seemed right to you from the evidence at the time, sir. I can't blame you."

As he rested in the sergeant's grasp his eyes watered, the tears washing the acid from his corneas. The shapes before him resolved themselves into rosebushes, a wall, and the pink gravel of the path, all swimming before him as if they were eddying in some dense fluid.

I'll see again. I'll work again. My friends are safe and innocent.

My marriage is safe. And think of what I've gained over these weeks. I've realised through those awful days of Alice's fever who I live to love and serve – not Helen's memory, not Antonia, but Margaret and the children. I've felt things with an intensity – a reality – which I've never felt since Helen died. I've experienced a deeper forgiveness from this good man who's holding me than I have ever known before. I know what my life is for from now on – to be an honest man, a good husband and father and a loyal comrade. He laughed, feeling a strange welling of joy from part of his mind that he hadn't known existed. Perhaps it was a form of madness, but if so it must be something like the madness which had made Patrick Slater want to pour out the remainder of his life in the service of the poor. It was the madness of grace, flooding his soul in a way he had never thought possible.

"Sir?"

Allerdyce could hear the sergeant's perplexity. What do I say, he asked himself? Is it too banal to tell McGillivray that I've seen the light, literally and morally?

"Nothing, Sergeant. Just that I'm seeing things more clearly than I did before."

"You still need help, sir."

"Yes, yes of course."

He let McGillivray start to lead him back into the house. As they paused at the threshold of the French windows Allerdyce spoke.

"Sergeant?"

"Yes, sir?"

"It would be my very great privilege if you would agree to serve with me again."

"And it would be my honour, sir."

"Thank you, Mr McGillivray. And may we be granted a fresh opportunity to protect the innocent and detect the guilty."

"Amen to that, sir."

Dalcorn House

9 November 1917

To: Dr Elsie Inglis

Scottish Women's War Hospital

C/o His Britannic Majesty's Consul-General

Odessa

Russia

My dear Elsie,

I think you will be very proud of me. I have followed your excellent example and given full use of Dalcorn House to your colleagues for use as a hospital. My only stipulations are that I should be allowed to retain my own modest apartment for as long as I require it, and that the hospital is solely for the treatment and convalescence of men of non-commissioned rank. I hold them to be the victims of this insane carnage. I believe the officer class – the aristocracy of this country, of Germany and of Russia – to be responsible for the holocaust which has overtaken Europe and I will not allow their admission to this house where their victims lie in agony.

I write, though, not simply nor chiefly to invite your praise. I am writing to tell you that I am about to die. A cancer has spread from my wasted womb throughout my body and my doctor says that in the next few days, when the pain goes beyond what I wish to bear and I have made a full disposition of my affairs, she will administer a fatal dose of morphine which will draw my life comfortably to a close.

Do not grieve for me, Elsie. I have lived for nearly eighty-three years and with my death the chief business of my life will, at last, reach its final and most satisfactory conclusion.

I think I know you well enough to believe that nothing I can say to you will shock you. If I tell you things which could, before this last illness, have seen me arraigned on capital charges I do so not out of any religious or superstitious feeling that I need to make some form of confession for the good of my eternal soul, but for the simple reason that I believe that, now that I cannot be harmed further, my actions deserve to be recorded and remembered.

I did not grow up with any notion that I should be the inheritor of the title and property of the Dukes of Dornoch, and my path towards that was a crooked and obscure one.

What I did grow up with though, Elsie, was a hatred for the hypocrisy and oppression which I saw every day. I believe we share that passion to redress injustice – it is a great blessing that you have been able to do so in the saving of lives, but for some of us our mission has had to be accomplished by the taking of life.

For as long as I remember I have burned with a hard anger against the cruelties of men. One of my earliest memories is of looking out of the window of my nursery at the back of the big plantation house in Louisiana. My black maid had just dressed me, and I stood at the open window hearing the deep, rhythmic singing of the slaves as they toiled in the fields. I saw my father ride up from the fields on his great black horse. He stopped outside the back door and shouted for his valet – Sam, a kindly man who was married to my nurse. He had to call twice before Sam ran out to take the reins of the horse. As my nurse and I watched he cursed the poor man and thrashed him over the head and shoulders with his horsewhip before dismounting and coming in.

I saw tears in my nurse's eyes as she turned me away from the window. My father ran upstairs to the nursery – as his only child I believe he was fond of me, even though I was a girl. He still had his horsewhip in his hand. He stood at the door, staring at the nurse and for a moment I thought he was about to beat her too until she remembered to curtsey and cast her eyes to the floor.

In retrospect, I believe that was the moment at which I realised that I was part of a class whose whole existence was oppression.

As I grew up I longed to escape. The life which was planned for me would have seen me marry the eldest son of a plantation owner, some bland young man of pleasant manners who would, without thought, kiss the hand of a lady in deference only minutes after having seen to the lynching of a disobedient slave. Our plantations would in due course be united by inheritance, to create an even greater wealth.

I thought that one day I might leave the house forever and find my way to New York or Boston, somewhere where a woman could live by her abilities and choose who or whether to marry. My dreams were interrupted, however, by a new proposal which my father found too advantageous to resist.

For over a century, since the failure of the Jacobite cause, my family had been sundered. On each side of the Atlantic Ocean the Bothwell-Scotts prospered from land and other peoples' labour, separated both by distance and by hereditary enmity. Now, it was proposed that I should marry William, Duke of Dornoch, the head of the Scottish branch of the family. His mother said that no dowry would be required – which pleased my father greatly – and that it would surely be to the advantage of the family that the wealth of both sides would finally be united when I inherited the plantation. The proposal, of course, did not need to say that as a married woman I would be deemed incapable of holding property independently, and that everything would therefore be vested in my husband.

And so I was sent, effectively as high-quality breeding stock, to Scotland. I had mixed feelings on my departure. It was not a change which I had chosen, but there was a strong relief in escaping from the heat and oppression of the plantation. On the voyage I relished standing on deck, the fresh wind blowing salt on my face, and imagined that I might enjoy living in the wild, passionate land of Rob Roy and Flora MacDonald.

Those two weeks crossing the Atlantic were the nearest thing to freedom which I was to experience for years. When I arrived in Scotland I was immediately put under the strict supervision and instruction of William's mother, who trained me in the vapid arts of hospitality and household management with which I was to occupy myself while producing an heir for the family. I was disappointed too in William who seemed from the outset to be resentful of me.

I endured a relationship which veered from disinterest to aggression. In one of his fits of sexual aggression I became pregnant.

For a few weeks William's behaviour to me was almost considerate. That changed when, on going into his dressing room to tell him that I had felt the child's first quickening, I found a telegram which he had left on a table. I picked it up and read it – 'I must see you. The well at midnight.'

Rather than confront my husband directly I went into the grounds that night to spy on him. I hung back in the darkness beneath the yews and saw him conversing with a hooded woman. He appeared to hand something over before walking away.

I had struck up some friendship with my husband's valet, Warner. He was a thief and a rogue but intelligent, and I think he hated the aristocracy as much as I did. I'd seen him, once, slipping a couple of William's cigars into his pocket when he thought no-one was looking. I told him I'd seen him, and he knew his job depended on me not telling.

I thought Warner, if anyone, would know if William had some mistress he was meeting or bribing. I summoned him and reminded him of his obligation to me. Of course, he claimed not to know anything but when he saw that I was quite determined to see him dismissed without a reference his resolution broke. At length he told me that he thought William had an illegitimate daughter and that it could have been her. He begged me to believe that he knew no more than that and never to let William know that he'd said any such thing.

I confronted William, saying that I'd been restless at night because of the child and had taken some fresh air in the gardens, where I had seen him with a woman. He denied it. I also said I'd heard talk below-stairs about whether he had a daughter. He said any such thing was a lie. I stood my ground and challenged him again. He grabbed me, thrust me against the wall, and slapped and kicked me before storming out leaving me, curled foetally around my unborn child, weeping and bruised on the floor.

That was when my contempt for him burned into hate. What, I thought, can I do which would most hurt him? What are the things which are most important to him?

The answer was clear. Money and heredity.

Well, I thought, I'm going to make sure I get all his money and cut off his heredity.

There is only one death for which I feel any guilt, Elsie. That poor unborn baby had committed no sin. It had lied to no-one, evicted no crofter, cut the wages of no miner. But it was the seed of William's heredity and it had to die. By rights it should have died from its own father's assault, but I had to do the deed myself with an oxytocic of aloes and tansy. I am grateful at least that William believed the miscarriage to have been the result of his actions and that his shrivelled conscience was affected. I made sure, with herbal infusions and douches of alum and sulphate of zinc, that I never conceived again. Perhaps my womb is suffering now as a result of the abuses I subjected it to, but I did what I had to.

William's death was easily enough accomplished. A telegram like the one I had already seen, an unwitnessed meeting in the grounds by the well, and a single shot from my little derringer – such a neat, ladylike little pistol – and let him fall down the well. I knew, indeed planned, that he would be discovered, but had already worked out my longer scheme for attributing guilt.

I did pause for reflection after William's death. His brothers had not afflicted me as directly as he had, so was it fair that they should die? On the other hand, each of them was an oppressor of their fellow man in their own way, with the exception of poor, weak Arthur. And until they had all died I would be a pensioner of the family, reliant on their charity for my comfort and subsistence.

Any indecision which had afflicted me was quashed by Brigadier Frederick Bothwell-Scott's decision, as soon as he inherited the title and estates, to expel me from Dalcorn House. He treated me with a contempt which even William had not been guilty of and would have exiled me permanently to Dornoch Palace, the last aristocratic house before the Arctic Circle, had it not been for Arthur's intervention. I was determined that they all had to die.

It never ceases to astonish me how intelligence and rank are so seldom related, and how easy it is to manipulate a man's mind through his passions. It was simplicity itself to make Frederick believe that I had become attracted to his choleric stupidity. From having wanted to get rid of me, he quickly came to regard me as his lover, or whore. I visited him in his apartments at Edinburgh Castle and led him practically to the point of abandon before insisting that he go to his private lavatory to wash his male member so that I could offer him a further pleasure. Unfortunately for him his ablutions were terminally interrupted when I took the sword from his desk and thrust it through his heart. It was a joy, Elsie, to see his expression fade from expectation to horror as he died, his member still erect.

George was the most intelligent member of the family. Of course, I knew he'd been attracted to me for a long time. To be honest, of all the brothers he was the one I found most sympathetic. He was no radical – if you scratched his veneer of reason you found the prejudices of his class – but you could at least have an intelligent conversation with him. His fascination with photography, and with the supposed spirit world, smoothed my path. I pretended to be able, like him, to hear the whispers of the spirits and to hear their message that he should re-engage with life, mourn his wife a little less and seek a new relationship. The job of persuasion was aided by my offer to sit as his photographic model to help him develop his art. I have to confess that I took some pleasure in the afternoons when we'd drink together, I'd undress for the camera and pose artistically, and then we'd make slow love on the floor of the studio. I always knew, though, that it had to end as soon as I'd set Arthur up to bear the guilt.

Poor Arthur. I felt that he was somehow predestined to be the sacrificial victim for the sins of his family. He'd suffered at their hands, as a child, almost worse than I had. When he told me of the beatings and humiliations he'd received I suppose I felt sorry for him, but only to the extent that perhaps nature feels sorry for the weaker species which fall by the wayside while the strong evolve. He was so pathetically in love with me that sealing his fate felt like killing a puppy. I do like to think that I brought some hope and pleasure to his constrained life before he died.

It was a careful task to make sure that the pathways of suspicion led to him. The pattern of teasing messages accompanying each death – the last one in handwriting copied from a letter he'd sent me. The fact of his being the direct beneficiary of his brothers' deaths. The careful deconstruction of the frail edifice of his beliefs, and my anonymous message to the prosecution counsel about that. The fuelling of his anger and jealousy against George. As I hid in the darkroom during Arthur's last visit to Rock House and heard his anger I hoped that Arthur would finish my task himself, but it sufficed that he had put himself in a position where that could be believed. A single shot from me finished the job.

And so, the powers of justice took Arthur's life without any need for further violence on my own part. I had a moment's concern on the morning of Arthur's execution, when I remembered that

George had set up a camera in the darkroom at Rock House which might, conceivably, have detected me. I was immensely relieved when Warner – whose loyalty to me as a lover was stronger than his sense of conduct as a servant – told me that he'd destroyed that evidence beyond all prospect of recovery.

Through my prison marriage to Arthur I came into the full inheritance of the titles and estates of the Bothwell-Scotts. I like to think I have done well, Elsie, through setting fair rents and paying fair wages to our workers. We have escaped the strikes which have plagued so many of our mining competitors, and through that have made tolerable profits which have helped me to build the lung disease sanatorium and retirement home for our workers. The glens of Sutherland will never be re-populated, but I have turned the wasteland of grouse-moors over to forests and stopped the gamekeepers from poisoning the eagles which soar over our hills. Our American plantations have been divided into smallholdings for the free negroes. In the great balance of things I believe I leave those parts of the world over which I have had power in a better condition than when I found them.

I must confess that recent events in Russia have quite impressed me – it must be a most exciting time to be there. Inspired by that, I have decided to bequeath the mines to the workers, to be held by workers co-operatives, or 'soviets' as I think they are called where you are. I am also bequeathing all actively farmed lands on our estates, both sides of the Atlantic, to their existing tenants. The remainder – Dalcorn House and Dornoch Palace and their associated lands, the forests and hills of Sutherland, I appoint to be sold by public auction, with the condition that the war hospital be allowed to occupy Dalcorn until hostilities have ceased and the patients have died or recovered. The proceeds of these auctions are to be divided equally to help your own work to promote women's medicine and the work of our friend Dr Marie Stopes to ensure that women may enjoy reproductive freedom.

And with my death, and with the disposal of these assets, the titles and property of the Dukes of Dornoch shall become EXTINCT.

Your affectionate friend,

Josephine